Mirrors & Mist

The Oxbow Kingdom Trilogy
Book II

C. M. SKIERA

ISBN-13: 978-1978343870
ISBN-10: 1978343876

Dedicated to my wife, Regina.

Tythania

The Land of Crimson & Cream

C.M. Skiera

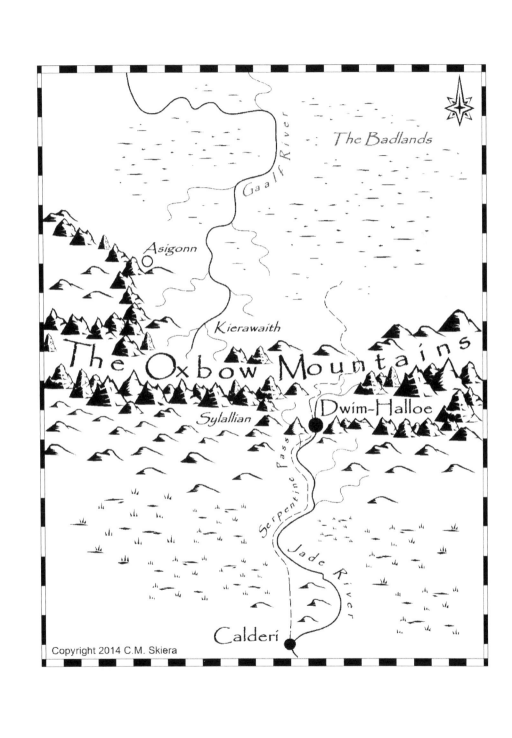

ACKNOWLEDGMENTS

Thank you to everyone who helped and supported me on this endeavor, especially my wife Regina and my mother Barb.

R. J. Blain toiled as my editor and helped me mold an aimless, flashback-laden story into something readable. Her insight and guidance continued to be invaluable in my development as a writer.

A huge thank you to my dedicated beta readers, reviewers, and fellow authors who helped me polish the manuscript; Jennifer Thompson, Brenda Perlin, Anne Carlson, Matt Carlson, Tony Jones, Lee Lyte, Gary Kacmarcik, Ray Nicholson, and Barb Skiera.

A special thanks to my cousin Ray, for unknowingly posing as the cover model for *Mirrors & Mist*. In addition, I'd like to thank the many friends from Facebook and Google Plus for motivating me and sharing their knowledge and experience.

Finally, thank you, dear reader, for giving this book a chance. I hope you enjoyed it. If you would be so generous as to leave a rating or review, I would sincerely appreciate it.

Prologue

"You impressed Princess Ioma, I presume?" Duke Daelis Vardan asked his son Valin.

"Of course." A game bird sat on the table with a loaf of wheat-flour bread. Valin broke off the end piece as he continued. "'Twas easy to see she was taken with me."

Seryn bristled at his sibling's misplaced bravado. *Liar.* Seryn bit his itching tongue. *The princess is right—this will get complicated. And ugly.*

"Excellent," replied Daelis, reaching for the fowl. "'Tis time Tygan narrowed the field. The Calderian relics may as well go home." He tore off a chunk of meat and continued while chewing. "Same for those fisher lords. Can you imagine, a sailor prince from Ost, or one of those *lakeling* lords wearing the crown?"

"Did you gain audience with King Tygan?" Valin asked.

"On the morrow, we'll meet to discuss the advantages our family brings to his southern interests. And I'll remind him of the depth of our coffers. 'Twas never a king that didn't fret about his treasury." A smug look on his face, the duke slid a slice of roast quail into his grinning maw. "Princess Ioma is a handsome lass. She'll make a fine wife."

"Even Seryn was smitten," Valin said. "Had a dance for himself." Valin's gray eyes burned through Seryn.

His ire from last night's confrontation diminished naught, Seryn feared.

"Campaigning on your brother's behalf, I hope," Daelis said.

Prepared for a fatherly reproach, Seryn fancied himself fortunate to get off with a disapproving glare. *Must be my lucky day.*

"M'lady is free to do as she chooses. She *is* a princess, after all."

Daelis narrowed his eyes, his thick white brows weighing them down.

"Do not shame each other," he warned. "For the shame will be on our house." Duke Vardan leaned forward, his frigid gaze reaching out to Seryn. "'Tis no game. Your brother can be king."

Seryn glanced at his plate and breathed deeply. *She deserves better.* The terse look on his face did little to hide his inner turmoil. *And I shall see that she gets it.*

"When will you see her again?" the duke inquired of his eldest.

"I'll call on her this eve," Valin replied.

"You've not sent a message yet?" Daelis frowned. "The princess is in high demand. She'll not sit idle awaiting your beckon." Daelis glanced at his unfinished plate, then at Valin's. "Get dressed. We'll go to the palace posthaste." Duke Vardan rose like steam from a boiling pot. Daelis hovered over his sons, as Valin shoved a final bite into his mouth. "The game's afoot. I'll not lose a step to those oafs. Now, move!"

Valin rushed off still chewing and Daelis followed. With his own plate empty, Seryn picked a bit of bread off Valin's and retreated to the library. He dozed with a book in his lap, dreaming of Ioma and his scheming family.

Seryn was surprised when a messenger returned but an hour later. Still groggy from his nap, he broke the wax seal, while the housekeeper peered over his shoulder. *How about that? She accepted my invitation to meet this very day!* Still in his morning robe, a rush of urgency surged through Seryn. "Alma, what should I wear?" he asked the housekeeper.

"We shall find something handsome," she replied. "And ye best take yer note," she nodded at the table. "Don't want ta leave *that* around for yer brother."

He smiled and raised his eyebrows, tucking the parchment in his pocket.

"Come," he said to her, "I must dress."

Alma followed Seryn upstairs and extracted an appropriate outfit. Seryn donned the clothes and bounded down the stairs before a glowing Alma could appreciate her handiwork. Through the window, he spotted her watching as he left. He waved a grateful goodbye.

Walking to the Granite Palace, butterflies danced on lightning inside his nervous chest. *I'd half expected an outright refusal.* Seryn entered the green palace grounds, sauntering across the royal bailey. *Alma chose well,* he thought, light and cool in his luxurious fabrics. Just past the lesser hall stood the tower where Dwim-Halloe's lord high wizard dwelled. In his wildest dreams, Seryn imagined someday, after paying his dues in service to the king, he might be considered a worthy appointment for the position. *I wonder,* he mused, *could I be both king and lord high wizard?* He chuckled to himself. *One pipedream at a time.*

Princess Ioma Tygan met Seryn at the Great Hall's front doors.

"M'lady, you look truly radiant this day."

"Thank you, Lord Vardan—you are too kind."

"Shall we stroll the garden, my princess?"

"That would be lovely. The hyssops are in bloom." Seryn wasn't interested in the purple-spiked flowers, or anything else besides the princess.

Ioma grabbed his arm. "I know a shortcut." She led him to an unassuming postern door behind the Great Hall. He followed her through the small doorway, and they snuck beneath the castle wall. The narrow tunnel left him to walk behind her, hunched to avoid rapping his skull. Trailing the princess, close to her backside in the confined space, Seryn's heart fluttered. *Don't even think it,* he admonished himself. They exited the curtain wall through another gate buried in ivy, into the walled garden.

Squinting in the sunlight, Ioma led Seryn to a whitestone bench outside the orchard, where they sat next to a bubbling fountain.

From within his tunic, Seryn extracted an ornate folding fan. "For you, m'lady." The colorful design mimicked peacock feathers. Wide-eyed and smiling, Ioma took the gift.

"Why, 'tis lovely! Thank you, Lord Vardan," she said, fanning herself. "Truly, you should not have troubled so."

"'Tis no trouble, m'lady, for next time the heat takes you, I may not be ready with a spell, so the fan must suffice."

"You certainly are the family jester." She mimicked his pose.

"Were you not roaring at Valin's witty repartee?" He faced her with a grin. Side-by-side on a bench, the free-spirited pair sat oblivious to the world.

"Your brother's a serious man, full of ambition." She feigned a pout.

"He is indeed. Yet, I can be serious as well, though, ambition is not my master."

"There's no disguising last night's purpose. Father intends I wed, and each one of my suitors surely has ambitions beyond winning my heart."

"I daresay, I must disagree with you, m'lady."

"Lord Vardan, you cannot dance with a princess without thinking of the throne." She leaned toward him as she spoke.

"'Tis true, Your Majesty, but, I confess, I was not even supposed to dance with you."

She stared at him, perplexed. "Lady Darksparrow scribed your name without your intent? How presumptuous!" Ioma halted and put her fists to her hips, elbows pointing wide. "I must have a word with my gentlewoman." The corners of her mouth curled to release a mischievous smirk. "Though, I can't fault her taste."

Seryn flushed. "You jest, yet, 'tis true," he replied. "My father and brother conspired for Valin to dance with you twice, after I excused myself due to a sudden queasiness. But, I knew I would not relinquish my chance."

"You flatter me, Lord Vardan. I fear your ensorcelling skills may be at work yet again."

"The truth holds a magic all its own, m'lady."

Her lithe hand floated towards his, grasped it, and squeezed.

"I fear you do not know what you're getting yourself into."

"'Tis half the fun." He tightened his grip in return.

"Father and Lord Nargul scheme to find me an advantageous match, with little care for my own wishes."

"I've not proposed *yet*, m'lady." She blushed and giggled. Her fingers felt soft and warm. *Am I squeezing too hard?* He released his grip a bit, only to feel hers tighten. *Relax,* he told himself, taking a deep breath. *Enjoy the scenery.* Seryn realized his hands were sweating, which turned out to be the least of his problems.

"Now more so than ever, I feel like the prize sow at the farmer's auction."

Seryn chuckled at the imagery. "You are no closer to a sow than I am a toad."

"Rib-bit," she said, her mouth curling upward. "You know what I mean." She flashed him an acknowledging smile. "I spend my days being courted and wooed by Tythania's nobles. Two Calderian lords are staying in the lesser hall. I fear they shall not leave till I'm wed." She chewed her lip in consternation before continuing. "And the fish-lords. Charming as longshoremen, those three. Oh, and lest I forget, the swaggering Dwim-Halloe blue-bloods. A dozen, if I count you among them."

"Please do, m'lady—though I do bleed red." His response elicited a royal chuckle that blended with the garden sounds of buzzing bees and rustling leaves.

"And this is after father and Lord Nargul culled the herd considerably."

"The politics of royal matchmaking. Do they hear your opinions at all?"

"I fear not. Certainly not Lord Nargul, and I further suspect he is no admirer of yours."

"Shocking—he was most hospitable while ignoring me at the harvest ball."

"Your sarcasm betrays you, Lord Vardan. Yet, it amuses me."

Seryn leaned toward the princess, placing his mischievous grin next to her ear.

"I shall tell you a secret, but you must keep it close," Seryn teased. "I suspect Lord Nargul is infatuated with my brother."

"Observant of you," she replied, inching closer to him, their shoulders rubbing. "He's made it clear that your sibling's his preferred choice."

Larks chirped in the branches above them, yet even as the princess sat hand-in-hand with him, Seryn felt only the sudden heaviness of disappointment.

"And what does her majesty think of this Valin Vardan?"

"I deem him charming and handsome." She smiled as Seryn failed to hide his chagrin. "Nearly as much as his younger brother."

"You toy with my emotions, m'lady."

"As you do with mine, Lord Vardan. If only we didn't suffer this pressure of my betrothal hanging over us. The thought of it is oppressive."

"And yet, 'tis the reason we are here now, so I cannot begrudge it."

"Though the year of mourning is passed, I still miss Mother terribly. If she were here, she'd navigate this chaos. Father needs her guidance."

"He still retains the counsel of a very wise daughter."

"A daughter he's grown deaf to, and is all too eager to marry off." Their knees touching, Ioma placed her free hand on his thigh. Seryn wiped his palm on his breeches and placed his hand atop hers. He could feel her pulse. *Her heart beats as fast as mine.*

"So, tell me of these other suitors—do they treat you well?"

"Oh, most certainly. Everyone is on their finest behavior when under the king's scrutiny. 'Tis what makes it so difficult—I see them only with their best foot forward. The Calderians are polished and polite—charming even. But they are both so *old*."

"I saw some local men my age dancing with you. Did they not impress?"

"'Tis *all* they tried to do—impress me. Success eluded them, however," she said with a wink.

And what am I doing? Seryn wondered. *Naught but trying to impress.* He unleashed a confident smile in spite of himself. "Good to hear it," he said, "for jealousy nips at me when you're entertaining the others." He instantly regretted admitting jealousy, but the words flew away, irretrievable.

"Seems like an occupation, really. Going through the motions until one or the other makes a gaffe serious enough for father to dismiss him." She waved her hand, mimicking the disapproving king.

"Being royalty sounds arduous, Your Majesty."

"'Twill not resolve itself today, so I shall enjoy my time with you and deal with the morrow when it comes."

For Seryn, the time *had* come. He leaned in and kissed Ioma softly. She floated into his embrace. The sun failed to match the heat of her lips.

Within the Vardan library, books covered the maple-shelved walls from floor to ceiling. The study breathed an aroma of candle wax, hardwood, and parchment. *This is my favorite room.*

"Seryn!" The comforting spell vanished. Seryn recognized the tone in his brother's voice. *He knows.*

"'Tis gone on long enough," Valin said. Fists balled, he planted himself in front of Seryn. His face a steely mask of determination, Valin reeked of the practice yard.

"What, exactly, do you speak of?" Seryn hoped it was other than what he feared. His brother's bulging neck veins told him it was not.

"This is your sole warning ere I take this to Father and Lord Nargul." His unblinking eyes burrowed into Seryn. "I *forbid* you to see her again."

Seryn held his tongue and comprehended Valin's consuming desire for the throne. He suspected his brother *was* fond of Ioma. Yet, it mattered not, for at that moment, he knew in his soul he *loved* Ioma. *I fear this will break him.*

"I'm sorry, brother. But I'm an adult, and Ioma's a princess. We'll not take orders from you."

Valin stabbed his rigid finger in Seryn's chest. "You've no right," Valin said. "I'm the eldest! 'Tis my birthright to take the throne."

Seryn chose his next words carefully, but doubted it mattered. "You speak as if the princess has no say in the matter."

"Little does she—for *she* serves the king. And the king's right hand favors me for the crown." Valin leaned in closer, and Seryn detected wine on his breath.

Seryn inched back from his brother's uncomfortable closeness. The enormity of the situation sank in. *I'm courting for a kingdom.* His mind churned as he scrambled for the words to respond. Though they had drifted far apart, guilt still crept from the corners of his mind. *He'll never forgive me.*

"Your selfish dalliances will not ruin this family," Valin said.

"Release her from your hypnotic ensorcelling."

Seryn stood stunned. "You think I cast a spell on her?" *What kind of monster does he take me for?* Seryn's shoulders slumped and his hands fell to his sides. "You cannot believe she could choose me of her own free will?"

"No—she could not. You and your mewling coven of unnaturals will not steal this crown." Valin's index finger shook, inches from Seryn's nose. "This is treason!"

"You speak nonsense." Seryn slapped his brother's hand from his face. With a fluid move, Valin clutched Seryn's tunic by the shoulders and shoved him. Seryn landed hard, as books rained on his head.

With a swing, Seryn swatted his brother's hands from his garment. Valin balled a fist and swung back. Seryn ducked as Valin punched a volume on Calderian farming, his fist but grazing the top of Seryn's head.

Seryn launched, tackling Valin over a bench, sandwiching his brother between himself and the furniture as they tumbled to the floor. Prone and grimacing, Valin glanced a fist off Seryn's cheek. Seryn responded with a rib strike—in precisely the spot where Valin landed on the bench. The wind left Valin with a futile whine. Seryn struggled to stand, but Valin, despite his gasping, grabbed hold and kept Seryn on his knees. *Just won't give up, will you?*

So Seryn reared back and hit him in the ribs again.

Valin wheezed, struggling to suck air into his empty lungs. He slumped from Seryn, buying time to catch his breath. Seryn used the bench to leverage himself to his feet. As Seryn stood over his fallen kin, Valin squirmed to the other side of the bench. *He's had enough,* Seryn thought.

Regaining his breath, Valin's gray eyes sparked. On his backside, the elder Vardan spun and kicked the bench into Seryn's shins, returning him to the floor. Valin swung wildly, and Seryn lurched out of harm's way. Valin swung again, before Seryn regained his balance.

Landing a fist squarely in Seryn's eye, Valin's punch knocked Seryn flat on his back. *Devil's luck, he's quick!* Valin pounced atop Seryn, pinning him to the ground.

"Warned you," Valin said, letting fly another blow as a knowing grin escaped his bloody lips. Elbow high, he cocked his arm again.

"Wouldn't listen," Valin chided. The next shot bloodied Seryn's nose.

Seryn writhed to unseat his brother, to no avail. *Devil take you!*

"Impertinent maggot-pie—now you'll learn!" Valin's next punch split Seryn's lip. *I'll not submit!*

Valin landed three more punches before Seryn blacked out.

Alma shrieked when she spotted Seryn and raced to his side, hopping over the strewn tomes. He stared at the ceiling, struggling to focus while tasting a mouthful of blood. Rather than spit in his beloved library, he swallowed. *Get up,* he urged himself.

His first attempt at standing landed him back on the floor.

"Oh, my," Alma said. "'Twas not yer clay-brained brother, was it?"

Seryn nodded.

"'Tis an ill omen fer kin ta fight like this." She shook her head, examining Seryn's injuries. "That logger-headed brother 'o yers done ye good this time." On her knees next to Seryn, elbows wide, she rested her fists on her narrow hips. "Don't move, pignut. I'll return in a blink with proper unguents."

I've no inclination to move. His head pounded and face throbbed. Even his ears rang.

Before he realized she'd left, Alma returned, hands full.

"This'll help," she said, wiping his split lip with a cloth dipped in her vinegar-based tonic. Seryn winced, doubting the efficacy of her homemade treatments. Yet, as far back as his memory reached, he recalled Alma treating him with her remedies. And it always seemed to help. *At least a little.*

"There, now," she said, her cloth now mottled with crimson. Alma tossed the bloodied rag aside and opened a clay jar. "This'll help the swelling." Her wrinkled fingers dipped into the container, extracting a dollop of ointment. Seryn grimaced at the sickly odor. "Hemlock and henbane," she replied. "Ye'll get used ta the smell, ninny-hammer," she said, wiping the balm on his puffy skin.

I believe her not one bit. "As if I didn't feel bad enough," he said, "now I smell of rotting flesh."

"'Tis that flap-mouth that earned ye this beating, I bet." She wiped a strand of red hair behind her ear. "Let's try an' get ye on yer feet." Knees popping, she stood and with a tug, pulled Seryn up. He planted a hand on the wall to steady himself.

"The room's in shambles."

"Don't fret, puttock," Alma cooed. "I'll tidy it up good as new."

Legs wobbly, he staggered to the stairway and, with her help, up to his bedroom. She ushered him in and promised to return with a healing elixir as soon as she brewed it.

Seryn shuffled to his mirror. Eyes blackened, lips swollen, his face looked twice its normal size. He wiped crusty blood from his inside his nostrils. *Alma had not ventured quite so far.*

Contrary to his training at Eh' liel Ev' Narron, he cast a spell to ease the pain and reduce the swelling. *Don't really know how badly I'm injured,* he rationalized. The illuminae instructed their students that magic was reserved for times of dire need. *This is dire enough for me.* The incantation provided a measure of relief, but drained his stamina. He stumbled to bed and dropped in a heap.

Alma returned with a steaming carafe, interrupting Seryn's attempts at slumber. As soon as his mind wandered from Valin's cruelty, his thoughts returned to Ioma. *It shames me to think of her finding out about today.* Alma poured a mug of her hot brew, distracting Seryn from his self-pity.

"Smells worse than the henbane," he whined, only half-serious.

"Will make ye see straight, dizzy-eyes," she replied. Seryn sipped the frothy concoction. He contorted his face, mostly for show. *Can't let her think it's anything less than horrible.*

"Finish that and rest till dinner. I'll summon ye when it's ready."

"Don't bother," he replied. "Food's the last thing I want." *I'll not give him the satisfaction of seeing me like this.*

"Yer gonna have ta face 'im sooner or later."

"Not tonight—not like this."

"Aye." She nodded, squinting. "'Tis yer father yer avoidin' ain't it?"

"There's hardly a difference. They're of the same mind."

"No father wants ta see his son suffer. Valin'll get a stern reproach for certain."

Seryn peered at Alma and shook his head. "Father'll say I was asking for it, and I got what I deserved. He'll probably hope Valin knocked some sense into me." Seryn chuckled half-heartedly. "You know I'm right."

"Drink up and get rest," she said, closing the door behind her.

The following morning, Seryn examined his reflection. *Feel worse than yesterday, and look it as well.* The swelling receded somewhat, but the coloring deepened. *If only I knew a spell to remove the bruising.*

Stiff and sore, Seryn shuffled to his desk. *I cannot face Ioma like this.* He opened an inkwell and dipped a quill, then put the dripping feather to fresh parchment. *Not my best penmanship.*

He summoned Alma to have his message delivered. *I'd rather she think me ill than know the truth.* Upon seeing his mottled visage, Alma covered her mouth. *Lovely,* he lamented. *I look the monster.* The startled housekeeper traded the rolled note for another serving of her steaming tonic. *Still pissing out last night's batch.*

Seryn skipped breakfast, and still neither his father nor brother called to check his condition. *It's as though I were dead.* Once his family left, he slunk to the kitchen, ravenous.

Filling up on soft foods and wine, he decided to stay home. *No school, no Ioma.* Despite his pain, his mind kept drifting back to the princess. *Who's courting her today? Is Valin feeding her lies about me? Is father conspiring with Nargul and the king to seal Valin's future?* His heart ached more than his battered head. Sprawled on the bed, he buried his face in his blanket.

Upon hearing soft knocking, he couldn't stand the thought of company.

"Go away!" When the door crept open, he glared.

"Seryn?"

His swollen jaw dropped as he watched Ioma slip in. When their eyes met, concern draped her face as she rushed to his bedside.

"What happened?" Ioma caressed his battered face, sliding on the down-filled mattress next to him. He winced at her touch, yet it sent shivers of pleasure through his wracked form.

"Long story," he slurred through his puffy lips.

"I'm in no hurry," she said, staring into his glistening hazel eyes. "Who *did* this to you?"

"Valin," he bullfrog-croaked. She stiffened.

"That jealous bastard. How could he look me in the face after doing this?"

"You saw him?"

"Yes, but not by choice. Father's pressuring me." She spoke the next words with difficulty. "Your father and Lord Nargul met this morning." Ioma looked ashamed. "He says Valin intends to propose."

Seryn's heart stuck in his throat as his heart raced. The blood rushing through his swollen veins ran red-hot.

"You cannot marry him!"

"I will not marry him!"

Seryn sat upright, failing to hide the discomfort the effort caused. He slid from the mattress and took one knee at her feet. *The time is now,* he told himself. He swallowed hard. "Ioma, I love you dearly. Will you do me the honor of accepting me as your husband?"

The princess paused not even a moment to consider.

"I *will* marry you, Seryn Vardan!"

He rose to the bed, no longer a pain in his body, took Ioma in his arms and kissed her. She returned the embrace, running her fingers through his long locks. His scalp tingled at her touch. Pulses accelerating, their hearts pounded in rhythm.

She unfastened her cloak, letting it slide off her shoulders, over the mattress edge, to the floor. The falling garment wafted her scent into Seryn's room. An aroma of rose-water and oil tantalized his nostrils as his eyes grew saucer-wide.

His fingers fumbled with her bodice strings while her warm hands slid inside his robe and caressed his aching ribs. Her soothing touch melted away his jitters, and her blouse ties fell victim to his now-nimble fingers. Encouraged by her fearless hands, his loose gown slipped from his shoulders and pooled around his waist. He kissed her neck, tasting her soft skin and inhaling her scent. Ioma took the lead, freeing him from all but the most pleasurable exertion.

They wound together, the warmth of their bodies spurring them on. Emboldened by youthful passion, they explored each other with inexperienced clumsiness. Were the heavens to rain fire, the couple would not relent.

Ioma did not leave until the morrow.

Chapter One

Jetsam noticed Tramp's pointy ears rotate. As the terrier charged toward the ridge crest, keening steel and battle cries reverberated on Jetsam's eardrums. Ground-hugging foliage stopped Tramp from advancing. With tan paws planted on rusty lichens, his low growl alerted the wizard Seryn Vardan to the faraway din as well.

Jetsam stepped over his four-legged companion and stood in the deep scrub. Gloved hands pushed aside the thick brush blocking his view. Winter retreated from the Kierawaith, but the dry devil's club branches still swayed barren of buds. Brittle flaxen spines dispersed with his touch, cascading to the mossy carpet at his feet. High in the spruce canopy above, prickly arms waltzed with the breeze.

Jetsam's palms opened a moon-lit portal through the splintery shrub. This high in the Oxbow Mountains, early spring temperatures demanded winter clothing. Jetsam wore the too-large gloves of the late bounty hunter Yduk Thiern. Even with space in the fingertips, the well-made gauntlets were a superior alternative to cloth mittens or Dwarven ringed mail, and especially bare hands.

With a calm command, Jetsam hushed his terrier, and peered upon the frenetic scene. On this cloudless night, the waxing moon illuminated the hillside enough to discern the forms below.

"Men!" Jetsam whispered. "And... *beasts!*"

Seryn leaned in over Jetsam's cloaked shoulder and searched down the ridge. As did Jetsam, the mage wore a fur-lined hooded cloak. Both faces were clean-shaven—Seryn's on purpose and Jetsam's because he grew no beard to shave.

"Too big for goblins, too small for trolls," Jetsam continued.

"*Grimions,*" Seryn said. "Bodes ill to see them this far south."

Jetsam recalled fireside stories Ratboy told in the underbelly. *Pitiless monsters,* he'd said, *head-hunters and flesh-eaters, that's what grimions are.* Jetsam envisioned Ratboy's serious gaze as he heaped fodder for the urchins' nightmares. *The gray-skins run with humpbacks and goblins, steal orphans in the violet hour, and fashion loincloths from human hair.* Though the tales frightened him as much as any of the orphans, Jetsam missed his friend's harrowing imagery. *They kidnap lasses for the Grimlord, and he breeds them to make more grimions.*

Or so Ratboy said.

From what Jetsam witnessed beneath him, his former companion's tales strayed not far from truth.

"They're *killing* them!" Jetsam said, turning to the sorcerer. Both he and Seryn saw enough to determine the caravan guards were not faring well. An aimless confusion undermined their efforts.

Then Jetsam's blue eyes spotted a girl, cowering beneath a woven basket in the rear of a breached wagon. The plunderers ripped open the canvas cover, exposing the lass to the onslaught. Jetsam swore on his life that this caravan girl would not carry a half-grimion child.

Before Seryn voiced an objection, Jetsam scrambled through the thicket, thorny brambles raking his long locks. Tramp barked in dismay and balanced on his hind legs, craning and ears erect, searching for a passage to follow. Only moments ago, Jetsam had contemplated setting camp and bedding down for the night. Now dinner would wait.

Adrenaline overrode Jetsam's rational thought as he descended the slope. His leatherwork boots kicked up dust from the landscape and sent stones and pebbles bouncing beneath him. He step-slid down the gravelly hillside, his left hand feathering the loose earth for balance. In his right hand, he held Enthran Ashvar's old staff, poking it into the ground as he worked down the bank.

Jetsam learned a plethora of spells from Seryn this past winter, and his mind reeled to select the most appropriate one for the current situation. A hundred paces below him, the caravan idled on the trail, its dozen guards battling the attackers.

Jetsam counted six covered wagons scattered in a crooked line along the trail. The raiders struck quickly, disabling the caravan before the wagons circled. Jetsam realized the grimions crippled at least one wheel or horse on each wagon. The war party overturned one of the smaller four-wheeled carriages—its well-oiled wooden wheels still spun in vain. The coachman and a pair of road horses lay dead. One sumpter bay bolted, its cargo strewn in its fleeing wake.

Horses neighed, stamped, and tangled in their harnesses as swords, clubs, and claws flew in a frenzied dance. The beleaguered guards made their stand beside the largest six-wheeled wagon; a beached whale in the mountain valley. Jetsam noticed an unfortunate passenger had been dragged out and gutted, but predominantly, the wily ravagers focused on the over-matched guards.

Halfway down the slope, Jetsam halted to scrutinize the vicious assailants. *The grimions outnumber them.* The war band wore a haphazard selection of what could most accurately be described as armor. A variety of cobbled materials fashioned breastplates, bucklers, greaves, and helms. The grimions brandished clubs and cudgels along with dirks for jugular slashes and scalping.

Jetsam contemplated turning around and racing back to higher ground. Glancing back, he saw Seryn hacking through the brush as it bit and grabbed at his cloak. Tramp hopped behind him, picking his way over the mage's hasty trail of crushed branches. Their rapid breath frosted in the cool mountain air.

Jetsam returned his gaze to the battle field and found the terrified girl. Upon spying a slavering monster turning toward the cowering lass, he dismissed the idea of retreat. *It spotted her!* The abomination released a banshee wail and bee-lined for the girl. Gore ran from its toothy maw and bloody claws. *My spell must be deadly.*

Jetsam focused and set upon an incantation. His outstretched right arm gripped his staff, leaving his left hand free to cast. As the Elven words fled his lips and his fingers danced... nothing happened.

Bugger!

In the brief time it took him to take a deep breath, recompose, and start again, the slavering mongrel reached the wagon. *Concentrate.*

Jetsam steeled his mind and repeated the incantation.

"Av-erif unan umine!"

A ribbon of flame erupted from his staff. The fire-tongue enveloped the rushing attacker. A screeching blur of arms, legs, and fire bolted headlong toward the screaming girl. She brandished the basket as a futile shield. The stumbling, burning cur crashed headfirst into the wagon with a thud and a crack. The lass fainted, and the smoldering mongrel slumped lifeless against a shattered wagon wheel as the girl's basket landed on its steaming skull.

Jetsam let out a sigh and took another deep breath, and heard Seryn release a spell. Jetsam gaped as the earth beneath three of the chargers magically changed to slop. Their clawed feet slipped and slid in the mud as the hard-packed caravan ruts transmuted to quicksand. The flailing beasts sunk to their bony knees in the morass.

Before the ensorcelled grimions slogged their way to solid ground, Seryn unleashed a second spell. The fresh mud cooled instantly as the earth froze hard around the raiders' submerged feet. Rooted in place, they squealed in pain and confusion. One off-balance monstrosity snapped his femur as he crumpled. The sound of cracking bone echoed like Dwarven blasting powder, startling the other two bound assailants. This trio was stuck firm—but they constituted a mere fraction of the problem.

Readying another incantation, Jetsam experienced his stamina waning. *Overdid it on that one.* He swayed light-headed as he watched a caravan guard chop the mud-frozen grimions like a stand of dry timber. Three more attackers fell as Seryn administered a fatal shock with a flickering whip of electricity.

By now, both the humans and despoilers were aware of the spellcasters on the hillside. The magical intervention swung the battle's momentum. A pair of carnivores pointed gnarled fingers at Jetsam, and charged toward him with clubs high.

As clawed feet shredded the embankment beneath him, Jetsam cast an incantation to animate the undergrowth. The vines and brush coiled around the marauders' feet and the gnarling duo stumbled. Undaunted, the creatures' muscled legs pulled against the entangling foliage, uprooting the binding creepers. Once again, the plunderers launched at Jetsam.

What've I got myself into? Jetsam raised his staff with both hands and braced for the onslaught. His magic reservoir was empty. *Now you've done it, fool.* As two bloody cudgels swung toward him, Jetsam recognized Seryn uttering another Elven phrase, then sensed a wave of magic rush past him.

Both grimions stood petrified like trolls in sunlight with their clubs halted in midswing, inches from striking Jetsam. He gaped at the dead monstrosities frozen in front of him. Hairless and gaunt, their mottled skin displayed every shade of gray-scale, from dusty silver to dirty charcoal. Scars and pockmarks covered them, while sinew and tendons protruded through their hide. Muscled skeletons dipped in ashen wax, the grimions carried nary an ounce of body fat. Their bloodshot eyes bulged, with ebony irises indiscernible from their black pupils. Jetsam fell to the sloping ground. As he rested, Seryn dispatched another ravager with his deadly casting.

When Jetsam saw the largest grimion throw the stone, he cried out in warning, but his shout was too late. Though Seryn tried to dodge the whistling projectile, the potato-sized rock clipped his knee. The sorcerer spun to the ground, dropping his staff. While Seryn clutched his knee, the raider chief charged him.

Even without his staff, Seryn released another spell as the sprinting grimion pounced. The beast exploded into bloody chunks of flesh, raining gore upon Seryn. This grisly display proved enough for the rattled attackers, and the remaining grimions retreated to the hills in disarray.

Jetsam released a sigh of relief, and hunched with his staff on his knees while he surveyed the carnage. Corpses littered the ground as nervous chatter and mournful wailing started amongst the survivors. Jetsam's head ached, and a single sob escaped his lips. Seryn shook the grimion remnants from his cloak and reached for his staff. The stunned guards inventoried the wounded and regrouped.

"Hack those two down," the captain said, pointing at the grimions Seryn petrified. "Don't know how long that spell will last."

"What about the unnaturals?" a redheaded guard asked.

"They'll come with us. Sorcery's illegal, no matter what."

"But, Cap'n, without 'em, we'd be dead!" said the bearded copper-head.

"*Never* trust an unnatural. They may attack *us* next. Now, grab the knave!"

Higher on the embankment, Seryn tried to stand, but his swelling knee failed him and he slipped back to the ground.

Too exhausted to scamper away, Jetsam wanted to run, but his foggy brain wasn't sending orders to his feet. As the red-beard approached, bloodied sword in hand, Jetsam recognized the Oxbow Kingdom coat of arms. *Of all the sodding luck.*

Then Jetsam observed a bewildered look wash over the guard's face. The man's vacant eyes glared right through him, and he strode past Jetsam, nearly stepping on him, but a foot away.

What happened?

The confused guard lumbered toward Seryn, who sat behind Jetsam, further up the slope.

"Don't move!" His sword tip pointed at the hobbled mage.

Cast a spell! Jetsam urged. *I've naught left, but surely you can save us from this mess.*

"You don't need to do this," Seryn said to the guard. "We can go our separate ways."

"Not another word. Drop yer staff!"

Seryn spun uphill from the man, regaining his feet. But the guard lunged, grasping the ankle of Seryn's gimpy leg as both tumbled to the ground. The spellcaster's staff slipped free as he fell. With gravity's help, the guard dragged him closer. Seryn struggled to break loose, but the redhead held the grimacing mage. As they wrestled on the hillside, two more guards clambered past Jetsam. The armored trio overpowered Seryn.

"Gag him and bind his wrists behind his back. Don't want him casting any more spells," the captain said. Seryn glanced in Jetsam's direction, and before they fastened his gag, yelled a warning.

"Run!"

With the aid of his staff, Jetsam rose. He knew in this state, he would not outrun the guards. Oddly, they paid him no heed.

"The knave!" the captain shouted. "Where's the knave?"

"Unnatural must a made 'im disappear," another said, shaking Seryn by the shoulders. "Where's the lad, unnatural?" Seryn didn't make a sound.

Jetsam held out his hands, and gazed at his feet. *Nothing. I'm invisible!*

Jetsam jumped when he heard a bark. Tramp was nowhere to be seen.

"You invisible, too, buddy boy?" he whispered.

The terrier's front paws planted on Jetsam's calf. *He can still smell me.* Jetsam bent to lift the dog. Even though he couldn't see Tramp, his groping hands found the furry terrier. Jetsam lifted his companion by the canine's warm midsection.

"Don't know how long this'll last," he murmured. "We should take cover." It pained Jetsam to abandon Seryn, but with his own magic depleted, he knew he shouldn't squander Seryn's selfless gift of an unfettered escape.

Jetsam crawled back up the slope. Footprints materialized in the dirt as if from a ghost. *Bloody strange,* he thought. He spotted Seryn's staff, abandoned on the dusty hillside. In the dark and in their rush, the guards had overlooked it. Jetsam snatched the polished wood. As soon as his transparent hand took hold of it, the staff vanished as well.

Once Jetsam reached the ridge top, he snuck through the line of brush. Despite his invisibility, he still made noise and rustled branches. He set Tramp down and plopped himself on the ground next to Seryn's pack—sitting right where he'd left it. Jetsam's mind spun. With his head in his palms, he brooded. *What do I do now?* His heart pounded against his ribcage. *Focus, fool,* he admonished himself.

From his elevated position, Jetsam maintained an unobstructed view of the stranded caravan. He spied Seryn bound to a wagon, gagged, with his hands tied behind his back. While Seryn sat immobilized, the guards and passengers worked like ants. They removed the undamaged wheels from the overturned wagon to replace the broken ones. Others separated the quick and the dead. Most of the manpower repaired the wagons and tended the wounded, though a few men sorted through cargo, while the merchant decided which goods would be discarded. An injured road horse received a mercy killing.

Jetsam wasn't sure how long he'd been invisible, but he could now see Tramp, and his own hands and feet.

"I made a bloody mess of things," he told the terrier. "We're on our own again, buddy boy."

Tramp tilted his head to the left, then right, his mouth open and pink tongue panting.

"Don't worry—we're going to get Seryn back. Soon as I figure out *how*." So far, his only ideas seemed absurdly dangerous, and he dismissed them. "Common sense," he told the terrier. "Better late than never."

Jetsam's eyelids drooped as he studied the caravan. The guards were busy treating the wounded and fortifying their perimeter. *Preparation is key,* he told himself. *Watch and learn.* His head jerked awake while counting the guards. *Start over. One, two...*

Despite his best effort to stay awake, sleep overtook him.

Jetsam suffered a fitful slumber. His dreams proved erratic and unnerving. One minute, he stood inside Seryn's cave, alongside his mentor, learning to cast spells. The next, he found himself in Dwim-Halloe, running from trolls. His twin brother Elvar appeared, but looked similar to Ratboy, and sounded like Mole. With dream-world swiftness, they attended a grand wedding in the Citadel garden, with coal-eyed goblins serving fruity mead. First, sunlight blinded him, then, in a blink, blackness blanketed the world. Next, the sky purpled and svelte firedrakes raced overhead. The bride materialized from the nightmare's shadows. It was Giselle, and the groom, Yduk Thiern, a pale, desiccated corpse.

Jetsam awoke in a sweat, icy beads running down his shivering back. Dawn had not yet broken. He bolted upright and felt Tramp cuddled by his side. Jetsam peered over the ledge and assessed the caravan. There was no movement now, but the fruits of a busy night's labor revealed themselves in the twilight. The survivors scrapped two disabled six-wheel wagons for parts to restore the remaining four large rigs, the wheel-less wooden carcasses left to rot, a somber monument to the acrimonious warfare. The rebuilt wagons sat overloaded with their accumulated burdens, and the caravan readied to crawl again.

Seryn was nowhere in sight. *Packed away in a wagon,* Jetsam hoped. He didn't want to consider the alternative. He didn't see the girl, either. *Hope she's all right, too.*

"We'll follow the caravan," Jetsam told Tramp. The terrier licked his lips and sat with one paw raised. "Maybe an opportunity will present itself." Jetsam regretted rushing to the caravan's rescue. He remembered an old saying of Elvar's: *No good deed goes unpunished.*

Jetsam removed the food from Seryn's pack. He carried enough of his own gear without lugging Seryn's as well, and Tramp wouldn't appreciate doubling as a tiny pack mule. Jetsam left the sorcerer's bedding and clothing in the sack and hid it in a cubbyhole beneath the briars for safe keeping. With gauntlets removed to reveal his pale hands, he dug a shallow trench in the ground near the brambles and buried Seryn's staff. With his sharp paring knife, he carved a few discrete symbols in the bark of the nearby trees to help him find the hiding place upon his return. Hopefully he'd be able to retrieve the belongings with Seryn soon.

Jetsam and Tramp followed the caravan the entire day. Head low and tail high, Tramp sniffed the ground. *Searching for Seryn's scent,* Jetsam suspected. Rocky and rough, the wagon trail looped with switch-backs and an arduous river crossing. It wasn't difficult for the pair to keep the sluggish wagons in sight, yet remain unnoticed. The spring day unfurled cool and overcast in the shadowy Kierawaith. Jetsam observed the caravan headed east. "Likely for the Serpentine Pass," he told his furry companion. The sun journeyed westward, dipped beneath the clouds, and painted the mountain in shades of orange, distracting Jetsam's tired eyes from the wagon train.

At sunset, the caravan stopped for the night. The wagons circled and guards positioned themselves around the perimeter. Even from a distance, Jetsam discerned high tensions. He watched and waited as the horses were tended, a meal prepared, bladders emptied, tents set up, and all but the sentry bedded down. *But no sign of Seryn, or the girl.* Jetsam crept closer and moved to within earshot of the watchmen on duty.

Side-by-side, the weary guards leaned on the battered wagon. The flickering campfire cast them in high-contrast silhouettes. The copper-bearded guard who tackled Seryn chatted with his moon-faced companion.

"Trader's happy the grimions didn't run off with his Dwarven goods," said the rusty-haired sentry.

"Aye, we got off with but a handful of dead. Guess that don't matter to 'im."

"Moneygrubber don't care 'bout a few corpses. Cheaper'n losin' his Dwarven treasures. He'll get good coin fer what he traded from them shortfolk."

"Aye, 'cept now we got six loads o' heavy crap stuffed into four wagons, plus a prisoner ta boot!"

"Ye get a look at the unnatural?" red-beard inquired.

"Not much o' one. Cap'n has got a close watch on 'im. Ask me, we shoulda finished him along with the grimions. Wagons are overloaded even without his dead weight."

"Aye, carryin' a spellcaster's dangerous fer all of us—even if he's bound and gagged. Odd that Cap'n wants to take him with us," said the redhead. "'Tis a long road to Dwim-Halloe."

"Might be he recognized 'im. Mebbe a reward out fer his hide?"

"Think that's the *kingslayer?*" copper-head asked. "Resembles King Valin, he does."

"Seryn Vardan? Cap'n could retire on *that* bounty."

"King'd prob'ly give Cap'n a little extra fer keeping 'im alive so he can watch his head fall in the basket."

"Aye, wonder if Valin'll use his headsman on the unnatural, or swing the axe himself?"

Chapter Two

Seryn sat on the floorboards of a covered wagon, hands behind him, iron shackles clamped around his wrists and a leather gag stuffing his mouth. His heart hammered and his extremities chilled. The piercing night breeze penetrated the cracks between the planks. No windows shed light into his wheeled cell, nor was a torch or lantern provided. *I'd welcome the heat, even without the light,* Seryn rationalized. *Got to escape, before I freeze.* He twisted and squirmed until his wrists burned raw and he gasped for breath. *Just like last time—I'll not wiggle free of these clamps, either.* He began to shiver.

How could I have let this happen? He rubbed his clammy palms with his freezing fingertips, trying to warm his hands. *Should've seen this coming. Yet, it happened so fast.* Knees to his chest, he stomped his boots on the floorboards and his achy knee punished him. *That's not helping.* Despite its ineffectiveness, he continued to clomp—his feet had turned as frigid as his hands. As he sat and stomped, his temper raised, boots pounding harder. *Why the bloody devil has this happened?* His arms tensed, pulling against his bonds. *Haven't I suffered enough?* His infuriated blood splashed a flush across his cheeks. *Try to help these superstitious ingrates and they turn on me.*

"Keep quiet, unnatural," a voice yelled from outside the wagon. "Any more racket and I'm beating ye to a pulp." The man slapped the wagon wall for emphasis, rocking the carriage and startling Seryn with the thunderous thump.

Are they posting a guard on me? Seryn rubbed his boots together in a quieter attempt to generate heat. The effort proved as fruitless as his stomping. *Can't believe I'm a captive again.* A panicked sweat coalesced over his forehead and his arms began to ache. He released a drawn-out sign. *Though, I couldn't fathom it last time, either.*

Seryn's chest lifted and fell as he collected his thoughts. His head ached from the guard's hillside tackle. *And my nose feels swollen.* He wiped a trail of dried blood from his upper lip onto his tunic shoulder. *Hope I didn't break it.* He swallowed a mixture of mucus and blood. *Guess that's the least of my worries.*

Seryn inhaled through his restricted nostrils, trying to slow his racing heart. A trace of campfire smoke mixed with the woody wagon scent. The crisp air triggered a sneeze, which sent pain shivering through his ribs.

Wonder what they'll do with me? Seryn entertained a few guesses, none of them encouraging. He tried to adjust his position, but he was wedged between crates and boxes, with no space to wiggle. Seryn sucked his teeth. *Even smaller than my last cell, and just as dark.* Seryn recalled a tiny, filthy room carved from rock, and a fist-sized drain that stunk of urine and feces.

His scalp itched in a spot he couldn't scratch, even when bending his head toward an adjacent crate. He bumped his bruised forehead and pushed a muffled moan through the gag as drool ran across his chin. *This is miserable, and it's just begun.* Seryn pondered his depressing surroundings. *We're in the middle of nowhere.* He recalled the view from the ridge and the wagons rolling eastbound on the trail. *That's not a good direction for men in Oxbow surcoats.*

Seryn slumped against his battered knees, feeling the pull of his bound hands. His empty stomach rumbled, igniting a wave of nausea. He hung his throbbing head in despair. *Maybe I'll see my old cell again.* He shuddered. *Don't even think it—just stay calm.* Seryn concentrated on shutting out the panic and anxiety, yet his rational mind fought a losing battle against his survival instincts. A noise from outside the wagon startled him, and thwarted his efforts. His head shot up, turning toward the distraction.

It's just voices. He focused on the muffled conversation. Words like 'dead' and 'repair' peppered the minced discussion. *I hear no mention of another captive. I pray Jetsam got away.* Thinking of his apprentice, Seryn shook his head.

Impertinent lad. If he'd let me assess the battle, I could've kept out of this mess, and still saved lives. Seryn tilted his stiff neck until his vertebrae popped. *Yet, I can't begrudge the boy for doing the right thing.* He rolled his shoulders, stretching the stiffening muscles to ward off the inevitable cramping. *I'm his teacher, after all, and* I *led us into danger.*

I've no one to blame but myself.

Seryn revisited the chaotic events of the caravan raid, retracing both his steps and Jetsam's. *The guards doubted us,* he suspected. *Maybe they saw me hesitate.* Seryn's chest heaved and fell, and rose again. *If I'd acted sooner, like the boy, they may've trusted us.* He recalled the terrified expressions on the guards' faces. *They feared us as much as they did the grimions,* he realized. *My reluctance introduced a shadow of a doubt, and now I'm a prisoner by the men I saved.*

Seryn's straining ears registered the activities outside his wagon. Staccato hammering echoed in the evening air. *They're repairing the wagons.* Pupils wide, Seryn tried to spot a flicker of light through the planks, yet he found naught but darkness. His numb fingers searched the floorboards beneath his rump, but discovered no cracks or holes large enough to grab. He explored his confines with his feet as well, but his boot soles encountered solid wood, resistant to his pushing. *I can't even stand.*

Seryn resigned himself to eavesdropping and listened to fearful, angry, confused voices. *Irrational voices.* Fear preyed on his vulnerable imagination and Seryn envisioned the worst. *'Tis but a matter of time until they drag me out and finish me.* He pulled and twisted on his restraints until exhausted, yet his efforts weakened only his stamina. *I've no way to defend myself.*

As his sweat chilled, Seryn wrestled with logic. *If they planned to kill, me, they'd have done it already.* He sighed in relief for a second, until an opposing idea confronted him. *Unless they're trying to lure Jetsam back to capture him.* Seryn's teeth ground into the moist rawhide gag. *Please, lad, don't be so foolish. Or brave.* Seryn imagined his apprentice pondering the predicament. *Jetsam will follow, I fear. The lad's too rash. And too loyal. If the guards spot him, he'll be doomed.*

Drained of energy, Seryn tried to focus on his options, yet his weary mind kept drifting back to his first capture, over a decade ago in Dwim-Halloe. *The parallels are too similar to ignore.* So instead of fighting the flood of memories, he dwelt on them in hopes of finding a way out of his current mess. As his mind wandered back in time, he searched his recollections.

Eighteen-year-old Seryn stretched inside the library of Dwim-Halloe's School of Sorcery.

"Enough for today?" a woman in charcoal robes asked him.

"I think so, Illuminae," Seryn told his instructor.

"'Tis been a long day."

She's being kind. I can't focus, and it shows. Too much on my mind, he lamented, his head pounding. *I'll not be able to concentrate until I sort out this mess with Valin.*

Seryn rolled his scroll and slipped it inside a case. As he closed the ivory container, a swooping bat zipped past his head. With a gasp, he jumped in surprise.

"Just a rafter bat," his instructor declared with a chuckle. "Good night, Seryn," she said as she waved.

"Till the morrow," Seryn replied, embarrassed for being startled.

Seryn gazed at the moon and strode down the staircase outside the school. His hand absentmindedly floated to his pouch. *Blast, I left my scroll inside. Damnable bat!*

Before he turned around, two forms lunged from the shadows. The assailants grasped his arms and contorted his limbs behind his back. He gritted his teeth and twisted in vain. Their grip held firm, and his futile struggling shot a sharp pain between his shoulder blades.

Behind him at the top of the stairs, Seryn heard the school's main entryway doors creak open. He craned toward the portal, but the men restrained him.

"Seryn Vardan, you're under arrest for the murder of the king."

What? Murder? "Wait! This is a mistake!" They silenced him with a gag and yanked a hood over his head. The captors lifted Seryn by the armpits, hauling him away as his boot tips scraped the cobblestone. An unseen third accomplice shackled his ankles as well.

Seryn tried to talk, to yell, to scream, but the gag muffled his attempts.

The king is dead? Absurd. He can't be dead!

Yet, the reality of his situation told him otherwise. *Maybe he is dead…*

Seryn felt his legs being lifted. *Surely they'll find out it wasn't me! I spent all day at study.*

With a toss, his captors dumped him into a wagon.

As the wheels bounced on the worn cobblestones, Seryn suffered every bump. Fearing his destination, he nonetheless yearned for the excruciating ride to end. But the route seemed long and winding. *Should have reached the Wizard's Tower by now.*

The wheel vibrations changed tone and the bumpy cobbles disappeared. *So they're not taking me to the tower dungeon?* Through the cracks in the carriage bottom, Seryn detected the faint sound of water. *We're crossing the Jade.*

Moments later, the cart returned to the unforgiving cobblestone. *We've rolled long enough to reach the outer ramparts,* he surmised. *If we haven't gone in circles, that is.*

Seryn's head lolled forward as the wagon lurched to a stop. A door opened, and, with a shove and a shuffle, the night air disappeared. *We're indoors.*

A stairway came without warning, and his aimless feet bounced on the descending steps. His pendulum mind swung back and forth.

Maybe these men aren't guards.

They're not taking me to the gaol.

Maybe I'll never see Ioma again.

I just need to talk to someone.

Anyone. Father. Even Valin.

Though Seryn's tender face still ached from the wrath of his sibling's blows.

He may hate me, but he won't let me be falsely accused. Regicide is certain death.

A metal door clanked and a squealing lock rotated. They left him shackled, with the hood and soggy gag in place.

Sometime during the interminable night, exhaustion overtook Seryn. He slumped to his side on the cell floor as slumber dragged him into a cauldron of nightmares.

He awoke stiff and achy to the sound of a female voice whispering his name.

"Seryn? Is that you?" The voice sounded familiar. "Uh-hung," he grunted, straining against the wet gag while nodding his hooded head.

"Don't worry," she said. "I'll get you out."

Seryn finally recognized the voice—his instructor from the academy. *She must have seen me being dragged away.*

He could hardly believe it. *Illuminae Lothyrn!*

Loud voices outside the wagon in the Kierawaith snapped Seryn from his recollection, dissolving the twelve-year-old memories of his first abduction. Seryn strained to hear the conversation through the plank walls. *They're right outside,* he realized. *Two of them.* An aroma of cooked meat wafted to Seryn's nose. *And they're eating. The bastards.* His empty stomach rumbled in jealousy while his deprived body shivered.

"Don't know why we ain't moving," a man said from the opposite side of Seryn's wall. "Those filthy grimions are still out there. Can feel 'em watchin' us."

Seryn recognized the voice of the first guard who tackled him. *Sodding redheaded lout. Two more steps and I would have escaped.*

"Horses need rest. We've no choice. Besides, the raiders won't regroup that quickly."

Don't recognize that voice. Seryn craned toward the sound, placing his ear against a crate.

"It's that bloody unnatural; I'm sure of it," the redhead replied.

Now what are they blaming me for? He slid his bottom on the rough floorboards to inch closer.

"Sure of what?"

"Them grimions—they've something to do with that mage."

Ignorant fools and their stupid superstitions. Seryn shook his head.

"Think so?"

"Worked this route for years. Never been attacked like that."

That part I can believe—I've not seen a grimion raiding party

29

this far south, either.

"Raiders was probably lookin' fer the warlock," redbeard said.

Why the devil would grimions be looking for me, you dolt?

"So ye think we're carrying live bait?" A hand banged on the wagon outside Seryn's ear. He jolted back in surprise.

Devil take me, I'm jumpy.

"Nothin' good can come of us keepin' an unnatural with us. He's sure to bring trouble."

Your wagons filled with Dwarven valuables would certainly never interest raiders. Seryn bit his gag. *Best blame the bloody mage instead.*

"No reason to keep him alive," the redhead stated through a mouth full of food. "We'll have to tend him and feed him and waste valuable cargo space on him."

Seryn ground his teeth and snorted. *Sodding rot.*

"Cap'n would hang us if we killed him."

Why does the captain care if I live? Seryn wondered. *Not that he's doing much to keep me alive.* He trembled in agony. *At this rate, I'll either freeze to death or die of starvation. Or both.*

"That's 'cause Cap'n will be the one getting the reward. That greedy bastard don't share. Killin' the unnatural's takin' gold from Cap'n's pocket, and he'd flay us for it."

"Only if his death was obvious," the redheaded guard said.

Guess I won't be eating anything they *give me.*

"Ye got something in mind?"

"Plenty of ways for a man to die in his sleep."

Starvation and freezing come to mind. Seryn fidgeted, and his frustration mounted. *I need to escape. I've no sympathizers here.* He tasted the leather gag wedged in his mouth and pushed at it with his tongue. *Not yet, at least, though, if I were to have a few words with someone, it would be a start.*

"Maybe we could help him 'escape.' Unnaturals been known to disappear."

Not when they're bound and gagged. Though, it's a trick I'd love to know.

"Not a bad idea. Dump him and wash our hands of it," the redhead replied. "But I don't like him going missing on our watch. Cap'n would tan our hides if we lost him."

The men fell quiet as Seryn's mind raced. *I've got to devise something quick.*

"Does he bring a bigger bounty if he's still alive?"

"Can't imagine the king bein' happy if he's deprived of a public spectacle."

The king?

"Think he's truly the kingslayer?"

By the devil, the bastards know who I am!

"Doubt it. But beheadin' any unnatural still thrills the mob."

"We could leave his head fer the king, but take his hands fer our safety."

"Aye—no chance o' castin' spells without his hands—shackles or no."

Seryn heard a distant shout, and the conversation halted as the men answered the call. *They're preparing to leave.* He slumped against the crates as his heart raced. *Disfigurement, disgrace and death.* His body's dull ache transformed into a spreading numbness. *They're taking me to Dwim-Halloe and there's nothing I can do about it.* Through his flaring nostrils, Seryn released a pent-up sigh. *Brother, I'm coming home.*

If I make it that far.

Chapter Three

Bloated clouds draped the crescent moon and a lazy breeze danced with the campfire smoke. Jetsam crept away from the circled wagons with the guards' ominous words rattling in his head. *Caravan's going to Dwim-Halloe,* he realized. *And they think Seryn's the kingslayer.* Jetsam swallowed a wad of phlegm as he completed another cautious step up the hillside. *They're taking him there to die.*

Despite his eavesdropping discovery, Jetsam focused on heeding his mentor's teachings. "Assess, evaluate, *then* act," was one of Seryn's mantras. *Don't rush into trouble,* Jetsam told himself. *At least, not again.* But the urgency of his dilemma pressed him. *Got to figure something out—and fast.*

Jetsam and Tramp climbed a pine-forested slope and picked their way through gloomy woods. Next to a granite tor, Jetsam surveyed the mountain pass below him. *From this elevation, I can stay hidden, yet see the wagons.* Although his main concern was Seryn's well-being, Jetsam knew he must consider his own safety as well. *With Illyassa's necklace, wolves and bears will leave me alone.* Goblins and night-hunting humpbacks, he recalled, resisted the dryad's ward, and should not be underestimated.

"You'll let me know if you smell a knuckle-dragger, won't you, buddy boy?" Jetsam glanced at his short-haired terrier. Tramp wagged and licked his snout. "Or a goblin." Tramp gazed up at Jetsam and the dog's mouth stretched in a toothy yawn. "I'm tired, too, buddy boy." Jetsam scratched Tramp's head, and ran his finger through the furry ridge between his brown eyes. "Have to find a spot to bed down." From the hilltop, Jetsam cast a wistful glance at the caravan in the valley. "The wagons will be rolling at daybreak."

Though the Kierawaith will be cold, I'll burn no campfire. Boots on and fully dressed, Jetsam wrapped himself tightly in his fur blanket and cuddled with Tramp to stay warm. Curled with his furry companion, Jetsam fretted over the fruits of his dire discovery. *I can't let Seryn reach Dwim-Halloe.* He scratched Tramp's belly while he struggled for ideas, but the puzzle of freeing the captured wizard remained unsolved. *I'm too tired to figure it out tonight.* "Might as well get some shut-eye while we can, buddy boy."

But sleep eluded Jetsam as melancholy crept into his head. He obsessed over Seryn's predicament, struggling to devise a way to free him. Beleaguered by guilt, Jetsam's rash actions haunted him. *Despite my training, I failed under pressure. Oxbow soldiers! How could I have been so stupid?*

Jetsam's conscious mind dodged dreamland while recollections of Seryn's calm voice instructed him, *Control magic with your head, not your heart. Patience is the difference twixt a good wizard and a dead one. Measure your foe before casting a spell. Use magic as a last resort.* Jetsam longed for those sun-starved days inside Seryn's grotto and realized he'd disappointed his teacher. *He must be furious with me,* Jetsam lamented. *I will right this wrong. I will save him.*

Jetsam's heavy lids fluttered as he stared into the purpling sky. *Seems like just yesterday the dragon flew us to Seryn's cave. And for once in my life, the future looked bright.* Jetsam floated in a hazy half-sleep as memories of better days filled his thoughts.

The night the emerald dragon Drahkang-roth left Seryn, Jetsam, and Tramp at the sorcerer's subterranean grotto, a new stage of Jetsam's life began. While the wyrm flew back to Asigonn, Jetsam entered the battle-weary wizard's cave for the first time as a houseguest, and not an intruder.

Although Jetsam trusted Seryn more than anyone outside the

underbelly, doubts still gnawed at him. But for now, he pushed his reservations aside. *Finding Seryn Vardan is what I wanted, and I'll be damned if I don't see it through.*

Seryn lit a stout candle and ignited a fire in the central pit. Once the flames jumped to life, the mage removed the thickest bearskin from his homemade rack and cleared a spot for Jetsam to sleep.

"Tomorrow we'll build you a proper bed," he said. "I'm dog-tired, and your dog *looks* tired, so let's call this a night, shall we?"

"Yes, sir," Jetsam suspected he'd spend the evening dreaming of questions to ask in the morn. For now, his battered body demanded rest. With his snout, Tramp flicked the bearskin, slipped under the fur, and snuggled next to Jetsam. The canine snored before Jetsam stroked him thrice.

Upon awakening, Jetsam squinted at the autumn sunrise creeping through the cavern entrance. The boulder sat beside the opening and Tramp and Seryn were nowhere in sight. Jetsam leapt into his clothes and scampered outside. Seryn was collecting dry wood for Jetsam's bed. Tramp sniffed at the base of a tree before lifting a leg and claiming it as his own.

"Still willing to be my apprentice?"

"Absolutely!"

"Excellent. Been out here alone too long. Give me a hand, will you?"

The morning passed while Seryn and Jetsam crafted a functional bed frame. They used sturdy Dwarven tools Seryn recovered from Asigonn.

"What about the scroll?" Jetsam implored. "Can you tell me what it says?"

"Tonight, after dinner, we'll look at it. We must finish this frame, cut firewood, and catch something to eat. Winter'll be here soon, so we'll spend every day till then preparing."

"Can't you just finish the bed with a spell?"

"A wise mage learns to never use magic unless he has to."

"Why's that?"

"Just as a man can run only so far before he tires, a wizard can cast only so much magic until it's spent. So a wise wizard never wastes his energy on trivial endeavors, or uses it at the expense of another option."

"Couldn't you use a little magic to help make the bed, then rest up to regain your power?"

"Suppose so. But what if I saved myself a bit of hard work, and an ogre came striding over that ridge? Is it worth the risk?"

Jetsam swung his head toward the hillside, scanning the landscape for the hypothetical beast. "Guess not."

Seryn lifted the wood pieces and strolled inside the cave as Jetsam followed.

"I saw you cast a *sunblink* spell at the bounty hunter," Seryn said. "What else did you learn?"

"That's the only one. Watched Enthran cast a healing spell and a *scrying* incantation, but I was never taught them properly."

"Healing spell's a must. We'll teach you that first."

"What about scrying?" Jetsam asked.

"That one's difficult and draining. It'll be a while before you reach that level."

"Can you teach me how to make salves, like the ones I used on you and Tramp?"

"Certainly—I'll show you everything I know, and suspect I'll learn a thing or two in the process."

"What's after healing?" Jetsam trembled with anticipatory energy.

"Since you've mastered sunblink, I'll teach you the related light spells—ones that are more useful than powerful," Seryn replied.

"Like what?"

"How to create light in darkness, on the tip of your finger or the end of your staff, or anywhere at all, for that matter. You've already cast a spell as bright as the sun, but light as dim as a flickering candle can also be useful."

"So healing and light, then what's next?" Jetsam oozed eagerness from every pore. Seryn scratched his stubbly chin.

"Logically, we'd move on to fire. Generating flame's similar to creating light, and more useful, in my opinion. Not only can it let you see in darkness, but keep you warm, cook a meal, even kill an ogre."

"And after that?"

"*After* that? How about you help me finish this bed? This

lumber's heavier than it looks."

Jetsam obliged, and idled his mouth for a few moments. His mind, however, raced ahead. "Light and fire seem a good start," he said, trying to coax more information from the carpentry-obsessed conjurer.

"I suspect those alone shall keep us busy all winter, but if you mind your lessons and practice, I'd probably move on to heat manipulation next."

"Heat manipulation?"

"Using magic to turn things hot as flame or cold as ice, or anywhere in between."

"You know so much! What else can you teach me?"

"Apparently, not a single thing about building furniture!"

Jetsam flushed, embarrassed at his lack of effort. He handed Seryn a Dwarven hammer and more nails. Seryn flashed him a knowing wink.

"I spent many a year at the most eminent school of sorcery in Tythania. I was bound to learn something," Seryn said. "Let me sleep on it, and I shall prepare you a proper lesson plan, worthy of the most deserving pupil of Eh' liel Ev' Narron."

Jetsam recognized the Elven name—a splinter of recollection from his long-ago childhood.

"You studied at the School of Sorcery in Dwim-Halloe?"

"Of course," Seryn responded.

"Did you know my parents?"

"I may have. What's your real name, Jetsam?"

"Eidryn," he said timidly. It had been so long since he uttered his own name aloud. His *real* name. "Eidryn *Lothyrn*." Uttering his surname, Jetsam observed Seryn's face soften. His reaction spoke volumes.

"Yes," Seryn confessed. "I knew your parents well." His gaze fell to the cavern floor, where he set his hammer. "I'd hoped they'd survived the rebellion."

Upon shaking his head in unspoken reply, Jetsam recognized pity in his host's eyes.

"Your mother was my mentor," he said. "They were wonderful people." He bit his lip and swallowed. "I'm so sorry for your loss."

"What were they like?"

"Kind and intelligent—truly fine people. They adored their sons.

'Tis such a shame." Seryn shook his head and recalled his former illuminae. "And your brother?"

"Gone, too," Jetsam said, his face darkening.

Seryn finished assembling Jetsam's bed frame in silence.

That evening, Jetsam retrieved his scroll case and slid out the rolled parchment. Somewhat reluctantly, he handed it to Seryn.

"I recognized this the first time I looked upon it," he told Jetsam.

In a rare display of patience, Jetsam bit his tongue.

"I worked on this scroll the night of my capture. This roll holds the framework of a new elixir I was developing."

"What does it *do?*" Jetsam entreated.

"Not sure it *does* anything—never been tested, and I've not had the proper materials to concoct it. But it's supposed to make a man live longer."

Jetsam's spirits fell. Not as exciting as he'd imagined, the writings had naught to do with his parents. And a cure for old age sat far down his list of pressing concerns.

"Will it make you live *forever?*"

Not forever, no—*longer.* Perhaps as long as an elf."

"How long does an elf live?"

"Much longer than a man, or even a dwarf. Hundreds of years, it's been said. But I've never met a pure-blooded elf, so I don't know if that's true." Seryn glanced at Jetsam and fidgeted. "When you showed me this scroll in Beggar's Alley, it gave me a strange idea. I'd like to resume work on this elixir."

"You're afraid of dying?"

"I fear dying without reuniting with my true love," Seryn confessed. "But that's a story for another day. Before winter sets in, we'll travel back to Asigonn. There, I may be able to find the materials I need."

A few weeks later, Seryn, Jetsam, and Tramp set out for the ancient Dwarven halls of Asigonn. During the interminable footslog through the unforgiving Kierawaith, Seryn revealed more of his past, if for no other reason than to pass the time.

"You believe me when I say I did not kill King Tygan?"

"Of course," Jetsam assured, though a kernel of a doubt remained burrowed deep within him. "But it wouldn't bother me if you had."

Seryn stopped and grabbed Jetsam by his shoulder. "It *should*," the mage insisted. "Murder is wrong."

"Maybe he deserved it. *This* king does."

Slack jawed, Seryn stared at Jetsam for a moment before speaking. "If you think I'll train you to be an assassin, you'll be sorely disappointed," Seryn said. "I won't teach you magic just so you can kill people."

A twinge of guilt assailed Jetsam. He knew King Valin was Seryn's brother, and he spoke out of line. Jetsam didn't want to alienate his mentor with disrespect.

"I believe you," Jetsam said. "And I'm glad you're not a murderer. But what does all this have to do with the scroll of long life?"

"Longevity," Seryn corrected. "This far-fetched idea of mine might allow me to someday reunite with my love, Queen Ioma."

"You're in love with the *queen?*"

"She was only a princess, then. Her father still lived. And she loved me as well."

"Why did she marry your *brother?*"

"Valin craved the throne like nothing else. He betrayed me, for marrying Ioma was his sole avenue to the crown. And I, his only obstacle."

Jetsam reflected on his deceased twin Elvar, and failed to fathom such treachery among kin.

"I cannot harm my brother, no matter how he's wronged me," Seryn said. "I would not dishonor my parents—*all* my ancestors. Though I will not hasten his passing, I can strive to outlive him. With such a potion, Ioma and I could be reunited after his death." Seryn stared Jetsam straight in the eye. "I know in my heart I can convince her I didn't kill her father."

"Your love is strong," Jetsam remarked, befuddled by the extraordinary patience the sorcerer proposed.

"'Tis better to live a miserable existence for a half century if it allows me to spend a year, a month, or even a week with my one true love." Seryn's hazel eyes fell to the moist ground. "I realize 'tis hard for a lad to comprehend, but once you've tasted love, and had it unjustly snatched away, your heart does not know its bounds."

"I know of love," Jetsam said. "There's a lass in the Citadel. We kissed." After a flash of unexpected embarrassment, Jetsam choked up. He'd not spoken of Giselle in some time. But the longing remained. Jetsam's cheeks burned, as the flushing blood seeped in. His shyness forced a concession and he changed the subject. "How will you make her drink the potion?"

"'Twill be a challenge, no doubt. But I must first make the potion before I worry about who drinks it."

"Is that why you were in Beggar's Alley disguised as a gypsy?"

"You're sharp, lad," Seryn said. "I need to stock up from time-to-time, but also make sure I learn what's going on in Dwim-Halloe. Check up on Ioma, albeit from afar." Seryn let his words drift. "And I hoped to find ingredients in the market."

"But you didn't?"

"Found a few necessary items, but not all, no." Seryn paused for a moment. "I also returned to speak with the former lord high wizard. Thought he may be able to help me."

"He's in Dwim-Halloe, too?"

"He fled after the failed revolt and lived in an Elven tree tower far south of the city. I discovered his corpse pinned against the tree trunk, a garrock through his neck."

"What happened?" Jetsam gasped.

"Killed by a crossbowman. The bolts were the same as those fired at you in Beggar's Alley."

Jetsam furrowed his brow. "The bounty hunter?"

"Afraid so. Like most of the mages who fled Dwim-Halloe, he wore a price on his head. My brother was ruthlessly diligent in extinguishing wizardry within his kingdom."

"I *hate* your brother."

Seryn shook his head. "Do not let it consume you. Hate can turn a true heart sour."

"But he's *ruined* our lives!"

"While we still breathe, our lives are not lost. We've the power to change things. But not with hatred. That kind of retribution will transform you into your enemy."

Jetsam gritted his teeth. He idolized Seryn, yet found this lesson difficult to accept. His wounded heart longed for vengeance.

"Tis difficult to heed my advice—I understand. But I've struggled with this battle longer than you, and my words are true. I've seen good men succumb to evil, starting with just one wrong step."

Jetsam swallowed hard. His heart drummed faster.

"Do not mistake me—justice *must* be served. But there's a difference betwixt doing what is right and blind submission to vengeance. Even though the end may be the same, the *reason* for your actions matters."

Jetsam gnawed his cheek. Though it vexed him, Seryn's logic irritated him. Yet, he acknowledged his mentor to be wise, and deep down, suspected Seryn was correct. He imagined Elvar agreeing with the sorcerer.

"I've lectured you enough today. Dwell on what I've said," Seryn instructed. "We'll reach the ruins soon, and I need you focused to help me search for the components I need."

"We can find these ingredients in Asigonn?"

"I hope so. They're essences the Dwarves may have possessed."

"What is it you need?"

"For one, I need powdered Eidulaar stone, which I hope to find in Asigonn—not powdered, of course. We'll do that ourselves."

"What's this rock look like?"

"A dark reddish stone with veins of goldish-orange. 'Tis quite rare, and found only deep underground. The Dwarves valued it highly."

"What else?" Jetsam compiled a mental list.

"Well, ideally, Elves' blood. But Dwarves' blood should also provide an anti-aging effect, just not as strong."

"But there are no Dwarves left in Asigonn."

"True, but perhaps I can scrape some marrow from a skeleton bone, at least to experiment with."

"That all?"

"I'll also need Sylallian pine sap and Elderberry pollen, which we'll have to wait until the spring blossom to harvest."

"Zounds! I hope that's everything."

"Enough to start with, at least. I expect a fair bit of trial and error."

"Say you find everything and mix your elixir, how will you *test* it?"

"An excellent question! I'll try it on Mayflies—they live brief lives, and are plentiful in the wet Kierawaith lowlands. Extending one's life to more than a few days would be an accomplishment."

"And you'd only need a tiny drop of elixir."

"Exactly," Seryn remarked. "Don't want to waste our precious ingredients."

Jetsam contemplated this plan as they trudged on in silence. He noticed the gloomy day darken even more. Shadows raced to cover the ground. Then Tramp stopped and growled.

Upon following the dog's gaze skyward, Jetsam gasped. The flood of darkness was not a black cloud, but rather the shading wings of a descending dragon. He swallowed hard and grabbed Seryn by his shoulder.

By the time Seryn comprehended the flying creature, Jetsam recognized the wyrm. *This close to Asigonn, it could be no other.* Yet, the specter of a soaring behemoth never failed to startle—regardless of your familiarity with the airborne lizard.

The emerald wyrm landed with the grace of a butterfly in a clearing half a furlong away. Tramp barked, and emitted another low growl. Jetsam hushed his little guardian and hurried along with Seryn to the landing spot.

"Greetings," Drahkang-roth growled in the voice of harnessed thunder.

"To what do we owe the honor?" Seryn inquired, a hint of nervousness in his tone.

"I ask the same of you," the one-eyed dragon rumbled. "Did not expect you near Asigonn so soon, yet your presence saves me a trip to your grotto."

"Afraid I don't understand. Were you looking for *us?*"

"I caught a familiar scent on the wind, and recognized you. I've news to share," Drahkang-roth said. "I am leaving Asigonn."

"*Why?*" Jetsam interjected.

"My lair is no longer a secret. Someday, your incantation will wear off," the dragon eyed Seryn as she rumbled, "and the squire will tell his story. Then more hunters will come. Once a dragon's lair has been discovered by one man, it is soon known by all."

"I assure you, great wyrm, the spell I cast on the squire will hold. His mind was ripe with fear, and the subliminal suggestion I planted took root."

"Seryn's as fine a wizard there is!" Jetsam said.

"'Tis true thou art a talented sorcerer, yet I understand the greedy hearts of men. 'Tis a chance I will not take. I've overstayed my welcome and my wanderlust grows unbearable."

"There is safety in numbers," Seryn replied. "I keep a keen eye for intruders, and always have your back."

"Your deeds shan't be forgotten, and I am forever grateful. But my mind is made. I leave on the morrow." Seryn and Jetsam gaped at the marvelous specimen, the melancholy of her impending departure just now setting in.

"We shall drink to our friendship this eve, and send you off with a toast," Seryn said. "We're heading to Asigonn to search for a rare stone I require."

"Then you shall be granted a final ride on these wings." Drahkang-roth lowered a flap for the three to climb on. In an instant, Jetsam once again flew high over the Kierawaith. The dizzying flight lasted but a short while, as Asigonn sat nearby. The descent through the collapsed dome of the legendary Dwarven hall stole Jetsam's breath.

"With your permission, great wyrm, we shall camp with you tonight," Seryn said.

"Granted," the gravel-throated voice replied.

"With your absence, these empty halls will teem with trolls and grimions and goblins," Seryn noted, more to himself than Drahkang-roth.

"The world is filled with vermin," the wyrm warned. "If you wish, tell the Dwarves their hall is empty, should they care to return."

Seryn rubbed his chin, as Jetsam fed Tramp by the hospitable flames.

"'Tis a rather excellent idea," Seryn said, warming his clammy hands by the flame. "The Dwarves may be grateful to hear the news. And I'd much rather have them for neighbors."

With the brimstone snoring of the slumbering lizard queen, the trio slept warmly in the ancient stone hall. True to her word, at dawn Drahkang-roth departed without flourish. With subdued fanfare, Jetsam and Seryn bid her farewell, while Tramp remained guarded. Sunlight trickled through the ruptured stonework as Jetsam gazed in wonderment at the flying wyrm disappearing into the morning sky.

"Let us break fast and begin the search," Seryn instructed.

"Do you think Drahkang-roth spoke true?" Jetsam wondered. "Will Kandris tell others about the dragon? About *us?*"

"I'm confident of my spell—but there are no guarantees. Drahkang-roth is wise, and though I cannot second guess her, I hope she's wrong."

"What if she *is* right? What if more men hunt us?"

"Men were coming for me long before Kandris Bayen and his ill-fated cronies stumbled upon Asigonn. As long as my brother keeps a bounty on my head, men will search for me. That is something you must consider. You've made a risky decision in staying with me."

"I'd be dead if not for you."

"And I the same."

As the explorers picked through Dwarven debris, searching for Seryn's ingredients, they worked their way outward from the dragon-renovated atrium.

"Asigonn's layout defies symmetry," Seryn explained. "Tunnels follow the mineral veins. Once a vein tapped out, stoneworkers followed the miners and converted the wormholes into halls and chambers."

Further from the central dome, they located remnants of Dwarven occupancy. Close enough to the great hall to have kept monsters and looters away, these rooms remained untouched since the Dwarven exile.

"When the ebony wyrm attacked the Dwarves, his breath scorched every passageway off the great hall." Wooden doors and furniture stood blistered and charred. "Although the Dwarves fled for their lives, they were not folk who left valuables behind." Seryn and Jetsam located little that proved salvageable in any branching room.

Although they eventually discovered sundry clothes and housewares in long-abandoned shelves and dressers, there was nary a valuable to be found. *Nor any of Seryn's ingredients,* Jetsam realized. By the end of a long day of fruitless trudging, the trio reached the outer radius of Asigonn. For Jetsam, the novelty of exploring the ruins expired hours ago.

"I'm afraid our search has not been rewarding," Seryn bemoaned. "We shall return home."

Jetsam recognized Seryn's thinly-veiled disappointment. Even with a stiff upper lip, there was no concealing the mage's dashed hopes.

"About what the dragon said," Jetsam asked. "Are you *really* going to tell the Dwarves?" The possibility of an excursion with his mentor thrilled him.

"I must," Seryn replied. "With my dreadful luck here, I still need to find ingredients, so a trip to *Qar Asigonn* seems prudent."

"*Qar* Asigonn?"

"Yes, the fleeing Dwarves built a new—*qar*—Asigonn far west of here, in a forested area near a river."

"How do you know?"

"The Dwarves require an abundance of timber and water for mining. They're necessities of the trade."

Jetsam nodded as Seryn continued. "It'll be a long journey, but we risk the safety of our grotto if monsters inhabit Asigonn. Those abominations breed and spawn like wildfire, and an abandoned Dwarven stronghold is a perfect lair for them."

"I'm going with you, of course," Jetsam insisted. "And Tramp."

"I expected as much, and welcome the company."

"Never seen a dwarf," Jetsam confessed. "You?"

"Encountered a few over the years. Gruff—no nonsense. But good folk, for certain."

"They as short as they say?"

"Indeed. You already tower over the tallest of them." Jetsam was lanky, but still growing. He'd gained an inch over the long winter, and now stood nearly even with the sorcerer. "But one weighs as much as three of you. They're mostly muscle, with a bit of belly."

"Can't wait to see Dwarves. When do we leave?"

"As soon as winter breaks."

"But that's months away."

"True, but early spring's a difficult enough time to travel."

"What's Qar Asigonn like?"

"No idea—don't even know quite where it is."

Chapter Four

The first captor Seryn saw was the redheaded guard. The pie-faced man peered through the open hatch with a lantern in hand while Seryn glared back. Flickering light cast shadows across the guard's pale face. *Could I ram him with my head and slip out?* The soldier appeared imposing, his frame filling the opening. *Devil take me, I can't even stand, much less knock him over, climb out, and run away.*

"Probably gotta piss by now, don't ye?"

Still bound and gagged, Seryn nodded as he shivered. *Though, the warmth might feel nice if I go right here.*

"Use this." The guard dropped a rattling pail at Seryn's feet. Seryn's brow furrowed as he stared at the man. "Slip yer hands under yer arse and around yer feet. I'll not hold it for ye." *I've already tried that maneuver, you dolt,* Seryn thought. *There's no room here for contortions.* The guard watched and waited, so Seryn struggled to prove a point. He managed to get his bound wrists under his rump before the binds caught on his boot heels and he listed to the side. *Still can't do it.*

"Not very agile, are ye? Lemme help." The redhead climbed in and manhandled Seryn enough so he could pull his shackled hands from back to front. The experience was not without pain.

"Ye're shivering," the guard said. "Thought unnaturals were cold-blooded."

Seryn shook his head, his eyes pleading for mercy while his mind admonished the guard. *You're dumb as a stump, aren't you?*

"Use the pail," the red-beard said. "I've orders not ta let ye out, and I don't want ye smearin' shite all over the wagon." When Seryn didn't move, the watchman reached for the pail. "Guess ye don't need to go."

Seryn grunted and shook his head, fumbling with his shackled wrists to drop his trousers. *Bloody devil, you're going to stand there and watch, aren't you?* Seryn's strained bowels and bladder held no shame as he squatted and filled the pail.

"I'll see if I can find ye a blanket," the guard replied as Seryn pulled his trousers up. "Now, step back over yer wrists and get yer hands behind your back." Seryn complied, but tumbled sideways into the crates as he stepped on his wrist irons.

"Clumsy sod," the guard scolded as he yanked Seryn's bound hands over his knees and across his boots. Seryn grunted in agony. "Yer useless without yer spells, ain't ye?"

The guard left Seryn crumpled in a ball and locked the wagon's door.

Take the stinking bucket, you oaf! But he didn't. *At least it's warm,* Seryn lamented while praying for the redhead to return with a blanket. *A bit of food wouldn't hurt, either, though this pail may suffice in ruining my appetite.*

Seryn moved his thumbs into his palms, curling his hands tight and strained against his shackles, twisting his contorted hands, trying to pull them through the irons. *Even if I broke my thumbs, I couldn't slip out of these.* The tight clamps claimed more of his chaffed skin, stripping his wrists bloody. He relented to the pain and abandoned the effort. *Try something else.*

Seryn slid his jaw and bit down on his leather gag. He ground his teeth against the cowhide, struggling to sink an incisor in. *I'm sure I could chew through it—eventually.* He worked against the restraint until his jaw ached and a cramp stabbed him from ear to chin. *But it'll take weeks, not days.*

Exhaustion overtook Seryn as he huddled hungry and shivering, waiting for the guard's return. He fell into a fitful sleep where memories from two decades past appeared as though they were yesterday's recollections.

"Valin, I've heard from Illuminae Daystar about your lack of attention," Duke Daelis Vardan scolded his son. "Though wizardry's a frivolous pursuit, a knight must know his foes." Ten-year-old Seryn's ears pricked at his father's choice of words. *Frivolous?*

"Just like a goblin or an ogre, you must study every opponent you may face," Daelis said. "No more complaints from your teacher. Understood?"

"Yes, Father." Young Valin looked up from his breakfast with puppy-dog eyes.

"Father?" Seryn asked.

"What now, boy?" The harsh reply caused Seryn to debate continuing, yet his youthful enthusiasm pushed him onward.

"Why do you think magic's frivolous? Illuminae—,"

"Illuminae Daystar's a charlatan—just like the ones that tried to save your mother," Daelis said. "Had the Reaper given me the choice, I would have kept *her* alive." Duke Vardan left the long table in a huff, his half-finished plate abandoned mid-meal.

"Today's Mother's birthday," Valin told his younger brother. "I'd steer clear of father if I were you," he said. "'Tis not a day he handles well."

I'm the last person in the world who needs that advice.

"He'll never forgive you for killing her," Valin taunted.

I didn't kill Mother, Seryn steeled himself. *Not on purpose.* He bit his tongue, trembling on the inside over the familiar accusation.

"Father never needed you," Valin said. "I'm his heir, and will become a knight and a noble and rule Vardenvaard one day."

Seryn ground his teeth. It was not the first time he'd endured this abuse. *And I'm certain it won't be the last.* Seryn avoided his brother's aggressive gaze. *Taunt me all you wish, for you shan't spoil this day for me.* The news Seryn bottled inside was bursting to escape. Thanks to Valin, he'd botched his opportunity at breakfast. *Now I must wait till dinner to tell father.* Seryn imagined informing his father, and couldn't wait to see the look on Valin's face. *Fill his breeches, he will.*

The specter of his mother's birthday hovered in Seryn's consciousness. *She'd be proud of me, I bet.* He clung to the stories their housekeeper had told him about their mother, Aleese. Alma's warm recollections countered the versions recited by Seryn's father and brother.

If only Father would speak of Mother, what stories he could tell.

"Bloody spellcasting's no use to me," Valin said, now that Daelis stormed out of ear shot. "Stupid Elvish words. Nobody talks like that anymore. Give me a good blade and I'll lop off your head ere you cast a single spell."

"'Tis not so difficult," Seryn replied. "I could help with your studies, if you wish."

The offer brought Valin's hand across the back of Seryn's head.

"Bore-ring," the older brother yawned. "A knight doesn't need Elven rhymes and finger dances to vanquish foes." Valin waved his hands and twitched his fingers mockingly.

"You'd be surprised at the spells you can cast," Seryn said. *Like turning you into a toad, perhaps.* He smiled at the thought. "'Tis truly fascinating if you give it a chance."

"Just begging for it, aren't you? First you anger Father, and now me. Wait till we're out in the yard. I'll break my practice blade on your skull." Valin chewed his lip. "Then mayhaps I'll get a *real* sword."

Mayhaps there's a spell to turn you into a slug.

Alma strode in, impatient as ever, and ushered them off to their lessons and out of *her* dining room.

"Waste of time, being chained to a desk every day. Much rather spend my days outdoors," Valin opined. "Archery, riding, falconry, weaponry. Those are the true studies for young lords."

The true studies for dumb *lords, perhaps.* Seryn kept his sarcasm bottled. *Speaking my thoughts aloud will only earn me another cuff, at best.* They would study inside for hours before getting to swing wooden swords in the practice yard. *Hope Valin cools off by then,* Seryn wished, yet he feared it was in vain.

A clanking lock awoke Seryn from his vivid childhood dream. The aroma of hot stew overpowered the stink of his excrement bucket and taunted his empty stomach. The rusty-haired guard stood offering a steamy mug. "Mostly broth," he said, presenting Seryn the stew. A second eagle-eyed guard stood outside the hatch, mace in hand, ready for any tricks.

They want me dead, Seryn remembered. *Could be poisoned.*

Seryn took the cup in his shackled hand anyway. *Nice and warm.* He stared at the guard and tilted his head. *I can't inhale it, genius.*

"I'll undo your gag."

I could toss the stew in his face and choke him with my chains, Seryn contemplated. *But his cohort would pummel me senseless.* Seryn eyed the armed sentry as his companion unfastened the gag. Seryn pushed the leather out with his tongue and licked his dry lips. *I'd never get a spell off in time, either,* he realized.

"You never brought me a blanket," Seryn said to the guard. "If you want to keep me alive to Dwim-Halloe, you shouldn't let me freeze to death."

"Just drink up. If I knew ye were so talkative, I'd of left ye gagged."

Seryn shook his head in refusal even as his insides rumbled in opposition.

"Fine," the redhead grumbled as he reached for the mug. "Believe it or not, I don't care if ye die. Starve or freeze, makes me no never-mind."

"We won't see a copper of that reward anyhow," said the mace-wielding watchman.

Seryn pulled the mug close and sniffed. *Don't smell any poison.* He glanced at the guard and caught his gaze.

"Think I'd waste a mug o' stew just ta poison ye? Easier ways ta kill ye then spoil precious food." He snatched the mug from Seryn, spilling hot liquid on both their hands. The redhead took a swig of the stew and swallowed it. "There," he replied, handing the mug back to Seryn. "Satisfied?"

I need to keep my strength, Seryn rationalized. *And it does smell good.* Upon draining the cup, Seryn wished they'd given him more. The guard took the empty mug from Seryn and refastened his gag. "Hold still, unnatural."

As the guard turned to leave, he groaned and crumpled to the wagon floor, clutching his stomach. Doubled-over on his knees, he stared at Seryn as if he'd seen a ghost. "Poison!" the redhead said.

Eyes wide, Seryn's hope vanished as he braced for the onslaught to his own system. *I should have known better.*

Then the red-beard rose to his feet and burst into laughter.

"Ye should of seen yer face, unnatural!" Both guards roared. "Ye thought ye was gonna die!" The redhead smacked his companion in the shoulder. "Wart's cookin' is horrible, but it ain't enough ta kill a man!" Tears rolled down his face. Seryn listened to their laughter as they left him locked in the dark.

Sodding fools. Enjoy your joke—you forgot to put my hands behind my back.

With his wrists bound together, Seryn lifted his hands over and behind his head and tried to loosen the gag strapped around his face. *If I can get this off, I can cast a spell.* With elbows over his ears, he struggled with the leather, stretching his fingers and twisting his wrists, yet the shackles prevented him from releasing the secure gag. *Bloody thing's on tight as a gold-lender.* Seryn wrestled with the restraint until his numb fingers burned raw and the irons scraped the remaining skin from his bloodied wrists. *I'll try again later when I regain some strength.*

With a pint of warm stew inside him and his head resting on his forearms, Seryn fell asleep once again feeling the victim. His troublesome dreams returned him to his youth.

The young Vardan brothers' weaponry instructor—Master Urry—was a dour old sod—the perfect temperament for curtailing the wandering minds of boys. A hoarse bulldog, Urry barked orders and pushed and pulled the lads like rag dolls, yet a more prestigious instructor Duke Vardan could not have found outside the Oxbows.

And, of course, the boys feared Master Urry.

"Today, more trainin' with the faux-longsword," Urry told them. "Grab yon pokin' sticks," he said, pointing at a battered weapon rack. "Ye'll practice combining the guards and steps into strikes, and how to defend 'em. Valin, ye'll start on the attack." The elder Vardan brother grinned ear-to-ear.

"Now, watch and repeat." With his own steel sword, Urry demonstrated the cross strike. The boys mimicked their instructor. "Again!"

After endless repetitions of slicing air, Urry paired the brothers against each other. Valin's gray eyes wide, he held his sword high, the wooden blade angled back. With a step, he brought the sword across his body, with the dulled tip swinging toward Seryn's head.

Seryn countered a shade slower. In trying to slide his strike under Valin's, he failed to protect himself. His mind drifted elsewhere as he rehearsed the important proclamation he'd reveal at dinner.

Like thunder, Valin's oak stick slapped the daydreaming Seryn.

"Ouch!" The iron helmet rang like a bell, stinging his skull and ringing his ears.

"Again!"

"Headless hobgoblin," Seryn said under his breath.

Once more, Valin proved quicker. He delivered his cross-strike to Seryn's padded ribs. Seryn dropped to the dirt, gasping for air. *Can't wait for this to end.*

"Shoulders too tense, Seryn," Urry said. "Yer grip is wrong. 'Tis a blade, not a hammer! Now get up!"

And so it went. For every three strikes Valin landed, Seryn was lucky to score a single hit. *Classroom smarts hold little sway out here in the yard,* Seryn lamented. *And Valin relishes nothing more than proving it.* True to his word, Valin battered and bruised Seryn even more than usual during the day's training.

Exhausted and aching, the thrill of the good news he wished to share all but evaporated. *They won't care anyway,* he told himself, while secretly hoping they'd prove him wrong.

"Father was a knight," Valin said, as they left the training yard.

For the hundredth time, I know already, Seryn thought. *I've heard the bloody story enough.*

"He fought the Grimlord's beasts with sword and shield."

"Wizards battled the Grimlord, too," Seryn rebuked, rubbing his bruised shoulder.

"They just distracted the stupid grimions and goblins with noises and lights while the knights did the *real* fighting," Valin responded. Chest out, Valin swaggered.

"Illuminae Daystar says the wizards *won* the battle," Seryn said. "Illuminae—,"

"Daystar's a charlatan—just like Father said. That old elf-lover just likes to hear himself talk. Probably hid in the library while Father hacked the heads off goblins." Valin strode a step ahead, as if reaching Vardenvaard first stood as another victory to claim.

Can't get a word in edgewise in this family.

"Father has a *medal* from the war. Betcha your *boyfriend* Daystar doesn't own a medal."

"*Illuminae* Daystar," Seryn corrected. "And if you paid attention, you'd know he's a hero."

"Smoke and mirrors," Father says. "Just old Elven tricks."

Incensed, Seryn tackled his unsuspecting sibling, yanking him to the ground and scrambling on top of him. They wrestled on the unforgiving cobblestone alley, rolling and grappling. Seryn's fresh bruises came to life, yet his fury hushed their screams.

"Liar," Seryn shouted. His surprise attack gave him the advantage as he pulled Valin into a head-lock. "Take it back!" With his hand gripping his brother's scalp, he squeezed Valin's neck in the crook of his elbow.

The elder boy squirmed, his face burning crimson. Seryn could almost feel the heat.

"Take it back, liar!" he repeated, trying to tighten his grip while his tired muscles burned, and Valin's ire weakened his hold.

A fierce elbow to Seryn's sore ribs allowed Valin to slip free. He rolled his younger sibling, squirming from Seryn's grasp and climbing atop him.

"You little bastard," Valin said, punching his brother. Seryn's head snapped back, his skull bouncing off the stone pavement. "Don't you ever think you can beat *me!*" Valin cocked his arm again, eyeing Seryn's nose.

"Enough!" Daelis bellowed. The roar halted Valin, his arm still raised. Seryn lifted his lids to see his father striding from the manor. Valin's punching arm twitched. Grabbing his eldest son by the wrist, Daelis yanked Valin to his feet.

Head throbbing and heart pounding, Seryn held back tears. Though his father dangled Valin by his arm, his fierce gaze burned through Seryn. *I've endured enough abuse.* Seryn twisted his joyous news into a venomous dagger, jabbing in the last word, and relishing its bite. "I got accepted to *Eh' liel Ev' Narron!*" Seryn shouted. "I'm going to be a wizard!"

Chapter Five

Jetsam awoke with a start, and Tramp with him. Jetsam's teeth chattered as men's voices floated up the ridge from the wagon troupe. His frosty nose sniffed the pinewood smoke from the doused campfires. Beneath dawn's hazy half-light, the caravan began to mobilize.

After yanking back his blanket, Jetsam lifted Tramp's toasty frame off his lap, and eased from his cubby. Tramp stretched lazily and shook off the night's sleep. The dense-coated canine seemed less affected by the morning chill than Jetsam. The infringing cold seeped into his shivering bones. *Moving about will warm me.* He rubbed his gloved hands vigorously and wiggled his icicle toes. A short-tailed shrew scurried past his leathered feet, scampering across the forest floor.

A slender shadow, Jetsam packed his makeshift camp, ready for another monotonous day of trailing Seryn's captors. The little-used trail the caravan followed would prove slow going until it intersected the Serpentine Pass. Jetsam surmised the wagons must be laden with valuables to make such a treacherous journey. *I can learn their routine, maybe spot a time when they're vulnerable.* As of yet, Jetsam didn't even know which wagon held his mentor.

Hidden amongst the shimmering columns of an aspen colony, Jetsam's sleepy eyes adjusted to the breaking daylight. From a safe distance, he studied the caravan's every move. After the grimion attack, only four wagons remained, each pulled by a quartet of draft horses. The mountain terrain, altitude, and heavy loads necessitated four horses per cart, and even then, the beasts of burden earned their oats.

Jetsam noted which wagon each guard returned to after he made his water. *Each cart carries one protector, along with a wagon master.* Jetsam deduced the most prodigious and ornate coach held the trader. He speculated *that* wagon least likely contained Seryn. *Wonder who the girl is, and why she's on such a dangerous journey.* He'd but glimpsed her since the grimion assault. "Maybe she's the merchant's daughter," he mumbled to Tramp.

As Jetsam tracked and scrutinized, Tramp followed, scouring the hillside for scents, never letting Jetsam out of his sight. Jetsam's gaze followed the wagon trail as it climbed eastward above the timberline. The disintegrating conifer canopy would allow warming sunlight to reach him. *If only the clouds would cooperate.* As it was, gray winds nipped at Jetsam's exposed skin and ruffled the short fur on Tramp's back.

Jetsam watched the caravan the entire day, memorizing the patterns of the guards and passengers. He inspected the horses from afar, assigned them names to help keep them straight. *Not sure what good that'll do.* But it passed the time and kept his conscious mind busy, allowing his subconscious the unenviable task of divining a solution to his conundrum.

When the sun slid behind the mountains, the caravan stopped for the night. Jetsam decided to investigate closer. He carried Tramp, not wanting to leave the dog alone in the Kierawaith. "We'll not separate, buddy boy," he said. Once the sentry manned their posts and the rest huddled around the campfire, Jetsam slunk toward the wagon circle. He located a decent hiding spot behind a thick hemlock stand, keeping as far from the guards as practical. From this position, he examined the wagons he'd trailed from a distance.

The caravan was a hodgepodge of different wagons, though all carried a cover, either of canvas or wood. Little cabins on wheels, they were designed for transport, not comfort. Some featured rear-loading gates, while others had ramp-doors on the sides. All appeared to be buttoned tight, keeping their cargo hidden from prying eyes. The windows, if any, were small and barred.

Still and quiet, he viewed the travelers eating. He noticed the girl, illuminated starkly by the firelight, sitting next to a man who Jetsam surmised must be the trader. His attire and demeanor set him above the rest. He shouted directions at the cook, and received his meal first, along with the lass. When they finished eating, the man and girl retreated to the ornate six-wheeled wagon. *I was right!*

Then Jetsam observed the redheaded guard fill a tin cup with porridge from the kettle. The bearded watchman disappeared inside a smaller four-wheeled wagon, and in a few minutes, returned with the empty cup.

Seryn's inside.

Jetsam engrained the covered cart's every detail into his memory; he would not lose track of the one carrying his mentor. *This one's smaller, with no windows and solid wheels—the rear larger than the front.* A strip of riveted Dwarven iron ringed each wheel. It proved a rudimentary—but sturdy—design, no doubt built with mountain hauling in mind. The haul cart's ruggedness also meant Jetsam identified no weak points. A hefty wheeled strongbox, this fortified wagon and its locked doors would not prove an easy breach. *I'll find a way,* he promised himself, not fully convinced. Eyes closed, he reconstructed the wagon in his head, piece by piece. Satisfied he could identify this wagon blindfolded, he scanned the campsite.

Jetsam tallied the passengers. Six guards and five coachmen survived the grimion attack, along with the captain. Jetsam also counted the trader, the girl, the cook, and what appeared to be a few other civilians. *Roughly a dozen and a half. Won't be easy getting him out of there.* One of the duty sentries stood outside the wagon that Jetsam earmarked as Seryn's. It was the copper-beard.

I'll need a peek inside. Watching and waiting, Jetsam devised a plan. He set Tramp at his feet and whispered "stay," then pulled out his sling and loaded a stone. With a flick of his wrist, the polished pebble sliced through the air and into the trunk of a stunted poplar, twenty paces in front of the sentry. With a hollow *thunk,* the projectile grabbed the guard's attention.

The redhead lit a torch, and with a low whistle, directed the other watchman toward him. Heads low, they approached the dead poplar, swords drawn. The guards plodded in the brush, squinting in the flickering illumination for the source of the noise, poking with their weapons, occupied for the time being.

Jetsam scooped Tramp up and crept toward the wagon. He approached from the front, and peered over the driver's seat. He placed Tramp on the wood plank and whispered "sit." Tramp complied and watched his partner join him. With a nimble hop and nary a sound, Jetsam climbed aboard the rig. Behind the coachman's bench, there sat a small door. Jetsam reached for the latch.

Locked. With no windows, the wagon was sealed tight. He wanted to get a glimpse of his mentor, but the locked door all but ensured Seryn sat inside. Tramp sniffed at the door and emitted a low whine. "*Quiet,* boy."

With a glance at the preoccupied sentry, Jetsam hopped from the wagon. His momentary diversion expired, and the guards' curiosity had sated. He lifted the sniffing dog from the wagon and slunk away.

As Jetsam retreated, sleep beckoned him. The evening grew late, and the wagons would roll at daybreak. He picked his way through the rocky landscape until he reached a safe distance from the caravan. Behind a low outcropping, he curled up with Tramp, fighting the cold till slumber took him. But before it did, he heard the shriek.

Tramp barked at the familiar noxious scent, the hairs on his back rigid spikes.

A moment later, Jetsam recognized the odor, too.

Knuckle-draggers!

To his dying day, Jetsam would be able to identify a troll instantly. Even if he lost his sense of smell, the imagery of the sunken eyes, misshapen skull, and raking claws—all wrapped in a gangly, humpbacked frame—forever etched in his memory. *One of my many curses.*

Despite the chill, troglodyte-induced sweat seeped from his pores. On his feet, Jetsam peered at the caravan. In the dark, he discerned only shadowy forms. By their size and shape, he identified several trolls. *A whole pack.*

Once again, the fated caravan fell under attack, and the cacophony soon reached Jetsam's ears. Terror rang out in shouts and screams. Horses stamped and pulled. A wagon sat overturned, a guard lay dismembered. Reminiscent of two days prior, chaos reigned. This time, Jetsam froze in place.

The speed at which the attackers tore through the guards astounded him. Jetsam recalled the Gaalf River ambush orchestrated by an ogre and troll pack that nearly dismantled Sir Prentice's party. Jetsam had never heard a rubber-skin speak a word, and he assumed speech was beyond these one-dimensional wrecking machines. But he remembered the coordinated assault, and how the ogre *must* have instructed the humpbacks in some manner. *The way Lohon Threll's plan came undone had to be more than mere happenstance.* What he saw here reminded him of that event. *The knuckle-draggers act in unison, with purpose—not just devouring their first kill.*

Jetsam detected a strange noise, a *hissing*, in harsh, short bursts. It wasn't a sound he'd ever heard a humpback make. *Almost like someone choking.* Depleted by the grimion raid, Jetsam realized these men would not defeat the ravagers. His spirits plummeted.

Seryn.

Jetsam's blood boiled. Without another thought, he picked up his staff and held it in his outstretched right hand, while his left molded the empty air. He licked his lips and spoke the familiar Elven words.

"Av-kier epira gwedath."

In an instant, the caravan trail drowned in blinding light. Though the power poured out of him, Jetsam feared his effort was in vain. Still, he stumbled toward the battle. As his conjured sunblink illumination faded and his sight returned, he held a shred of hope. The raiders scrambled in retreat. He ran toward the demolished wagon train, Tramp at his heels. A stone waylaid his step, and Jetsam crashed to the dusty ground, catching a mouthful of dry dirt. The nimble dog lunged at Jetsam and nipped at his cheek. *It's not playtime, buddy boy.* Jetsam pushed Tramp aside, and the rebuffed dog waited for him to regain his feet. They jogged off, while Jetsam shook the gravel from his shirtsleeves.

As Jetsam raced to the wagons, he discovered horrible carnage strewn about the caravan. His pace slowed, and he observed no movement. The marauders killed the horses and littered the ground with dead watchmen. Body parts dotted the trail. An arm. A hoof. A bloody head with a red shock of hair.

In the dark, Jetsam raced straight for Seryn's wagon. The paneled cover had been ripped open. Jetsam thrust his head into the breach.

No one remained inside.

Aghast, Jetsam swiveled. *Sodding, fobbing, piss.* As Tramp sniffed the bloody soil, Jetsam searched the bodies. *Please not Seryn.* Crouched next to an unmoving form, Jetsam turned a moist head to reveal its face. The trader—dead. Not bothering to stand, Jetsam crawled to the next body, and the next. A guard, a coachman, the cook—all dead. The landscape held more blood and gore than Jetsam had ever seen. He gagged, and fought the urge to vomit. Unaware of his condition, he slipped into shock, but kept moving. A groan rang out, followed by muted, gut-wrenching crying.

The trader's ornate six-wheeled wagon lay on its side, the driver pinned beneath its bulk. Muffled sobs emanated from within the battered carriage. With swift steps, Jetsam approached the man.

"Where's the mage?" Jetsam demanded. Glossy-eyed, the coachman stared back at him. Tramp licked his bleeding head.

"Prithee help," the injured man pleaded.

"Of course," said Jetsam in a trance-like tone. *He has no idea what happened to Seryn,* Jetsam told himself, analyzing the man's predicament. Jetsam crouched and grabbed the wagon with both hands. Pushing with his thighs, he grunted and strained, yet the cart moved naught.

Unable to free the driver, Jetsam cast a healing spell to stabilize him. While he released his incantation, Tramp spotted a hint of movement and rushed toward a prostrate guard. Seeing the pinned wagon master react favorably to the restorative sorcery, Jetsam left him and followed the canine.

Tramp sniffed at the bloodied guard, sprawled on the ground. The man still breathed, but appeared gravely wounded. Jetsam surmised he held but one more spell. Healing the watchman would render him defenseless. *Should I save the men that captured Seryn?*

Jetsam walked away toward the next body, shaking his head. A watchman. The next—another driver. And another; the guard captain. *You brought this on yourself,* Jetsam mentally admonished the corpse. *You locked up the one man that could've saved you.*

By the time Jetsam checked the fifteenth bloody corpse, he knew Seryn wasn't among them. *Maybe he escaped?* Thinking of his mentor, and this possibility, Jetsam returned to the injured guard, who still labored to breathe.

It's what Seryn would do, he told himself, wondering if it was true.

With his staff extended toward the fallen guard, Jetsam spent the last of his magic reviving the man. Dirt and blood caked the victim's face, and his head bobbed as he struggled to regain his senses. His unsteady gaze on Jetsam, the wounded watchman licked his crusted lips as a look of comprehension washed over him.

"Grammarcy, lad."

Stalled by indecision, Jetsam bit his lip and squinted, before speaking. "You gonna try and capture me, too?" Jetsam observed the battered guard's eyebrows elevate in surprise.

"Nay, lad," the man replied. "'Twas yer spell that chased away the knuckle-draggers, weren't it?"

A lithe marble statue, Jetsam stood motionless and silent.

"Ye saved us twice. 'Twas the Cap'n made us do it," the grounded watchman confessed. "We wanted ta let yer friend go after th' grimions." Jetsam glared at the man, not a hint of trust in his azure eyes. "Name's Prescote." The sentry struggled to sit, propped himself with one arm and extended the other toward Jetsam, who left his callused palm feeling the breeze.

Despite Jetsam's healing spell, the guard remained in shock. Turning from Jetsam, he surveyed the battlefield in a daze. He gaped at the carnage that a short while ago constituted living, breathing companions. Jetsam pulled him from his stupor.

"Can you stand?"

"Think so," Prescote said, swallowing hard. With much effort, his actions answered Jetsam in the affirmative. With a wave, Jetsam motioned for the upright guard to follow him.

"Over here. We've got to lift this wagon." With the caution and concern he spared the watchman, Jetsam poked his head inside a breach in the wagon's side. "Lass? Come on, we need your help."

The terrified girl peeked out. Nose bloodied, her eyes held terror. In the last few days, she'd witnessed more bloodshed than most Oxbow soldiers. His hands under her armpits, Prescote lifted the traumatized lass to the ground, and swiveled her away from the corpses.

With the girl teetering beside them, Jetsam nodded toward the overturned wagon. Prescote bent into a proper position and he and Jetsam tried lifting together. The wagon remained too weighty to budge.

"Let's lighten the load," the guardsman suggested. He set about removing a handful of strategic bolts that sealed the loading hatch. Once Prescote opened the breach, Jetsam clambered inside the broken vehicle, hoisted a toppled crate, and handed it to the watchman. Together, Jetsam and the fatigued guard emptied the cases and crates from the disabled cart. As they tossed the payload aside, Jetsam prodded the weary man.

"What happened to the mage?"

"No idea. Ye didn't find his corpse?" Prescote asked.

Jetsam shook his head. He could only hope for the best. As Jetsam collected the strewn cargo, he discovered a few crates opened from the spill. One box held oiled axe heads, and another, shiny ring mail gauntlets. The craftwork on the armor reminded Jetsam of his own Dwarven hauberk.

"Where were you coming from?" he asked Prescote.

"Qar Asigonn," the guard replied. "Trading with the Dwarves."

How ironic, Jetsam mused. He considered asking for directions to the Dwarven stronghold, but he knew his trip with Seryn was sidetracked indefinitely. Besides, every word from Prescote's mouth required a concerted effort from the battered watchman. *Describing the path back to Qar Asigonn is beyond his capability.* They continued their labor, emptying the wagon in a silence broken only by the occasional sob from the trader's daughter.

With the cargo removed and the load lightened, they finally freed the wagon master. When Jetsam and Prescote lifted the burden, the man slid from under it. Once he was clear of danger, they dropped the overturned wreck and it fell with a creaking thud. The feeble coachman writhed on the ground with an injured leg. The girl continued sobbing. Jetsam wanted to join her.

Grimly, Prescote staggered away from the wagon to put a struggling horse out of its misery. Exhausted, Jetsam plopped on the dirt next to the disconsolate lass. She'd seen her father's corpse. *Like me, she's alone in the world.* The first rays of sun lightened the sky beyond the mountain peaks, foretelling daybreak's approaching arrival.

"At least the humpbacks won't return tonight," Jetsam said to no one in particular. With his arm around the girl, and Tramp in his lap, Jetsam dozed.

In his dreaming, he no longer rested in the Kierawaith, rather, he sat on a stump in Seryn's grotto. Elvar reclined across from him, cloaked in ebony, looking Jetsam in the eyes. Elvar's lips moved, but no sound came out. Expressionless, he glanced over his shoulder. A woman stepped from the shadows. In a tone mimicking the lagging rumble of thunder, Jetsam heard his brother's voice inside his head. *She has something important to say.*

Mother, Jetsam realized. Her visage fluttered, soft and hazy, familiar and foreign all at once. She spoke to him through her blue eyes, her full lips remaining closed.

"So, you've met my student," she said to Jetsam. Inside his dream, Jetsam struggled for lucidity. A tiny, isolated part of his consciousness urged him to stand, to run and hug his mother. Yet, his subconscious left him rooted on the stump, across from his dead brother, who gazed longingly at their mother. Jetsam presumed she spoke of Seryn, but in this blurry world of flickering clarity, he couldn't even remember the wizard's name, though he managed to nod.

His mother stood in front of him, her hand on Elvar's shoulder. Her silky hair fluttered and danced as though in a gale, yet Jetsam detected no breeze. His gaze returned to his brother, and it reminded him of looking in a misty mirror. Elvar's long locks resisted the netherworld wind that wafted his mother's tresses in waving strings.

Behind them, Jetsam discerned movement—a translucent silhouette. He knew it was his father. The entire family gathered once more, as bittersweet lava surged through his veins. Tight-lipped, his mother spoke again.

"Now my student is the teacher, and you, my son, learn from him." Jetsam nodded again, squinting to see her blue orbs. But all he saw were dark, hollow sockets. Yet, his mouth widened and stretched into a timid grin.

"Eidryn," she said, addressing him by his birth name. "I need you to speak with him—to set him straight." Her eyes re-emerged from the smoky caverns astride her nose. Their gaze grabbed Jetsam. "Seryn needs to know the truth. Will you tell him for me, dear?"

Still silent, he repeated his nodding, hanging on her next words.

"You must convince him that—"

Jetsam awoke to the guard shaking his shoulder. The risen sun shone bleakly through the Kierawaith haze. He clamped his eyes shut, trying to slip back into slumber.

"Two of the horses yet live!" Prescote said. "Can ye heal 'em?"

Jetsam struggled to shut his ears—to close off the real world's intrusion to return to his dream.

But it was too late. The vision evaporated.

Groggily, Jetsam rose to his feet. Irritated by the untimely interruption, he fumed. Teeth clenched, Jetsam glared at Prescote. Seeing the wounded man's pleading eyes, Jetsam's heart softened. *'Twas just a dream,* he assured himself, trying to shake the sensation of being robbed.

"I'm pretty well spent, but I'll see what I can do," he said. In the daylight, the campsite appeared beyond gruesome. Prescote stayed busy, dragging corpses to a somewhat respectful arrangement near the overturned wagon. Still, the smell of death was oppressive.

The short slumber returned part of Jetsam's restorative power, and against his better judgment, he healed both the horses. Prescote gaped as the animals regained their feet.

"Me mum could cast a bit o' magic," he confessed. The guard viewed Jetsam with glassy eyes. "Ne'r thought it was fair what happened to them spellcasters." Jetsam held his tongue and resisted sympathizing. *This man is still the enemy.*

"I think I can mend the driver's leg as well, enough to get him on his feet." Jetsam surprised himself with his offer. *Seryn must have gotten inside my head.* He nearly smiled at the possibility and prayed Seryn somehow escaped. *At least he's not among the dead.*

The wagon master's name was Sollers, and he proved as grateful as Prescote. Jetsam became a hero in their eyes. *Today, there are two less wizard-haters in the Oxbows.*

"He healed two horses," Prescote told Sollers. "We may make it ta Dwim-Halloe yet." The guard sifted through the wreckage. "Gonna leave a fortune on this hillside," he said to Sollers. Jetsam glanced at the shattered crates and ruptured boxes. Iron ingots, gems, jewelry, sharpened blades of every size, ornate flambeaus, stone bowls and ewers—a veritable Dwarven treasure, abandoned on a blood-soaked trail in the Kierawaith.

"S'pose we should burn 'em." Prescote nodded toward the bodies.

"Proper thing to do," said Sollers. The two men constructed a funeral pyre with lumber from the wagons. Jetsam wanted none of it.

When he returned to the girl, she sat cross-legged, petting Tramp, the terrier curled in her lap. She looked at Jetsam, her upper lip crusted with blood, and her bloodshot eyes met his. Her voice quivered, quiet as a field mouse and hoarse as sandpaper.

"Monsters took your friend."

Chapter Six

Inside the impromptu prison wagon, Seryn awoke from his dream with a pounding head and aching joints. Stiff and coated with chilling sweat, he renewed his resolve. *I must escape today.* When he lifted his arms above his head to resume his assault on his stubborn gag, his muscles screamed in opposition. *Spirit of the devil, that hurts!* His leaden arms slumped into his lap. *Got to be another way.*

Seryn ran scenarios through his mind, searching for a method of escape. *Next time they feed me, they'll release the gag,* he surmised. *If I had enough time to recite a spell, I could turn invisible.* He shook his head. *They'd pummel me as soon as I started chanting. It would give them an excuse to kill me.*

The guards' conversation repeated in his head, sparking an idea. *Except for the captain, they all want me dead. What if I pretend I'm sick and delirious?* Seryn rolled his shoulders, stretching his painful tendons. *If they undid my gag, could I mutter a spell and have them think it incoherent gibberish? Even bound, I could move enough to trigger a spell.* His hands wiggled, testing his theory.

But what spell? It must be short as possible with gestures I can manage while shackled. His greasy brow furrowed. *That limits my choices.*

Seryn reviewed his options. *If I turn invisible, they might still shut the hatch before I escape.* He examined the sturdy wagon door and envisioned scrambling past two guards before they realized what he'd done. Seryn frowned and shook his head. *I don't like those odds.*

Eyes closed, he chewed his gag and mulled over his known spells. *Killing them instantly would be tricky in such tight quarters. Fire and lightning are out of the question—I'd likely kill myself as well, or set the wagon aflame.*

His rumbling stomach turned his thoughts toward food. *They fed me after the wagons stopped for the night,* he recalled. *After everyone else ate.* As Seryn's face softened, a hint of a smile crossed his chapped lips. *I could put them to sleep and sneak out while the rest are slumbering.* Seryn pantomimed the *slumber* spell gestures and recited the Elven trigger words in his head. *It just might work!*

The day proved interminable as Seryn waited for the sun to set. As the cargo wagon bounced and jostled him, he envisioned every step of his plan. *What if they don't release my gag?* He gnawed the inside of his cheek. *I must act coherent enough for them to think I can eat.* He imagined himself lolling on the floor, fever-stricken and moaning, and wondered if the guards would be compelled to remove his gag. *Or could I mumble a spell with a mouthful of food?* Stuffed inside his dim cabin, he evaluated the feasibility of this scenario. Through the slivers between his wagon planks, he noticed the daylight waning. *We'll be stopping soon.* His stomach churned with excitement and anticipation. *What's the worst that could happen? I suffer a beating before I die? I've nothing to lose.*

Seryn rehearsed his act in silence as the wagon rolled. *When Redbeard opens the hatch, I'll be ready.* He made retching sounds through his gag and feigned spastic agony. *Have to be convincing.* He recited the words to the slumber spell through his head, accelerating the cadence each time. *It's been a while since I've cast that spell. Got to spit it out fast as I can.* With each silent repetition, he moved his fingers and hands. *Think I can pull it off.*

Focused in his preparation, Seryn didn't notice the wagon slowing until the abrupt halt alerted him. Bathed in darkness, his ears tuned to the sound of the camp setting up. He slowed his breathing to calm his trepidation. *I'll only get one shot at this.* As the wagons emptied, voices shouted orders, and the nightly tumult began around the campfire, Seryn remained in his trance. Ignoring the guard's banter and the fireside chatting, he honed his senses for his pending performance.

As the aroma of dinner wafted inside Seryn's wagon, a

cacophony erupted outside. *What the devil's going on?* He shook himself and focused on the caterwaul. *That's Redbeard yelling.* The noise re-ignited the pounding in his skull. *Is there a fight?* Seryn tensed as he sorted out the sounds. *Horses, shouting, clanging. More than a fight—we're under attack!*

He sat at attention. *The grimions are back! I should have guessed they'd return for the rest.* Dehydrated and shivering, he collected his wits.

If they find me, they'll kill me, he realized, pulling on his shackles. The irons bit his raw wrists. The creaky wagon rocked as an unseen force impacted the wall next to Seryn. *What the gods was that?* The wagon shook again and a plank broke loose near his head. *Something bigger than a grimion. And it smells awful.*

Seryn's stiff, numb fingers pulled on the gag, but his effort proved futile once again. He cursed silently in frustration. *Can't cast a spell with this bloody strap in my mouth.* Grunting and groaning, he struggled with the restraint until his wrists bled and hands cramped.

Think it's coming loose.

As Seryn's cracked fingernails dug into the cowhide, something burst through the wagon wall, splintering the planks and knocking him on his side. Stacked crates of Dwarven loot tumbled upon him. The slippery gag slipped from his aching fingers. *Devil take you! I almost had it!*

Seryn struggled to sit, shifting the crates off his battered body. He stared at a gaping hole in the wagon's side. *I'm free!* With the accompanying surge of adrenaline, his hands attacked the leather gag with renewed vigor. *Turn invisible and sneak away.*

As the gag came loose, Seryn saw two massive hands grasp the roof. In the moonlight, their ebony claws shredded the wood and ripped the wagon open. He heard a thunderous crash before the first Elven word left his lips, and everything went black.

"Put that foolish notion out of your head," Daelis Vardan said to his son.

Though sore and bloodied, announcing his acceptance into Eh' liel Ev' Narron washed young Seryn's pain away. Yet, his father stood determined to bring it all back—immediately.

"You'll not be going to sorcery school." He shook his head, a mask of disgust covering his face. "You'll follow your brother to the Academy and squire when the time comes."

"But, Father, Illuminae Daystar says I'm his best student. That I've enormous potential."

"You've the potential to follow in your brother's footsteps. Vardans have been a prominent bloodline since the beginning of Dwim-Halloe. Your forbearers and I worked hard to give you the opportunity to be distinguished citizens—leaders of men. You'll not squander that on convoluted Elvish tricks and useless knowledge."

"But, Father—I *want* to!"

"I said no. Once your lessons with Daystar are finished, you're through with sorcery." As Seryn groped for a counter to his father, his brother broke the temporary silence.

"Father?" Valin asked.

"What, lad?"

"Seryn's no challenge for me. His skill with blades and bows will never match mine."

"What's your point, lad?"

"I need to train with older boys. I'll not improve practicing against *him*." Valin's heavy eyes glowered at his prone brother. "Let him go to this school and be out from underfoot."

Seryn wanted to hug his brother and slug him all at once.

Duke Daelis Vardan gaped at his oldest with a slack-jawed expression. His frosty brow tightened.

"You honor your brother to take his side, but I shan't give up hope on him. With more training and practice, he may mature into a young warrior like yourself."

Seryn watched in awe, nearly as stupefied as his father. *Valin never takes my side,* he pondered.

"I'm ready for the Academy *now*, Father," Valin said. "Surely you can convince them to bring me in early, can't you?" Daelis Vardan wore his pride like a badge, and Seryn knew he considered himself one of the most influential men in Dwim-Halloe. For his own son to doubt his ability to pull strings was absurd. *Valin knows Father well,* Seryn realized, comprehending his ploy.

"Of course I can," Daelis said. "That doesn't mean I *will*." Seryn suspected the idea appealed to his father. *A son entering the Academy at such a young age would be a proud accomplishment—for both Father and Valin.* Yet, Seryn feared Daelis would never allow his decision to be dictated by his sons. *If any such idea would be enacted, the world must know it came from him, and not his offspring's clever manipulation.*

"Don't challenge me, Valin. I'll decide when you're ready for the Academy and what your brother's path shall be. Now, stand up, boy," he told Seryn. "Wash yourselves and prepare for supper."

Daelis Vardan spoke no more of this subject. Valin and Seryn trained together the rest of the semester. Seryn was not pleased with his decision, and suspected Daelis recognized it. *And I know it sits ill with Valin. Every day he rambles about the Academy,* Seryn agonized. *It'll be a blessing when he finally goes—for none other than an end to his complaining.*

When the new semester arrived, Daelis spoke to his sons.

"Valin, I've watched your progress and seen the strides you've made. I deem you ready for the Academy."

Valin shot from his seat, his chair teetering. A flicker of hope grew in Seryn's mind, but it was tempered with dread. *Not me, too, I pray.*

"Thank you, Father, thank you! I shall make you proud." He lunged and hugged his father, who endured the embrace for a moment before shrugging it off.

"You're still younger than the Academy allows, but I pulled some strings. Make certain you don't disappoint."

Seryn sat, timid as a mouse, staunching his hopes, lest they be dashed.

"And you, lad." Daelis turned to his young son. "You're not ready for the Academy, and may never be." Daelis' chagrined face bore a look of utter disappointment. "I've enrolled you in the sorcery school— for *one* semester."

Seryn's heart beat faster, his stomach tingling. He tried not to smile, but failed miserably.

"But you'll be on a short leash," Daelis said. "If I receive one complaint or if you cannot excel above your contemporaries, that will be the end of it. Understood?"

"Yes, Father. Thank you—I shall be the best student they've ever had."

When Seryn departed his childhood dream and regained consciousness, he couldn't see a thing. *Where am I?* He blinked and squinted, but his crusty eyes detected no light. In response to the hammers in his skull, he clamped his ineffective eyes shut to ward off the pain.

Am I still in the wagon?

For the first time in days, Seryn realized he wasn't shivering. The crisp mountain breeze was absent. The stagnant air hung cool and clammy, but not nearly as frigid as inside the wagon.

Am I underground?

Then Seryn noticed the leather gag back in place, tighter than ever. His jaw ached and his nape bit where his hair caught in the knot. *What the devil?* A tug on his wrists confirmed his hands were bound. *Still can't cast a spell.*

As his disoriented senses reluctantly awakened, so did his pain. His aching body rocked, but unlike the rumbling wagon, this new bouncing felt rhythmic. Blood rushed to his pounding head and his drool ran backwards, running down his cheeks and into his eyes.

How long have I been out?

Something pushed at his abdomen as he hung from his midsection, legs dangling and head upside down slapping against a rough hairless hide. *Am I being carried?* Sharp claws dug into his ribcage, securing him in place. *And by what?*

His gag forced him to breathe through his nose and endure a fetid aroma wafting off his captor. Between the knobby shoulder squeezing the breath from him and the rank stench of his abductor, Seryn's bilious stomach lurched as bile rose in his throat.

It's not a grimion.

Seryn kicked his feet and his toes connected with a solid slab. In response to his insolence, a baritone growl and a violent squeeze rebuked him. Seryn bit hard on his gag as the creature's pointy claws pierced his tender skin.

Spirit help me! Don't do that again!

While the fresh pain in his rib cage receded to blend with the overall throbbing of the rest of his tormented body, Seryn assessed his surroundings. Good as blind, with his sense of smell overwhelmed, his ears became attuned to the environment. He heard stomping through water and felt a rogue droplet hit his forehead.

There's a pack of them.

As the thump-splash sounds of tromping feet assaulted his ears, Seryn searched for other sounds, but found none. *No one's talking.* He detected an occasional hissing he couldn't identify. *It's coming from the front, whatever it is.*

Seryn pushed at his gag with his tongue, but it only caused him to cough. Snot pooled in his sinuses and he swallowed hard to evacuate the mucous. Dizzy and nauseated, questions peppered his tormented brain.

Where are they taking me? What do they want with me?

A single answer tortured him. *Back to their lair.* His useless eyes clamped shut. *To eat me.*

After seven years as a student at Eh' liel Ev' Narron, Seryn had achieved unprecedented success. Yet, every accomplishment he earned at the School of Sorcery had been matched by his brother at the Royal Academy. Neither brother shared any joy in the other's achievements.

"King Tygan has declared the mourning period over," Daelis told his sons. "Tygan will debut Ioma at the harvest ball. With the queen dead, and no male heirs, he must accept suitors for the princess."

Seryn's stomach churned as his father's words filled him with despair. *I feared this day would come.*

"Do you understand what this means?" Daelis asked.

Seryn and Valin glanced at each other.

"There'll be a feeding frenzy of every half-blood noble at the harvest ball," Valin said. His smirk vanished beneath his father's stern glare.

"The competition for the next king has begun," the duke stated flatly. "Tygan knows she must wed to carry on his bloodline. 'Tis the opportunity of a lifetime. You shall be at your most charming and win the princess' heart," Daelis said, with no hint of emotion. "It will make it easier to convince Tygan you're the best match."

Seryn viewed the expression on his brother's face change from cocksure to timid in the blink of an eye.

"But, Father, surely there will be dozens of suitors."

"There certainly will, which is why I'll take no chances." Duke Daelis Vardan stared at his eldest. "You are to woo the princess while I impress upon the king your many virtues. And, I shall remind him of our holdings in the south, and how advantageous a Vardan marriage would be to his relations with the Freelords."

Seryn felt invisible. *I shouldn't be so astonished by the arrogance of these two.* The image sent a shiver down his spine. He could not envision Valin as king. Nor Ioma as his queen.

"And what of me?" Seryn asked. "Should I entreat the mages of Eh' liel Ev' Narron to prepare a potion to brainwash Ioma into marrying my oafish brother?" Seryn failed to discern which of the two resulting glares was icier.

"Jest now, brother, for when I am king, I'll throw you in the *donjon* for such disrespect."

"'Tis no joking matter," Daelis said. "Generations of Vardans have waited for such an opportunity. 'Tis time you both acted like men and made your mother proud." Both brothers lowered their eyes to their food. When Daelis invoked the name of their dear departed mother, he was not to be trifled with.

"Seryn, you'll accompany your brother to the ball and ensure Valin has adequate opportunity to impress the princess."

He shall have me poison the other suitors, I suspect, Seryn lamented, but dared not speak. "As you wish, Father."

The night of the ball, Seryn dressed in his finest stamped velvet tunic, black linen hose and shiny boots. *They may wear dancing shoes in the Southern Freeholds,* he thought, *but even at a royal ball, mountain folk wear boots.* The brothers left the estate together in body, but not mind. With a glance behind as the carriage rolled away, Seryn glimpsed his father on the manor steps, his eyes following Valin.

Still invisible, I am.

The Vardan carriage was one of many crossing through the

Granite Palace's gatehouse this eve. Glowing lanterns lined the royal bailey, swaying in the breeze. As the gloaming gave way to night, the lanterns cast a golden glow on the palace structures, dancing off the ashlar faces and disappearing in the spaces between the blocks.

Can't believe I'm going to a royal ball.

Abuzz with activity, the Citadel's Great Hall became the center of the Oxbow Mountain universe this eve. Every eligible blue-blood who entertained even the remotest hope for the throne attended *this* harvest ball.

It's chaos, Seryn thought. *I pity the princess.*

Upon entering the Great Hall, Seryn surveyed the ballroom; the chandeliers cast a warm glow on the mingling nobles. The blue-gray Oxbow marble floors shined clean and polished. A long crimson and cream banner sporting the royal heraldry hung from carved corbels and blanketed the room's north wall.

"And you must be Valin Vardan—I recognize you from the tourneys." Though the deep voice addressed the brother at his side, it startled Seryn from his sightseeing. "Allow me to welcome you to the ball—I am Lord High Chamberlain Nargul." The lord stood erect, chest puffed out, bearded chin jutting. A decade older than Valin, Tark Nargul was nonetheless young for his lofty position at the king's side.

And he knows it.

"'Tis an honor, my Lord." Valin said with a perfunctory bow. "Please, allow me to introduce my younger brother, Seryn," he said.

"Ah, yes, the *magician.*" Nargul offered Seryn the mildest of acknowledging nods.

"I'm certain the princess will be delighted at your presence," Nargul said to Valin. "For she and King Tygan are regulars at the tournaments and have noted your accomplishments. See Lady Darksparrow to schedule your dance. The princess is in high demand this eve." With a wave, he directed Valin toward a matronly woman recording the list of suitors who would dance with King Tygan's only child tonight.

As expected, Seryn supposed. *At least I'm accustomed to being ignored.* He experienced an odd sensation while standing near the lord high chamberlain, but dismissed it as a reaction to his chilly greeting.

At the rear of the ball room sat the elevated throne of King

Tygan, who reclined, goblet in hand, surveying the scene while nobles waited to greet his majesty. Next to him hovered the fair Princess Ioma. *She's more enchanting than ever!*

"Come on," Valin tugged Seryn's shirt sleeve. "We'll both sign up so I can get two dances." On the way to the ball, Valin instructed Seryn to defer any opportunity to dance with the princess to him, who would then double his time with Ioma. Seryn realized he would surrender no such opportunity. The siblings Vardan added their names to the list, Seryn allowing his brother to go first.

"Don't go right behind me," Valin instructed. "I don't want to dance twice in a row." Seryn stepped out of line briefly, letting a few other zealous young men add their names. When *Master Seryn Vardan* was scribed onto the parchment, he was surprised to see he grabbed the last spot. He was doubly relieved. *Nearly missed my chance,* he realized, *and the last dance will limit the time Valin can stew for being deprived of his encore.*

With his evening schedule now set, Seryn had time to kill. *I've no desire to mingle with the competition,* he decided. *They're Valin's ilk, not mine.* Seryn claimed a high stool near the wine cask and planted himself. *So much to study.* The steward filled his goblet. *Better take it slow, the last dance is a ways off.*

Chapter Seven

Surrounded by fresh corpses in the dim Kierawaith, Jetsam stared in shock at the caravan girl. She sat in the dirt, holding Tramp in her lap, as Prescote and Sollers toiled behind her.

"What do you mean, monsters took him?" Jetsam asked the hollowed-out lass.

"I saw them drag him away," she said, her voice raw from screaming and weeping. "The stinky monsters and the *ghost-man*."

Jetsam stared into her vacant eyes and considered believing her. Though her body survived the two horrific raids, Jetsam wondered if her mind fared as well.

"Ghost-man? What ghost-man?"

"He led the humpbacks—told them what to do." She spoke through chapped lips, draped by dirty tear streaks and crusted snot. Her blond hair sat akin to a wig put on sideways—matted and wild at the same time. "He moved, but looked dead—like a ghost."

Jetsam pitied the lass. In a matter of days, he witnessed her life unravel. *Don't blame her for seeing ghosts—she's seen enough dead.* Jetsam understood the merchant's daughter would never be the same. Her upturned predicament mirrored his ill-fated life. *Another orphan in the Oxbows,* he lamented. *And I don't even know her name!*

He peeled off his leather glove and extended a clammy hand

toward the girl.

"My name's Jetsam."

With a look that questioned whether she possessed a name at all, her brown eyes gazed through him. If she had an ounce of moisture left, she would have shed another tear. From the pit of her stomach, she forced out a word.

"Dydera," she said, reaching for his hand. "My name's Dydera."

Her fragile hand trembled inside Jetsam's. As he executed a polite handshake, he felt her holding on. For a second, their eyes met. A crashing of broken wagon pieces startled the lass, and she released her grip.

With the last armful of kindling on the pile, Prescote and Sollers finished stacking the debris shards and deadwood over and around the corpses.

"Soon as we set the fire, we got to leave," Prescote said. "The girl can ride with me, and you with Sollers," he told Jetsam, thumbing toward the wagon master. "Them knuckle-draggers'll be back at nightfall. They'll come fer the horsemeat, if'n the wolves don't get here first. Either way, the further we get from here, the better."

"How many'd you count?" Jetsam asked. Prescote squinted and tilted his head.

"Hard ta say—they was on us so quick. Swear a half dozen at least. Prob'ly more."

"Don't know what's goin' on in these parts, but I ain't never seen mongrels and humpbacks attackin' in packs," Sollers said, shaking his scabbing head. "I've taken this route to Qar Asigonn half dozen times, and never run into unnaturals organized like this."

"But they hardly took anything with 'em," said the guard, turning toward Sollers. "The prisoner and mebbe some horsemeat. They didn't even raid the cargo."

Prescote stopped scratching his head and set the fire ablaze. Then he and Sollers loaded their harried horses.

"Let's go, lass," Prescote said. "Gotta move." The tentative girl rose, and the sentry lifted her on the dapple-gray.

"Come on, lad. Yer dog can run 'longside."

His jaw set, Jetsam squinted at the Oxbow soldier.

"I'm not going with you."

"Don't worry, lad. Yer secret's safe with us," Prescote said. "We ain't gonna tell no one yer a spellcaster."

Prescote's dull gray eyes appeared confused by the lingering silence. Jetsam decided it couldn't hurt to reveal his plan. *These men are harmless, now.*

"I'm going to find my friend."

Prescote's eyebrows floated and Sollers' jaw dropped. "Lass said the knuckle-draggers got 'im. He's dead by now, lad," Prescote said.

"I'm not going back to Dwim-Halloe." The two men glanced at each other, sharing a mutual failure to comprehend Jetsam.

"Are ye daft, lad? With the smoke and the corpses, this place'll be crawlin' with vermin afore ye know it."

Knew they wouldn't understand, Jetsam told himself. "Come on Tramp." He spun and walked from the camp. "In the daylight, the rubber-skins' trail will be easier to follow," he told the terrier.

The two men shook their heads.

"Change yer mind, ye can still catch up with us," Prescote said as Jetsam strolled away. Jetsam forced an acknowledging half-smile and caught Dydera's longing gaze. *Nothing else I can do for her.*

The trio rode away on the horses Jetsam saved. *They owe me everything.*

Jetsam surveyed the camp site's wreckage. *Wagon contents strewn everywhere.* He seized the opportunity to stock up on essentials. The perishables would be eaten by wolves and whatnot come nightfall, so he filled his sack with apples, dried venison, and half a loaf of bread. He discovered a cracked-open crate of Dwarven-crafted torches and took as many as he could carry. Of the many talents the Dwarves possessed, Seryn once told him, they were masterful at lighting dark caverns.

Jetsam recalled the direction the raiders fled, so picking up their trail proved easy. Footprints, crushed foliage, and broken branches marked the way. Tramp picked up a scent, and Jetsam suspected it was Seryn's.

"You know we're gonna find a cave, don't you, buddy boy?"

Jetsam realized Tramp wouldn't relish another trek underground, but he also recognized the troglodytes must flee the dawn. He held out hope that the sunlight beat the marauders to their lair, and he'd find them frozen in place, and Seryn none the worse for wear.

But he knew it was a pipedream.

In a few barren spots, when Jetsam couldn't find any evidence across a patch of rocky terrain, tracking the creatures proved tricky. So he trusted his dog, as Tramp sniffed the way and Jetsam tromped behind him. Upon reaching a swale full of scrub, Jetsam identified more signs of the humpbacks' passage, and he knew the terrier would not lead him astray.

Feeble sunlight poked through the mid-morning gloom, and Jetsam noted the bleak glow overhead. Troll tracks stood like craters in the muddy soil, moistened by meandering rivulets of spring meltwater. As the fresh footpath descended into a ravine, Jetsam noticed the crevice. *Big enough for trolls.* A triangular slice in the rock, the troll's trail led him to this ominous breach. Tramp hesitated at the opening, glancing at Jetsam.

"Sorry, buddy boy, we're going in."

Jetsam entered the foreboding maw, stepping where resilient mosses and plants encroached upon the deepest reaches of daylight's touch. An unfortunate snail crunched under his foot. A startled Tramp barked at the sound, then followed Jetsam to sniff the crushed shell.

Three steps past the last fingers of vegetation, Jetsam left the daylight behind him. A cave salamander darted along the wall, skirting the twilight from dark to light. Tramp's keen eyes caught the movement, and he leapt toward the lizard. The salamander slipped away as Tramp stood on his hind legs, front paws on the cave wall. He barked, and relented to follow Jetsam, who had slowed while allowing his eyes to adjust.

After a few minutes of creeping into the crevasse, even the weakest trickles of light abandoned the pair, leaving them in utter blackness. Jetsam holstered his staff in a strap across his back and fumbled to light a torch. This far underground, the air languished, lifeless and humid. Jetsam caught a whiff of bat guano as his flambeau took flame. He glanced at the terrier, who appeared oblivious to the stink.

The steep, narrow cave brightened with the pine-wood glow. Crystalline deposits of calcium carbonate glistened on the cavern walls. Overhead, Jetsam observed a blanket of bats coating the ceiling. At his feet, their droppings caked thick beneath his boots, confirming his sense of smell.

"Sorry, buddy boy," he said, envisioning the dog's paws slogging through the excrement.

With his flickering brand lighting the way, Jetsam led Tramp across the uneven footing. Rocks jutted as they trudged deeper into the bowels of the Oxbow Mountains. Centuries of moisture left clusters of onyx cave coral, built up in rough knobs on the walls and floors. *Not a single Dwarven pick ever touched this stone.*

Still floating unresolved inside his head, Jetsam reflected on Dydera's vexing words. *What did she see that made her think of a ghost-man?* His head pounded.

The scant path proved steep and winding, ever downward. Several times Jetsam stooped to scoop up Tramp and carry him down a drop too daunting for the terrier. *Wouldn't want a troll to drag me through this.* He envisioned Seryn's rough ride, hoping his friend still lived. He suspected the humpbacks were none too careful with their baggage.

Jetsam imagined the route was a tight squeeze for that many trolls. Water trickled and dripped on and around the pair and the air grew moist and foul. Jetsam detected the lingering stench of troll. *We've probably stepped in that, too, buddy boy.* The descent was arduous, but the acrid scent heartened him. *We're on the right trail.* And still the question nagged Jetsam. *Why'd they take him?*

Jetsam's lungs grew heavy and his thighs burned. His torch flame dwindled to a flicker. Tramp snapped at a millipede racing across his path, but the pale insect escaped the dog's half-hearted bite.

"You didn't want to eat that thing, anyway," Jetsam said, peering at the terrier in the fading light. A drip of hot pitch fled the torch and landed on the terrier's furry rump. Tramp released a startled yelp.

"Sorry, boy!" Jetsam wiped the sticky goo off the fur as best he could. The tar blackened the fingers of his leather gloves. Tramp sat in a curl, licking his bottom while Jetsam fished out a snack from his pack.

"Here you go, buddy boy. This beats a stinky, old bug." The aroma of dried meat distracted Tramp for a few seconds, and he devoured the chunk of jerky. While Tramp licked his chops, Jetsam lit a second torch, and discarded the original on the wet cavern floor. It landed with a hiss.

The new brand illuminated a wider radius than its dying

predecessor, and Jetsam saw the cavern open before them. Cave crickets and spiders fled the intruding illumination. Smooth flowstone sheets sparkled in the hand-held firelight. Slippery stalactites reached to stumpy stalagmites, and a few consummated their patient union in narrow-waisted columns.

Rivulets of water streamed at Jetsam's feet and he heard lapping ahead. He picked up Tramp to spare him the wet floor. While navigating the glossy, uneven rock, Jetsam noticed the ceiling rise and the walls fall away. They stood in a spacious cavern, barely illuminated by the hand-held flambeau. As Jetsam inched forward, surveying the carbonate icicles dripping mineral-laden drops into the pool below, he lost his footing.

Still holding Tramp in one arm, Jetsam slid down a submerged embankment. He slipped underwater before he could react. Tramp squirmed loose, dog-paddling to the surface as Jetsam's rump hit the hard bottom. As fast as he could, Jetsam regained his feet, standing upright with the water around his belly. Coughing and spitting the stale fluid, he rubbed his eyes and opened them to darkness.

The torch was out.

Jetsam shook his head, trying to drain the water clogging his ear canals. With a slick glove, he pushed his hair back out of his face. He heard Tramp paddling nearby. After a moment of panicked groping, Jetsam found his companion and lifted him from the water. Tramp licked Jetsam's wet cheek. With the dog cradled against his shoulder, Jetsam worked his way backward up the slick slope. He detected a subtle current in the water.

Jetsam slipped once, banging his knee on the stone, before conquering the bank. He set Tramp on a flat patch and plopped beside him. The terrier shook off the wet and sprayed Jetsam. Although water soaked Jetsam to the bone, the entrained air inside his pack kept it afloat, so his belongings were moist, at worst. *Still, lighting another torch will be a challenge.* As Jetsam shivered and Tramp shook, he reflected on Seryn's advice. *Don't use your magic unless you absolutely have to.*

Cold, damp, and blind, sitting in an unknown cave, Jetsam rationalized that he *had* to. Though he spent the morning healing horses and men, Jetsam suspected he could force out enough flame to light the pitch-soaked brand.

So he did, and the cavern flickered to life.

No more spells for me.

With his dense coat and vigorous shaking, Tramp dried in no time. Jetsam, however, suffered. He took off his boots and dumped out the water. The cavern stayed warmer than the chilly air in the Kierawaith above, but to the drenched Jetsam, it was freezing. Barefooted, he backtracked up the tunnel until he located a dry spot, free of drips and rivulets. Jetsam stuck the fresh torch in a crook above the alcove, careful to place it so it wouldn't drip on Tramp again. *Or me.* Jetsam stripped naked, dried himself with the blanket from his pack, and wrung out his clothes. Sapped of magic and of strength, he curled up on the dry stone, wrapped himself with his damp blanket and pulled Tramp close. The canine's warmth offset his wet odor. Jetsam ate a handful of fruit and nuts, and shared more jerky with Tramp.

Despite the food, despair set in as Jetsam shivered. *Wonder if I'll survive the night?* Then he contemplated the cavern water. *We've lost the scent, that's for sure.* Jetsam feared relenting to his exhaustion. He dreaded succumbing to an endless sleep.

If I hadn't healed those horses, I could cast a spell to warm myself. Deep down, he knew he'd done right by the caravan survivors. He'd never feel sympathy for an Oxbow soldier, but the girl and coachman were another story. *Without the horses, they'd be dead.* As it was, they had a difficult road ahead to reach Dwim-Halloe, but at least they had a chance. Jetsam could hear Seryn: *those three are alive because of you.* Jetsam prayed his generosity wouldn't cost him *his* life. Once again, his ruminations returned to the words of his deceased brother. He recalled Flotsam reminding him that 'no good deed goes unpunished.' Despite his best efforts and racing mind, his exhausted body succumbed to slumber.

Jetsam opened his eyes to darkness; the torch had burned out. Curled in a ball, Tramp snored beneath the blanket, wedged between Jetsam's shivering thighs and rumbling stomach. In his sleep, Jetsam coiled his lanky frame, mimicking the canine.

Groggy and chilled, Jetsam unwound and sat up. He ached everywhere—especially his damp neck. His throat burned raw and his head sloshed full of snot, while the inside of his skull pounded. He sneezed and woke Tramp. The dog poked his head out from under the blanket and stretched, his front paws reaching in front of him with his bottom in the air. Jetsam scratched the terrier's backside as he tried to clear his head.

"Feel like dung, buddy boy."

Jetsam fumbled to retrieve a fresh torch. *Hope that was enough rest to let me cast.* With a few Elven words and a finger dance, the brand burned bright. Jetsam stood, his muscles screaming, and replaced the dead torch in the nook. He surveyed the cramped alcove. His clothes remained damp, but no longer drenched. "Must have slept longer than I thought," he told Tramp. "Think I can cast another spell."

Still wrapped in a moist blanket, Jetsam focused. Foremost, the practical Seryn taught him survival spells. Jetsam concentrated, remembering the words, and moved his hands, creating a pulsing cerulean light that grew to pumpkin size. The energy gave off heat, and Tramp backed away, growling. Warmth radiated from the conjuration, heating Jetsam's chilled flesh and damp clothes. He maintained the spell, letting the warmth spread. Beads of sweat coalesced on his brow. *This'll be the last spell I cast for a while.* The warmth felt so good, he fueled the cyan sphere until he was spent. *I'm sure I'll regret that later, but sod it, I'm not shivering.*

Jetsam slipped into his dry-ish clothes and Dwarven hauberk, and feared a daunting path lay ahead. *Don't relish getting back in the water.* He packed his meager camp, grabbed the torch and continued on his way, Tramp by his side.

Upon returning to the site of his spill, Jetsam worked the spacious cavern's perimeter, staying dry by hugging the walls where the water ran shallow. While encircling the hollowed-out space, Jetsam sensed an aura of energy ahead. *Like Ashvar's magic stones.* Jetsam allowed his sixth sense to lead him, and soon spotted glistening woodwork extending into the water. Several barrels sat atop the low dock, but no boat was anchored. Jetsam walked out on the creaky structure, snaking between the containers. *The magical energy is intensifying.* He balanced his burning brand on one of the barrels and opened another. Jetsam found the container full of arrows. *Nothing magical here.* He scratched his head and opened a second oaken container. A variety of weapons filled the barrel—hand axes and short swords, with a smattering of daggers and maces.

Jetsam extracted a blade and examined the ricasso under the torch light. He recognized the maker's stamp. *This is from Dwim-Halloe!*

With his mouth contorted in a troubled expression, Jetsam inspected several other weapons. The markings were the same. *Fine craftsmanship—but nothing emanating magic.*

"What do you make of that?" he asked Tramp. "Smugglers, maybe?"

He pried the lid off a third barrel with his new dagger.

Scrolls!

Packed with no regard for the delicate cargo, the barrel held rolls of vellum and parchment. "There's magic in here," he told Tramp. Jetsam's first instinct was to dig in and examine the writings, but his blossoming restraint allowed him to pause and reconsider. *Humid air and smoky torch flames are the last thing these scrolls need.* He picked up the drum lid and flicked a flatworm off with his index finger. *And I've no time to waste,* he reminded himself, thinking of Seryn.

Jetsam tried tilting the barrel, and the container's mass surprised him. *Too heavy to just be parchment,* he rationalized. *Maybe I need another look.*

He again removed the lid, and while holding the torch high, pushed aside the scrolls, wiggling his free hand deeper. His fingertips tingled, sensing the mysterious energy at the barrel's bottom. As his armpit neared the barrel rim, his index finger poked something hard and smooth. A surge of magic rushed up his arm, and he recoiled, knocking a scroll out of the barrel, onto the dock and into the drink.

Bugger!

Before he finished considering dropping the torch and reaching for the sinking scroll, it slipped beneath the rippled surface.

It's gone now.

Jetsam steadied himself, and forced the lost scroll's image from his mind. He crouched with one hand holding the torch above his head and the other shoved deep in the barrel. *That magic radiated stronger than Regret, or even Seryn's staff.* He inhaled to recompose himself, stretched deeper and grabbed the mysterious object. His hand groped to take hold of the stone, yet it resisted, too large and heavy for him to extract. His torch arm wearied while his fingers probed the surface for a hand-hold. By pinching an irregular protrusion between his thumb and three fingers, Jetsam again tried to lift the troublesome object.

This time, the chunk broke off in his hand. He slid out of the barrel, careful not to spill more scrolls. Beneath the torchlight, he observed a milky crystal. *A pretty gem, but nothing special, except for the power coming from it.*

Jetsam slipped the stone into his pocket and pondered the barrel.

I'm coming back for this, he promised himself, envisioning a plethora of magic crystal hiding beneath the neglected scrolls. After sealing the container a second time, he searched for a hiding spot. *That'll do,* he decided, finding a small alcove not far from the dock. By tilting the heavy container, he rolled it on its bottom edge, maneuvering it off the dock and into the concealing nook. Every second he spent hiding the barrel, he feared Seryn slipped further away.

With his booty well-hidden, Jetsam retrieved his torch and strode to the end of the dock, extending the flambeau over the water. The light crept across the timid ripples, but did not reveal the other side. Still enjoying the warmth of his dry clothes, Jetsam entertained an idea.

"We'll make a raft, buddy boy."

Jetsam removed a section of the dock, and by scavenging materials from the barrels, fashioned a flat skiff, wide enough to hold himself and Tramp. He affixed his torch in a makeshift holder at the front of the craft.

"This'll keep our feet dry, and let us move faster." Jetsam slid the craft off the dock, and grinned at the seaworthy vessel. *At least it floats.* Jetsam kept the Dwim-Halloe dagger. He didn't need another knife, but it was a decent blade, and he resolved to keep *some* evidence from the cache.

Jetsam boarded his craft and lifted the wary canine aboard. With his staff as a guide pole, he pushed off, and the current led them across the cavern. As they floated southward, the torchlight illuminated a tunnel ahead. The vessel entered the slender passage, leaving the dock and sprawling cavern in its wake. Tramp curled and set his chin on his front paws as Jetsam guided the raft through the subterranean river. With the assisting current, he used his staff to accelerate the skiff and guide it from hitting the glistening walls.

"We've got to go fast to catch the trolls, buddy boy."

Hours after the immense cavern disappeared behind them, the duo floated into an intersection. Three passages lay in front of them. Water trickled along the walls, following folds and curls that reminded Jetsam of the curtains in his childhood home. He planted his staff on the river bottom, holding the craft firm against the current. A few stowaway springtails scampered across his makeshift deck.

"Bloody," he murmured. "Which way do we go?" Panicked, he gnawed the inside of his cheek as he waited for the dog to answer. Jetsam scrutinized each passage, but discovered no sign. *Two out of three chances we lose him.* He wracked his brain, trying to determine his best bet. Confounded, he lifted his gnarled staff off the cave bottom and let the current lead them.

Ten feet ahead, the skiff dawdled, and came to a stop before reaching any of the three branches. Jetsam saw the life of his torch drawing near as the indecisive skiff bobbled in the stagnant stream. He ignited a new brand, and flung the failing flambeau into the center passage. It spun through the humid air and hit the water with a hiss.

Jetsam ground his teeth. "What do you think, Tramp? Which way should we go? Pick the wrong one, and we never see Seryn again."

In frustration, he slapped the water with his hardwood staff. Tramp recoiled from the noisy splash. "Damn it!" Jetsam swung the staff again, hard into the river bottom, rocking the skiff. The canine barked at him.

Jetsam slammed his staff onto the raft, and plopped next to Tramp. The skiff rocked and water bled onto the deck, washing the uninvited springtails overboard. The dog trembled and licked himself. "Sorry, boy, I just don't know what to *do*." Jetsam petted Tramp behind the ears, and stifled a sob. Tramp licked his lips and raised his paw.

Jetsam stuck his other hand into his pocket, fingering the magic crystal.

Then, he heard a whisper.

Chapter Eight

Seryn rode on the knobby shoulder of his hunchbacked captor. *Bound, gagged, and hoisted like a potato sack,* Seryn lamented. *How the devil can I escape?* He spared his raw wrists and refrained from tugging on his restraining irons. *I'll not get out of these.* Like his aching body, Seryn's mind suffered exhaustion. *Spirit knows the last time I've eaten, who knows if I can even stand?* His dangling feet itched to touch the ground. *Are they ever going to stop?* His damaged ribs and swollen knee anguished with every bounce and breath and his full bladder suffered every motion. *Still can't see a bloody thing and all I smell is god-awful troll stink.*

Onward into the blackness the pack lumbered, splashing Seryn with every step. *Wonder how many there are?* His wet hair hung in strands as he listened to multiple sets of legs wading through the water. *May not have to worry about being eaten—doubt I can survive much more of this marching.* Seryn's pain, hunger, and physical abuse pulled him into a state of feverish delirium. And the sloshing tortured his strained bladder. *I can't hold it any longer.* With a sigh, Seryn released his water and the warm liquid ran down his legs and into his wet boots. A slurry of river water, sweat, and urine soaked his shriveling feet. *Maybe it's a blessing I haven't eaten in days. Certainly can't make the stink any worse.*

The relief from his empty bladder evaporated as his litany of other ailments filled the void. And yet his physical discomfort paled compared to his mental anguish. *Why haven't they eaten me?* He coughed a ball of phlegm that stuck on his gag. *We've been traveling far too long. Trolls don't range this far from their lair.* Other than the splashing, no sounds, besides an occasion grunt or hiss, reached Seryn's ears.

Trolls don't hiss. Seryn gnawed on his leather gag. *And why the devil would they tighten my gag?* Seryn lacked an obvious answer. *I've got to get free.* Seryn catalogued his options, and none of them were promising. *I've no chance of escape until they set me down.* His limp body bobbed in unison with the troll's lumbering motion. *If they set me down.* A wiry troll hair poked his damp cheek. *And if I don't drown.*

With ideas on his own survival muddled, Seryn's mind wandered to his apprentice. *Wonder if the lad tried to follow me?* His last image of Jetsam flashed in his mind. *I pray he didn't trail me, but I fear he did.* Seryn realized the odds that Jetsam still tracked him were slim. *Even if he followed us, he couldn't keep up through this water.* The trolls' long legs strode at a tireless pace. *And what chance would he have?* Despite his fear for Jetsam's safety, the thought of being abandoned still saddened him.

Seryn recalled tutoring Jetsam last winter, safe and warm in the grotto. *All the good I hoped to do for him, and it's for naught.* The lad's companionship had been the lone bright spot in Seryn's lengthy exile. *Now Jetsam's alone again, his hopes dashed once more.* Seryn shook his inverted head. *I was a fool for encouraging him.* He chuckled in despair. *No good deed goes unpunished.*

A gouging agony in his rump yanked Seryn from his wallowing. He writhed and screamed through the gag, releasing a muffled howl. *Devil's luck, they've finally decided to eat me!* Seryn thrashed and kicked, pulling from the bite only to suffer the suffocating squeeze of the beast's sharp claws. He yelled again, to no avail. Warm blood ran down his leg and into his boot. Though breath abandoned him, Seryn kicked even harder when teeth touched his rent flesh.

No!

As an incisor pierced his rump once again, Seryn heard a whistling hiss that stung his eardrums. *What the devil was that?* Shrill and sharp, the whistle-hiss halted his hungry captor. The creature released Seryn's buttock from its maw and growled. *Whatever it was, the troll obeyed.* He moved his bound hands to his injured rear. With the back of his hand, he felt his rent trousers and his raw, wet flesh. Seryn explored the throbbing wound with his fingers and shuddered. With a grimace, he pushed the torn fabric over the bite to staunch the bleeding. *Going to get infected.* To take his mind off his newest injury, Seryn forced his thoughts to recollections of Ioma.

At Dwim-Halloe's Royal Harvest Ball, Seryn observed the first nervous suitor take the floor with Princess Ioma. Relieved he wouldn't be the first one in the fish bowl, Seryn spied the young noble's sweating brow and self-conscious countenance. *Poor bastard.* He was the first of many, and Seryn scrutinized these men, seeing them as competition. But it proved difficult to keep his eyes off Ioma.

When the princess took her infrequent breaks, Seryn watched Lord Nargul. One minute he whispered in the king's ear, the next, he chatted with a potential suitor. After a while, Seryn discerned which nobles Nargul favored. *Valin's one of them.* Now, the lord high chamberlain stood shoulder to shoulder with Valin, sharing a laugh. The more Seryn saw of Tark Nargul, the less he liked him. *The sycophant.*

As Princess Ioma took the floor with another hopeful suitor, Seryn's promised last dance seemed eons away. He swallowed another mouthful of Calderian red. *She plays the part well.*

When Valin's turn arrived, Seryn neared the bottom of his second goblet. His eyes focused on the dancing pair. *My brother and the princess.*

A curdling nausea rumbled through his gut as his brother took the princess' hand and kissed it. Seryn shook his head as the couple began. *His dancing's improved,* Seryn noted, before finishing his wine. As they graced the floor, Valin's lips moved more than Ioma's. *Go on and bore her to tears, you oaf.* And yet Seryn spotted Ioma's ivory teeth shining through her red-lipped smile.

A fake smile, he tried to convince himself. *She's just being polite.*

With a wave, Seryn begged off another refill. Watching his brother and Ioma, he lost his desire for drink. *This bloody song goes on forever.* Seryn suspected Valin shielded his view on purpose, as if he knew Seryn's eyes lingered upon them. *'Tis just my imagination,* he mused, glancing at his empty goblet. *Or the red.*

When the number finally concluded, Seryn thirsted for another drink. Though loathe to admit it, he feared Valin made a decent impression on the princess. Seryn relented to his craving and refilled his goblet. *I'll nurse it until my turn.*

As the last dance approached, Valin hovered near Seryn, who pretended not to notice. *He'll not take this well.* The princess floated toward the Vardan brothers, her fingers outstretched. Seryn endured Valin's heat as he accepted Ioma's hand and strode onto the dance floor.

From the corner of his eye, he saw Valin lurch.

"Good evening, Your Royal Highness," he said, forsaking the presumptuous kiss his brother bestowed upon her fair hand. *Start dancing, ere Valin tackles me.* "You are a vision of loveliness this eve, as ever."

"You are gracious, as ever, Lord Vardan, but I fear I shall be a poor dance partner, for the weight of this gown has sapped my stamina."

"Fear not, for the song is slow, and despite the wine, I retain enough strength to keep us both upright." He glimpsed a flash of her smile and his heart fluttered.

"Hold tight, for I am so warm I fear I may faint in your arms. I've not danced so long in my life, and you were unlucky enough to draw the last dance." Her forehead glistened with moistness and her cheeks flushed. *She speaks true,* Seryn lamented, gauging her fatigue.

"I have never felt more lucky than I do at this moment," he gushed.

"You're the perfect gentleman, and witty, too, but the heat grows too much to bear. I fear I must take my leave and find a chair."

What? No! Think of something, you dolt. "If I may be so bold, m'lady, would you allow me to relieve you of the heat?"

"Were your hands of ice, it would not cool me enough."

It may have been the wine, or the moment, or even the moon, but Seryn swaggered. With whispered words and a subtle wave of his fingers, he cast the mildest of incantations on the unsuspecting princess. *If anyone notices, they'll drag me to the donjon,* he thought, only half in jest.

From the perimeter, Tark Nargul and Valin glared.

Ioma's eyes grew saucer-like as a refreshing coolness enveloped her and seeped beneath her skin. Her jaw dropped, yet she kept pace with the dance.

"I feel kissed by an ocean breeze." She cocked a thin brow at her partner. "Did you ensorcel me, Seryn Vardan?"

"I fear I did, m'lady," Seryn confessed. "But only to rid you the burden of that debilitating heat. For, if you were to leave me alone on this floor, my heart would break."

"Father warned me about wizards," she teased. "I should have heeded him."

"Your father is wise, for we of Eh' liel Ev' Narron are scoundrels."

"Do I stand a chance against your insidious wizardry?"

"You've already fallen prey to my mystical charms, for unbeknownst to you, my magic has shielded you from the worst dancing you've ever known."

When she laughed, Seryn's heart leapt.

The dance ended too soon, yet Ioma appeared more refreshed than before she stepped on the floor.

Seryn held her hand high and bowed with a flourish. "'Twas an honor, m'lady."

"The fates smiled upon me by saving the best for last." She winked and waltzed away, leaving Seryn to melt onto the polished floor.

"Think you're clever, don't you?" Valin said over Seryn's shoulder. Seryn turned toward his brother, expecting the worst, while still floating on butterfly wings.

"I do, yes. Thought you knew as much."

"Don't fancy yourself a suitor—you're out of your league."

"I rather think you're wrong. I'm right in my element with the princess."

"I warn you, don't cross me again. You'll not stop me from the throne."

"Ah, the throne you seek, is it? Then we have no quarrel, for all I wish is to spend time with Ioma."

"You know damn well this isn't about romance," Valin steamed. "Besides, the princess adored me, and Lord Nargul himself said I made an excellent candidate."

"Have no worries. For if the princess chooses me, you and Lord Nargul shall make a dashing couple."

"You're not fit to be king," Valin said. "No unnatural is!"

A bestial grunt snapped Seryn from his daydreaming as he bounced along on the troll's shoulder. *Why's life so difficult?* With every step the monster took, Seryn's organs suffered an agonizing blow and his bloodied backside stung. *What've I done to deserve such hardship?* He kept his eyes closed, protected from the errant splash. *I've not been a bad person, I've done no harm, and yet, all I endure is suffering.* The beast beneath him coughed a phlegm-laden rumble, sending a tremor through Seryn's floppy form and flaring his rump's fresh wound. *From the day Mother died, it's been an uphill battle, and I keep sliding further backward.* The troll spit a glob of mucus and Seryn heard it plop into the water. *My brother's king, married to my true love, and I'm branded a murderous outlaw.* He smirked at the irony as snot bubbled up from his nostrils. *And I was always the* good *one!*

Seryn ignored the unusual sensations he detected in the tunnel. *I'm feverish and delirious.* But as the troll pack plunged ever onward and his body grew numb, the mental sensations grew, prickly and invasive. *I'm not imagining it.* He chased the painful imagery of Valin and Ioma from his mind and heeded his sixth sense. *There's energy in this tunnel.*

Seryn craned his head, gazing sideways into the blackness, searching for a clue to the emanation. *Is that a hint of light?* He doubted his overwhelmed senses. *I'm just imagining things.* Blood pounded in his upside-down head and his eyeballs ached.

He closed his eyes and held them shut as his captor lumbered ever forward. *There's less splashing,* he realized. *Pace is quickening— water's shallower.* When Seryn reopened his eyes, he detected a subtle difference. *There's light ahead.* His neglected pupils adjusted. *And the magic's even stronger.*

His battered body fed off the supernatural emanation. *If I could cast a spell, this aura would magnify my power.* The sensation stumped him. *Never read about such a phenomenon at Eh' liel Ev' Narron.*

Seryn enjoyed no time to ponder, as each troll step carried him into the light and onto dryer footing. *One more secret left unsolved before I die.* Inverted against a troll's shoulder blade, Seryn suffered a compromised view of his surroundings. *Where the devil are we?*

Seryn spied a wall-mounted torch struggling to illuminate a sprawling cavern. The light reflected off his sinewy captor. *He's huge!* Seryn counted six other trolls, led by a shambling human. *Is that the hisser?* Seryn could only see the man's back, and in the flickering rushlight, his form was a silhouette. *He's heading for a door.* Seryn's fatiguing neck cramped and failed, leaving his skull to bounce off the troll's leaden ribcage.

To what horrors does it lead?

As if in reply, the door creaked open, spilling lantern light into the cavern, bathing the trolls in a brighter illumination than the sputtering wall torch. A bulky pair of armored men stepped through the portal. *Soldiers?* As the light fed color to their surcoats, Seryn recognized the sigil. *Crescent moon over the Mirrored Peaks and Wizard's Tower.* He scrutinized the shining mail. *Are they royal guards?*

A third figure stepped through the subterranean entrance and onto the cavern floor. *It can't be.* The regal man spoke the first words Seryn had heard in days, and they chilled him to his soul.

That voice! Seryn's head spun as he tried to discern the speaker, yet there was no mistaking his ears. Though the exact words eluded him, the voice sliced Seryn like a blade.

Father?

Chapter Nine

Bobbing in the stagnant stream, Jetsam scrutinized the three passages in front of him. As if scarred by a giant trident, the ominous voids in the rock stared back at him, tight-lipped and protecting their secret. Jetsam gnawed his lip as his gaze covered every inch of the panorama, seeking a clue as to which passage the trolls selected.

Left.

"Left?" Jetsam repeated. He glanced at Tramp. "Hear that, buddy boy?" Tramp lifted his head, oblivious. But a faraway whisper from somewhere deep inside, Jetsam understood the gravity of heeding the instruction. His only doubt was whether he heard a voice at all, or imagined it in his desperation. "Whatever you say, Elvar," he agreed, acknowledging his brother's signal from the afterworld. "Left it is."

A subtle smile graced Jetsam's face. Where moments ago, doubt and despair taunted him, the spirit-voice filled him with a calming confidence. His sibling's single word laid bare the path ahead. Jetsam grasped his staff and launched the raft forward.

Either way, we'll accomplish nothing by sitting idle, Jetsam assured himself.

Into the leftmost passage the rickety skiff ventured. *Short of a dead-end, there's no turning back.* He felt heartened, if but slightly. Direction decided, he believed his brother's spirit guided the way. *To*

Seryn, I hope.

With the burden of decision lifted, Jetsam released a weighty breath and admired nature's subterranean artwork. Eons of trickling water painted a mosaic of mineral deposits that reveled in the rare illumination. The flickering flames cast iridescent splashes and dancing shadows on the glossy cavern. Combined with the moving raft, flowing water, and dripping stalactites, the static cave appeared animated. From the corner of his eye, Jetsam caught an ivory spider darting across his glistening web. Tramp spotted it, too, and released a sharp yip.

"Speedy little bugger, eh, boy?"

A few furlongs into the snaking passage, the current revived, and Jetsam no longer needed to push. From his pouch, he retrieved a handful of ligonberries for himself and a strip of pickled venison for his furry companion. Tramp devoured the meat with nary a bite before Jetsam even swallowed his first sour berry.

"You even taste it?" he asked. Tramp licked his chops and stared at Jetsam. "That's all for now, buddy boy." Jetsam's words did little to discourage Tramp's pleading stare. "Just a bit more, then." Jetsam tossed another red berry in his mouth and tore off one last nibble for his terrier. Jetsam finished with a bite of the deer meat. The peppercorn flavor tempted a sneeze, but he held it back.

The underground river's flow moved them at a deceptive pace, and Jetsam added speed with his staff. *We must be gaining on them,* he thought, imagining a pack of trolls sloshing through the water. As he rode the winding river, gazing at the cavern features, Jetsam spied something floating. "See it, Tramp?" Guiding the skiff toward it, he retrieved a torn piece of cloth. Tramp sniffed the wet fabric hanging from Jetsam's fingers.

"Is it Seryn's, buddy boy?" Jetsam lifted the sopping cloth to his nostrils. Even in the saturated fabric, he recognized troll stink. Tramp's wagging tail told Jetsam the terrier identified more than just a knuckle-dragger. Jetsam fingered the strip of fur-lined wool. "Could be Seryn's cloak." Jetsam's confidence grew, yet he failed to conceive how to free his teacher from the humpbacks, if he caught up to them. *Do trolls sleep?*

As the hours passed, the monotony grew. The torch-lit cavern walls captivated Jetsam, but even their natural beauty grew familiar. He glanced at the terrier, ears at attention, and a sliver of pink tongue poking out. As always, Tramp's nostrils twitched, cataloging the world.

"Too bad you never got to meet Elvar, buddy boy." Tramp tilted his head. "You would've liked him. He loved dogs." Jetsam's memories slipped back to Dwim-Halloe and the underbelly. "We could never keep a pet, though. Barely had enough to feed ourselves. Besides, the strays liked the underbelly even less than you." Jetsam remembered his brother playing with the feral mutts—the friendly ones, at least.

Jetsam held but fuzzy images of his life before the underbelly. Besides cherished memories of his parents and home, he recalled their family dog. "Brute," we called him, he informed Tramp. "He was bigger than you. Black and brown and white and furry." Jetsam recollected wrestling with the floppy-eared mountain dog. "Never saw him again after we ran away." The recollections of his harried flight intruded on his warm memories. Jetsam feared the worst for the protective hound, knowing the fate bestowed upon his parents. He imagined Brute growling and snapping at the intruding guards. *Poor old Brute.*

Lips sealed, he petted Tramp, and the raft-bound terrier grew restless. He nipped at Jetsam's hand and flopped on his back, mouthing his thumb. Jetsam wiggled his fingers and circled his hand around Tramp's head. The panting dog's attentive eyes glued to Jetsam's hand. He scratched the blissful canine's belly and rolled him around on the raft floor. Somewhere between a scratch and a massage, Jetsam worked his fingers into the dog's fur, eliciting a contented murmur. Tramp's enthusiasm raised Jetsam's spirit, and took his mind off the eventual unpleasantness ahead. The pair played until Jetsam's arm grew weary and Tramp submitted to a nap.

With his dog dozing, Jetsam's lids grew heavy. He struggled to stay awake, but was too stubborn to sacrifice more time to the leading trolls. Yet, somewhere along the way, he succumbed to slumber.

The inky cavern and bobbing motion imprinted themselves on Jetsam's uneasy dreams. His body conceding to exhaustion and tedium, Jetsam's subconscious visions played out as an incoherent jumble of wavering images. Faces flitted in and out of focus and ominous shadows taunted him. He swam in a pool of sticky black cotton, binding his every movement. The ebony spider webs in his abstract nightmare changed to gravel, scratching his bare skin.

With a start, Jetsam awoke to the scraping of wood on rock. The raft lurched, and he rolled on Tramp. Despite the consuming blackness allowed by the expired torch, Jetsam knew they'd run aground. He fumbled blindly on the raft deck until his fingers located another brand amidst his belongings. Unnerved by waking sightless on a beached raft in an unknown cavern, he lit the torch with a spell. Once the flambeau took flame, Jetsam confirmed his suspicion. The river ran low and split around a higher slab of rock between the two branches.

A foot-worn path meandered across the stone surface. Jetsam knelt and tried to discern fresh tracks, but the rocky terrain revealed none. Upon standing, Jetsam noticed Tramp picked up a scent. "Is it Seryn, boy?" *If only he could answer.* Tramp lifted his snout and checked Jetsam, then licked his lips. Jetsam considered his options. *I'll follow the path, at least for a short while, or until Elvar tells me which river branch to take.* For now, he noticed nothing but trickling water and Tramp's attentive sniffing.

"Magic feels strong here," he told the terrier, as they worked their way up the dank passage. *Where could it be coming from?* He brushed his fingertips along the coarse wall. Tramp held steady on the trail and Jetsam observed enough of a trodden path to keep faith in his partner. *Wonder how close we are?* He couldn't imagine the trolls using a water craft, and guessed they slogged knee-deep through the shallow river.

Jetsam's adrenaline surged, while the diligent terrier scanned the stone floor, locked on a scent and visibly excited to be off the water. Senses on high alert, Jetsam's eyes darted from the tunnel ahead, to the floor below, to Tramp, and back again, cycling his concentration to detect any clue. He perceived the magical sensation growing as they delved, but with his concentration focused at the task at hand, the magical pulse remained an afterthought. But he stored it in the back of his mind and fingered the crystal in his pocket. *Wonder if there's a connection?*

Tramp emitted a rumbling growl, a tone so low and deep, Jetsam didn't think it came from his terrier. Tramp stood at attention, fur on end. Jetsam inhaled, and he, too, smelled the odor. *Troll.* With a finger to his lips, he quieted the canine.

As he set the burning brand against a jagged protrusion, Jetsam discovered bits of crystal clinging to the cave wall. *What's this?* His hand prickled at the magic emanating from the fragments. He retrieved the shard from his pocket and compared it to the residue on the stony surface. *Both milky-white,* he confirmed. *Looks like somebody's harvesting the stuff.* He considered trying to scrape off the residual crumbs, but realized the sand ran low in Seryn's hourglass.

With his burning torch wedged by the crystal flakes, Jetsam crept into blackness. The stench lingered as he tiptoed away from the fading light. He detected a faint glow in the passage ahead, crouched lower, and signaled Tramp to stay silent.

With his dying torch abandoned, he and his companion wore a cloak of shadow. Soft-footed as the dog, Jetsam slunk forward, focusing on his stealth, while wondering what he'd find, and what he'd do. Momentum was on his side, as he allowed himself to be pulled toward the inevitable action. With each step, the light ahead grew brighter. Jetsam suffered the icy breath of death tickling his nape. *This day, death smells of troll.* The reaper commanded fear, but Jetsam resisted.

Jetsam detected movement in the blot of light. He breathed deep and checked his faithful partner. If possible, the terrier focused even more than Jetsam. Blue eyes squinting, Jetsam discerned forms ahead. Towering, humpbacked, gangly forms—several of them.

And two humans.

Jetsam halted, resisting the urge to rush ahead. *Seryn would be proud,* he thought, reflecting on his budding self-control. He lifted the terrier and Tramp licked his chin. Jetsam tallied muted shapes in the distance.

Five, six... seven! Seven knuckle-draggers. No wonder they decimated the caravan. One of the beasts lumbered out of eyesight, giving Jetsam a better view of the two men silhouetted by a wall-mounted torch.

One man appeared gagged and bound, shoulders slumped and head hung low. *Seryn?* After scrutinizing the captive's height and physique, Jetsam grew certain. With Seryn's fur cloak missing, the restrained spellcaster sat shivering in his gray tunic and breeches. Jetsam conceded his teacher would be little help in his own rescue.

At least he lives.

Jetsam felt Tramp trembling against his own pounding chest. Step by step, Jetsam drew closer, gauging his own visibility in the flickering rushlight. Satisfied with the concealing darkness, he pushed forward.

Something about the man next to Seryn made him uneasy. While hugging the cavern wall in front of a concealing bend, Jetsam decided further progress risked revealing himself in the dim light. Knees bent and back bowed, he peered around the corner.

The two men stood next to an imposing door. Thick oak planks crisscrossed reinforcing braces, held fast by iron straps and secured with iron studs. The fortified door was shut, and Jetsam saw no handle or latch to open the portal from this side. The trolls mulled around the general vicinity. They seemed invisibly tethered to the unsettling figure next to Seryn. *Like wild dogs on long leashes.*

The low moan of creaking wood echoed through the cavern as the door swung open. Lantern light spilled from beyond, illuminating the bound Seryn and the man next to him.

Kandris Bayen!

Jetsam couldn't believe his eyes. Craning and squinting, his chest tightened. *It is Kandris!* Jetsam's dislike of the craven squire blossomed into a full-blown hatred. *Drahkang-roth was right! But how? That weasel would soil himself before getting that close to a knuckle-dragger, let alone seven!*

Jetsam glared at the former squire to Sir Prentice Imoor. *He looks like death.* Jetsam recalled Kandris' fastidious attire from their days tending camp, but now the lanky squire appeared as if he still wore the same outfit since Jetsam last saw him. His cloak ragged and faded, Kandris reminded Jetsam of a moth-eaten blanket flung atop a coat rack. Though his tattered clothes bleached from the sunlight, the squire's pasty skin looked as though he'd spent the last six months in a sarcophagus. *His hair's not grown an inch.* The shoulder-length locks hung matted and knotted.

Can't imagine how awful he smells.

Before Jetsam took it all in, two more men stepped through the doorway, oblivious to the humpbacks, who returned the favor. The armored men wore the crimson and cream surcoats of Dwim-Halloe.

Jetsam's head spun. *Oxbow soldiers ignoring trolls? And trolls ignoring them…*

A third man followed the guards. Cloaked in a luxurious ermine fur cape, the man wore a velvet mantle over an ivory tunic, with a gemstone-studded belt fastening his striped breeches. A feathered cap and pointy boots completed the outfit. Despite his extravagant attire, he also looked familiar.

"Been a long time," the regal man said to Seryn, who made no reply. "Finally caught you, after all these years." The duo shared many features—oval faces, auburn hair, and piercing eyes. Though their outfits could not have been more different, the regal man's face reflected an uncanny similarity. *Like an older Seryn!*

Like the king, a familiar voice echoed on the fringe of his consciousness.

Jetsam's stomach churned as Kandris handed Seryn over to this man. *This king,* he fumed. *This king, who killed my parents, betrayed his own brother, outlawed sorcery, and consorts with trolls!* Jetsam ground his teeth.

This king must die!

As Jetsam's fury boiled, the king nodded to his men and turned back toward the open door. The two guards grabbed Seryn and pushed him behind the king. Jetsam's mind raced for a spell. He dropped Tramp, extended his staff, and initiated a chant. The terrier skirted behind Jetsam, ears pinned and head low.

"Av-erif unan umine!"

As the Elven words leapt from Jetsam's tongue, Seryn, the king, and his men headed into the tunnel. As the hefty oaken door swung shut behind them, Jetsam's spell came to life. A bolt of crackling fire jetted from the hardwood staff, across the cavern, toward the closing door and the king disappearing behind it. The scent of brimstone permeated the humid air. A meandering troll stepped in the ribbon's path, and cooked to the core. The concentrated inferno melted the creature's skin, tore into its broad chest, and boiled the abomination's heart in its own blood.

Before the smoking carcass hit the ground, Jetsam realized he'd made a grave mistake. *You fobbing fool!* In trying to save Seryn, he'd failed him again. Now his anger and rash decision revealed himself to seven—nay six—charging trolls.

And his magic was gone.

The bloody cavern reeks of burnt humpback. Jetsam choked down the bile upturning his stomach.

With no other option, Jetsam secured his smoking staff in his back harness, scooped up Tramp, and ran back the tunnel. *I'll not vomit,* he promised himself. He knew the underground river lay ahead, and he didn't need to look behind to confirm the troglodytes trailed him. He recognized their grunting, slapping, claw-foot on stone sound all too well. *To think, I'd never seen a knuckle-dragger 'til a year ago.* No more prepared than he was then—he'd wasted his sole advantage. *Now, they're everywhere I go.*

"Just like old times," he told Tramp, tucked in the crook of his arm. Jetsam's eyes tracked a dim light as he retraced his steps. He rushed past the torch he discarded moments earlier, its embers still radiating enough light for his eyes to detect. By the time his long legs carried him to the raft, he suspected several—if not all—of the trolls followed.

Raft's too slow. They'll catch us for sure.

Jetsam barreled headlong into the water, sticking to the wall and the river's shallowest part. Still the liquid reached his thighs, and his pace slowed to a crawl. He recognized that in the water, the towering monstrosities would gain on him. As his boots filled, his burning thighs churned. Thunderous splashing told him the knuckle-draggers reached the river's edge.

Invisibility would help, he concluded. *Too bad I haven't learned that one. Not that I could cast anything now,* he lamented. He caught a whiff of Tramp, the soaked canine now as wet as he was. *Humpbacks' would still smell us.* Despite his empty reservoir, Jetsam's mind flooded his head with his litany of learned spells. *Sunblink might slow them.* Recalling the ogre ambush at the Gaalf, Jetsam realized his fire spells would be counteracted by the water. *Wet rubber-skins are hard to cook.* As the water fought his every step, Jetsam considered turning the liquid to ice. *No way I could freeze the whole river—and I'd be stuck, too.* This deep underground, there was no vegetation to animate. *Not that it would stop them.* As his saturated leather boots slipped on the hard cavern floor, he debated another tactic. *Guess I could turn the river bottom to muck—if I had any magic left.* He adjusted his grip on the growling terrier, as his bad ankle throbbed in the frigid river. *Have to try that next time.*

Jetsam used his left hand to guide along the slippery wall, while he held Tramp tight in his right hand. His heavy wet boot landed on a loose stone, and before he could react, his mouth filled with sour liquid as he sunk beneath the surface. Tramp slipped away as Jetsam's hands shot forward to break his fall. The confounding water thwarted the attempt, and he landed face-first on the river bottom, once again soaked to the bone. As the liquid pushed the air from his lungs, Jetsam struggled to hold his breath. He'd swallowed enough stagnant water and wanted no more.

The water burned his nostrils as he scrambled to regain his feet. He coughed out the vile liquid, only to have more surge back into his lungs. Still submerged on hands and knees, he sensed gravity reverse. His tangled head broke the surface and cool air filled his tortured lungs. Spit from the water, Jetsam hovered in space, arms and legs flailing.

He had no clue what happened.

"Tramp?"

A slavering brute held Jetsam aloft, shaking him as he showed off his prey to the other humpbacks. Jetsam heard the bloodthirsty grunting as the pack closed in on him.

His head swirled and he vomited a quart of river water sprinkled with chewed lingonberry down the assailant's sinewy arm.

Chapter Ten

As the tunnel door slammed shut behind him and his captors, Seryn heard a crackling explosion on the other side. The oaken door rattled on its hinges, but held firm. *What* was *that?* Seryn's head jerked back toward the tunnel while the two royal guards pulled him up the stairs, his numb legs dragging. *Sounded like a fire spell.* He heard a troll's anguished roar from the cavern opposite the door. *Jetsam?* As Seryn's wet boots dragged on the stairway, he smelled a hint of brimstone. *I swear it was a spell. But there were* seven *trolls.* An image of Jetsam flashed in his brain. *Pray, lad, don't get yourself killed.*

"Lock it," the familiar voice said, and the hissing man slapped the heavy bolt in place. When the guards glanced at the door, the man scolded them. "Ignore it! Move faster."

Could it be him?

The armored duo complied with solemn nods. As the pace accelerated, Seryn scrutinized the leader from behind him. *His hair's not gray.* Seryn's head spun in confusion. *He's too young.* The regal commander craned back at his soldiers. Even after all these years, the face remained unmistakable. *Of course, he sounds like Father.*

"Faster, I said!"

The guards ascended the spiral staircase in a careless rush, following the king and jostling Seryn as much as the troll. He bit his gag in anguish. Behind Seryn and his tandem escort, the hissing man followed. No more words were spoken.

Are they taking me to the executioner? Seryn wilted in the guards' grasp. *Will he even grant me a trial?* His bloodshot eyes glared at the back of his brother's head. *I'm his own blood, for spirits' sake.*

Weary of his toes stubbing the stone stairs, Seryn moved his leaden legs in rhythm with the guards, and spared his feet more pounding, though aggravating his wounded rump. After days of inactivity in the wagon and on the troll's shoulder, his atrophied muscles fatigued. *I'm so weak.*

Before long, his swollen knee ached and his cramping legs once again dangled while his bruised feet slapped the stone stairs. *I've no strength to keep up, much less escape.* Seryn closed his eyes and struggled to lift his aching feet. *Please, let it end.*

Well beyond the point Seryn imagined he could endure, the party reached a landing. With a cell-lined hallway before him, he guessed his location. Though he recalled stories of the infamous prison beneath the Wizard's Tower, he'd never set foot there.

But instead of depositing him in one of the cramped cells, his escorts hauled him through the corridor to another room. *What is this place?* As Seryn glanced around the circular chamber, his spirits crashed further than he thought possible.

Fates curse me!

His captors held him upright against a granite pillar. Seryn's unsteady legs wobbled as the guards pinned him in place. He scanned the chamber, his eyes wide and nostrils flaring. The king's hissing creature clamped a choker around Seryn's neck, pinching his wet hair in the hinge. The pale hands fastened the heavy choker chain to the column. *He looks like the Calderian squire,* Seryn thought, as the deathly-looking man locked the chain to an iron ring. *But he's not alive—not human.*

"Hands and feet," the king instructed his minion.

The undead Kandris Bayen attached another chain to Seryn's wrist shackles and locked him to a floor ring. *Please, brother, let me speak.* The creature yanked Seryn's sopping boots off and restrained his chaffed ankles well.

How strong do they think I am? I haven't eaten in days.

Seryn felt the creature's frigid hands loosen his gag. *They're as cold as the floor.* As the leather strap fell away, Seryn stretched his mouth and jaw while staring at his brother. The king averted his pleading gaze.

"Where are the other unnaturals?"

"Valin, listen, I didn't kill Tygan."

"*Your Majesty*, kingslayer," corrected the king's guard with a backhanded slap to Seryn's aching jaw.

"*Where* are the other unnaturals?" The question rolled off the royal tongue without a hint of emotion.

What other unnaturals? Haven't you killed them all? "Please, hear me out."

"Turn him 'round," the king said.

Kandris Bayen grabbed Seryn's shoulder and yanked him. Seryn's front smacked against the pillar as his chains twisted and pulled. *He smells of death.* Seryn wrenched back toward his brother, shrugging off the former squire's icy hand.

Now what, Valin?

As he swiveled, Seryn spied Kandris' fist streaking toward his face. A ball of stiff flesh hammered Seryn's nose before he could dodge. Cartilage cracked and blood gushed from his nostrils as his watery eyes clamped shut.

Seryn collapsed, but before he reached his knees, his choker chain pulled tight, hanging him from the pillar. The iron collar bit into his jaw while his stinging eyes dripped tears and his nose bled. One of the guards jerked his chains before Seryn could find his feet, turning him sideways as a whip slashed across his back.

Fates have mercy!

Seryn grunted and spat blood onto the floor as the whip bit him again. Pain clouded his mind as he braced for another blow. Kandris cracked the leather and sent it snaking across Seryn's blistering ribs.

Should have killed that bloody squire back in the Kierawaith. Seryn contemplated the abomination Kandris Bayen had become. *Would have been better for both of us.*

The king spit out his question, enunciating each word. "Where are the rest of Dwim-Halloe's wizards?"

Seryn raised his swelling, bleeding head toward his brother. "Dead. Thanks to you."

He convulsed as the whip tore another strip of flesh from his back.

Just like old times.

"Not all of them," the king said. "Not yet."

Kandris fed him the leather again.

"Where. Are. They?"

"Gods' sake, Valin, I don't *know!*"

"Your Majesty," the guard corrected, repeating his slap to Seryn's cheek. The gauntlet blow sent a spray of blood from Seryn's nose. The crimson droplets splattered on his bare feet. "Don't make me tell you again."

"Finger." The king nodded at Kandris, who exchanged the bloody whip for shears.

"No!" Seryn shouted as the former squire grasped his shackled hand. "We're kin!"

Kandris bent Seryn's little finger at an odd angle and applied the shears. *And to think I feared the executioner!* Seryn clamped his watering eyes and gritted his teeth as the blades sliced.

He groaned as his finger fell to the floor, followed by a trail of blood. Seryn felt lightheaded and held his thumb over the wound to staunch the flow. He tore his gaze from his bleeding knuckle and focused on his brother.

"Damn it, what the devil are you doing?" His petulance earned him another slap, this one loosening an incisor.

"I'll ask once more, where are your cohorts hiding?"

"I've no cohorts! Your *Majesty.*" Seryn sucked his loose tooth, tasting blood. *Who is he looking for?* "I've lived alone in the wilderness for a decade."

King Valin Vardan's icy gray eyes examined Seryn, who saw no reflection of pity. *What the devil happened to you, Valin?* "I'm telling the sodding truth! Your Majesty."

"Where did you hide?"

Seryn dropped his head and sighed. "In a cave in the bloody Kierawaith!" He braced for another slap, but received an unexpected reprieve. *His hand must hurt.*

"And the dragon?"

Seryn's jaw fell faster than the blood from his hand. *How does he know of the dragon?* Seryn scrutinized his stoic brother. *He's bluffing.* "What dragon?"

"Take one from the other hand," Valin instructed.

"No—wait!" Seryn slumped as gravity pulled against his restraints. "The dragon's gone. She used to dwell in Asigonn, but I don't know where she is now." Seryn's legs wobbled and his bare soles slid an awkward dance in his own blood. *His heart's a frozen stone.* From the corner of his eye, he saw his finger in a vermilion pool, and his knees buckled. Bereft of strength and hope, he collapsed, hanging from the wall chain clamped around his neck. *I can't breathe, and I don't care.*

"Hold him up."

Kandris lifted Seryn under the arms. *I'm as dead as he.*

"If anyone knows of the remaining rebels, it's you, and I shall have that information before I remove your head."

I'm already dead to you. Seryn's fiery gaze burned into his brother's emotionless orbs. *As you are to me.* Seryn licked his slippery gums and forced out his reply. "One of your bounty hunters killed the lord high wizard." The words fell from his parched lips in a strained whisper. "He was the last I knew of."

Before he could spit out 'Your Majesty,' Seryn's head dropped, and he fainted.

"Move toward my voice," Vellae Lothyrn said.

Eighteen-year-old Seryn Vardan attempted a reply, but the soggy leather in his mouth prevented a response. He tried to stand, but with his bound hands behind him, it proved no simple task. With each torturous movement, the wrist irons chewed his raw skin. He backed against the stone wall and pushed himself up, scraping his back along the way. On wobbly legs he shuffled toward the voice.

"This way," she urged. "Careful."

Blind and mute, with only his ears to guide him, Seryn slid toward her.

"Come here—I'll remove your hood." Seryn leaned into the iron bars, bumping his forehead.

"Turn 'round—slowly. 'Tis knotted in back."

His head jerked while she untied the knot, her thin hands

working between the bars. A cavalcade of questions queued in his mind, while he waited for his mouth to be freed. *Did you see the men who abducted me? What did they look like? Where am I now? How did you get in here? Who would do this? And why?* After a long minute, the hood peeled off his damp head. His auburn locks stuck matted to his scalp in knotty strings.

Though the air in the cell lingered dank and musty, after breathing through the hood for so long, it tasted fresh to Seryn. A torch outside his cell cast weak illumination into his room. He gazed upon the tiny chamber, a dirty square, every surface save the iron bars was rock. With no windows, the only orifice besides the cell door was a fist-sized floor drain for excrement. A smattering of straw covered the rear of the room.

"Let me get that out of your mouth."

When Seryn obliged, he observed no one in front of him—yet an unseen force pulled the slimy leather from his mouth.

Am I dreaming?

Seryn licked his lips and gums, trying to moisten his arid mouth. "Where are you?" The first words he'd spoken in hours rolled out like a dusty rug.

"Invisible," she said.

"What happened?"

"I saw you taken and followed you here," she said. "But other than that, I've no idea."

"Where are we?" Cow hide lingered on his swollen tongue.

"Hush—we've no time to waste. Turn back around—I'll remove your shackles."

The lingering questions in Seryn's head piled into each other, forced to wait their turn even longer. Vellae whispered an Elven phrase and a familiar pulse of magic energy tickled his skin. His restraints loosened and hands slipped free. Vellae's voice emanated from the empty hallway.

"Making you invisible, too. Hold still."

She recited another incantation. Seryn watched his hands and feet fade to nothingness.

"Take off your clothes and stuff them with straw—make it appear you're lying in the corner."

Seryn did as told, with as much haste as possible. Cold and coarse, the rock floor rebuffed his bare feet, while wet straw clung to his tender soles. *She has a plan*, he convinced himself, stripping to his smallclothes.

Until he met Ioma, he'd harbored a crush on the married mage. Now he disrobed in front of her. *But I'm invisible*, he reminded himself.

On his bare knees, Seryn filled his clothes and hood with straw, set his boots inside his trouser legs, and posed the flimsy rag doll in the back corner. *I suppose*, he deliberated, *in the darkness, it could pass for a curled-up man.*

"That lock is glyphed against sorcery, so we'll need the guard to unlock it for you to slip out." Before Seryn asked her how they'd convince him to do that, she told him. "You must scream—but make it believable. As if you've been stabbed."

Hands at his sides, he cleared his scratchy throat, took a deep breath, and recalled Valin pummeling him over the death of their mother. Seryn let out a blood-curdling howl, and backed to the side of the door.

Seconds later, boots stomped on the stairs.

"Keep quiet, unnatural," the guard scolded, a hint of nervousness in his voice. Seryn watched the man peer into the cell.

He wears Dwim-Halloe garb.

"Damn it," the guard said.

Seryn waited, his invisible hands covered in transparent sweat. His bare back pushed against the chilling masonry.

The guard swore under his breath, squinting at the decoy. "Get up!" He waited a few beats. "Don't make me come in there," he warned. "If this is some trick, I'll beat ye bloody senseless."

Seryn saw the man pull an iron mace from his belt. The guard raked the heavy weapon across the bars, making a clamor to rouse the dead. Seryn plugged his invisible ears with transparent fingers. The flustered soldier harnessed his weapon and fumbled with a key chain.

With the click of a lock and the squeal of a rusty door, the armed guard entered Seryn's cell as if expecting a ghost. He passed within a foot of Seryn. *He's been drinking.*

Seryn didn't wait to see if the guard kicked the straw man or hit him with the mace. As soon as the door swung wide, and the watchman stepped past, Seryn hurried out. From behind, he heard a thud and the guard's furious cursing a moment later.

A clarion rang out as the duped sentry called for reinforcements. The alarm horn caused Seryn's heart to skip a beat. Up the stairs he bolted, his bare feet slapping on the frigid blocks. From a blind turn at the first landing, a descending watchman appeared in his path. *Look out!* Seryn lacked the time or space to avert a collision.

Back pressed to the wall, Seryn avoided a direct impact, and clipped the responding sentry as he raced by, knocking both men off balance. Seryn stuck out a leg and tripped the wobbling sentry, sending the man tumbling down the unforgiving stairs in a litany of profanity.

Seryn pushed on, ignoring his stinging shin. In the stairwell behind him, shouting echoed.

"Bloody unnatural escaped!"

Seryn stepped into the mountain air as his eyes adjusted to the creeping daylight. Dwindling hearth fires polluted the morning breeze as the majority of Dwim-Halloe still slept. The news of yesterday evening had not yet escaped the palace, and the general populace slumbered oblivious to the fact they no longer had a king.

Chapter Eleven

Held aloft above the underground river, foul troll breath slapped Jetsam's cheek as his arms and legs flailed. *Lemme go you sodding wretch!* Exhaled spittle covered his pallid face. *I'll claw your bloody eyes out.* The disgusting maw hovered close enough to taste. Contorted upside down, Jetsam swung for the troll's face.

And missed.

But gravity grabbed Jetsam, accompanied by the sound of fabric tearing. Falling for but a moment, Jetsam hit the water. *I'm free!* The wailing assailant held naught but Jetsam's pack as its yellowed incisors bit into the torn sack. The knuckle-dragger shook its head like a dog, shredding the pack and strewing its contents around the cavern.

With his staff, Regret, and bloated pouch still strapped to his lithe frame, Jetsam sunk. *Hold your breath!* But without his cumbersome pack, he gained more mobility than moments prior. Energized with the stomping of rubbery legs, the turbid water turned frothy. Jetsam's ankle hit something solid, and he lurched away from it, crawling on all fours, holding his breath. His hands clawed the rocky floor and his feet searched for foot holds as he scrambled from the chaos, all the while submerged. *Need air.* He stuck his head above the surface long enough to exhale and refill his lungs. Behind him, the trolls stomped and clawed in the river, searching for their lost minnow.

Tramp! Where's Tramp?

Jetsam slipped back under water, hoping they wouldn't catch the scent of *his* breath. He swam-crawled from the confounded troglodytes, holding his breath until his lungs blistered. He stayed submerged, knowing the water hid his odor from the beasts.

When Jetsam popped above the surface, the unrelenting darkness remained. His ears informed him he'd maneuvered out of the trolls' reach, but they'd soon be on him again.

Then barking echoed throughout the cavern—terrified, angry, confused barking.

Hush, boy, knuckle-draggers will hear you. Jetsam headed toward his noisy companion, high-stepping through the slick wetness. Chasing Tramp's voice, he stumbled up a dry passage, water running off him to the smooth stone floor. Jetsam reached out to the walls. *They're cut stone, too.* His fingers guided him from the underground river into the corridor.

Where'd this come from? Jetsam remembered he'd dozed on the raft, and must have floated past the off-branch in his slumber. *This is like Gwae Gierameth.* He yearned for a torch to light his way, or enough magic to make his staff glow. *Nah, that would just make it easier for the humpbacks to follow.* Undaunted, he trudged on sans light when a yip at his feet stopped him.

"*Good* boy!" Jetsam reached and patted the sopping dog. Tramp licked Jetsam's wet wrist, and they both heard the noisy trolls regrouping. "Come on, buddy boy." Jetsam detected the briefest of lights in the misty passage ahead and resumed his flight with Tramp at his heels.

Jetsam shuffled through the tunnel, chasing the dim glow. He passed a diluted beam of light, reflecting off a mirror set high in the tunnel. *A mirror, here?* Jetsam's brow rose as an anguished squeal erupted behind him, followed by another tortured howl.

Sunlight!

"Must be day time," he told Tramp. Despite the troll screeching, Jetsam and Tramp maintained a steady pace. His wet clothing chaffed his damp skin, and the caterwaul continued behind them, but Jetsam discerned he widened the distance between himself and the carnivores.

They're afraid of the light.

Upon looking up, Jetsam discovered another thin beam, feeding the mirror he had just ambled past. This light led to a third mirror, perched to catch the daylight trickling down an old Dwarven mining vent.

Are the mirrors for the humpbacks, or just a coincidence? As he contemplated the mirrors, he recognized a calm silence in the tunnel behind him. Beyond the overhead vent, the passage again grew black.

"What do you think, buddy boy? Did we lose 'em?" The panting at Jetsam's feet assured him Tramp stood beside him. "Think I can eek out enough to make my staff glow, just a bit." Jetsam pulled the gnarled rod from his back and released the tiniest drop of energy to light his staff. Seconds later, faint blue illuminated the tunnel. It proved adequate to navigate with, albeit at a water-logged pace.

"Looks like Gwae Gierameth, doesn't it?" he said.

The silver-speckled granite appeared just as he remembered the Dwarven walls of the long-dead city beneath Dwim-Halloe. His staff light animated the ivory veins that grew like crystalline cobwebs in the smooth architecture.

"Look, boy," Jetsam said, pointing. "A Dwarven glow-stone." Tramp's night-eyes followed Jetsam's finger, but the dog scanned for a squirrel or coney—not the inlaid phosphorescent gemstone his two-legged partner directed him toward. A few feet later, Jetsam spotted an ornate wall-mounted oil basin. "I *know* we're somewhere in Gwae Gierameth."

Jetsam pushed on, hoping for a familiar sign. At every stairway or upward-sloping passage Jetsam encountered, he chose the incline, longing to reach the surface. *How deep we are, I've no clue.* He moved at a cautious pace, ever aware of the potential for more trolls. Of the pack that abused him in the river, though, he had heard nothing from them since the mirrors.

Wet, cold, and tired, Jetsam suspected he would not breathe fresh air before failing to exhaustion. He discovered a collapsed doorway—another remnant of the powerful quake that devastated Gwae Gierameth all those years ago. The fallen rock left naught but a narrow hole to the room beyond.

"Trolls won't squeeze through that," he said. With the terrier in the crook of his arm, Jetsam ascended the crumbled rock and wiggled through the tight opening. His staff illuminated a storage room, filled with rotting barrels, long since emptied of perishables by vermin.

"We can rest here." By pushing aside crates and containers, he cleared a spot on the stone floor. Without his pack, their blanket and food floated somewhere in the subterranean waterway. Jetsam sighed, shivering in his dampness. He conjured another blue ball of radiating heat, and kept it glowing until once again his magic depleted. *How did I survive so long without casting spells?*

Jetsam awoke stiff and sore with a rumbling stomach. Tramp waited by his side, alert as ever. With a sharp bark and a spin on the floor, the terrier let Jetsam know he was hungry, too. "Got nothing left, buddy boy." Jetsam fastened his sword belt and slung his staff across his back. With a grunt, he lifted Tramp and climbed out of his hiding spot. His knees popped as he landed on the granite-floored corridor.

"Today, we find our way out."

He and Tramp climbed every stairway and rising passage they found. Dead-ends taunted him, as they backtracked through several tunnels, retreating to the next unknown wormhole. His staff lighting the way, Jetsam scrutinized the walls and passages for something familiar. The size of the Dwarven infrastructure astonished him. As an underbelly boy, he figured he knew every inch of the caverns beneath Dwim-Halloe. *How wrong I was.*

As their search dragged on, time taunted Jetsam. He realized with every backtracked step, he lost precious minutes. He imaged a burly executioner seated beside a spinning whetstone, sharpening his long-handled axe, while Seryn sat waiting as the next victim.

And then Jetsam heard *the voice*. A hypnotic suggestion, perceptible on the edge his consciousness, the otherworldly whisper directed him.

Right... left... left.

Jetsam and Tramp strolled into an expansive round room. As his magic light extended its bluish glow to the high-vaulted ceiling, Jetsam recognized where he was. He stopped under a sweeping archway supported by granite columns and surveyed the soaring vault. Rusted chandelier chains hung draped in gossamer and coated with dust. The toes of Jetsam's leather boots rested on the perimeter of a swirling tile mosaic. His staff revealed marble statues staring from sheltering alcoves.

This is where Baldy killed a troll, and left its burning carcass. A pile of black soot still soiled the tiles. With a whiff, Jetsam confirmed his suspicion. *Definitely humpback. Even the ash stinks.*

From this room, Jetsam remembered the way aboveground. *Dwim-Halloe, here I come.* Retracing the familiar path to the surface brought a rush of bittersweet emotions to Jetsam. *Giselle. Ratboy. Elvar.* Then he envisioned Seryn, and wondered if he still breathed.

"We need help, buddy boy."

By the time he reached the infamous hole on the Jade River's bank, darkness covered the Mirrored Peaks. *Everything looks the same.*

Under the concealing cover of pre-dawn, Jetsam and Tramp moved as shadows, and soon reached a sewer entrance to the underbelly. Once again, the authorities sealed the inlet with a grate. Jetsam considered his options. With only a sword and staff, removing the obstacle would prove a long, noisy affair, so he initiated a spell.

The grate heated as Jetsam focused his energy on the softening metal brackets. As the iron fasteners glowed, he pried the grate free with the foot of his staff. After gently setting the red-hot barrier on the cobblestones, he lifted Tramp. They slipped through the sewer drain and hurried toward a reunion.

"Can't believe I'm nervous," he said. "Think they'll recognize us?"

Jetsam's heart beat faster while striding the familiar tunnels. *I miss my friends.* The anticipation brought a sweat to his palms. His hardwood staff felt slick in his grip. His feet moved quicker. Even Tramp seemed excited.

"Sure is dark." By this time of early morning, the nocturnal urchins usually bustled around the campfire, returning from their scavenging before the sun breached the horizon. This morning, everything remained quiet.

Blue staff light leading his way, Jetsam peered into his former home.

It's abandoned!

Heart sinking, Jetsam spun in a circle, seeking signs of life. The central fire pit was but a smudge of trodden ash, trampled and tracked around the cavern. There were no sleeping mats or stores of food, no torches, pots, or hanging coney carcasses. Even his old cubby hole sat empty.

But most of all, no orphans.

A lump tightened in his throat.

Tramp released a protective growl and a high-pitched bark. Quickened footsteps echoed behind Jetsam. As he swiveled with his lighted staff toward the on-comers, he glimpsed two forms springing toward him. *Bounty hunters?* He was tackled to the unforgiving ground before he could dodge. The back of his head smacked the hard stone, and he dropped his staff. *Or guards?* Tramp barked as Jetsam's head whirled.

His attackers rolled him over, face down on the rock. They forced Jetsam's arms behind him and bound his wrists. A dirty finger slipped into the side of his mouth and fish-hooked his cheek. Mouth agape, someone stuffed a rag in his maw.

"Bag the dog."

With his staff extinguished, Jetsam saw nothing. Tramp growled and barked.

"Bugger! Bloody biter got me."

Jetsam heard the struggle, and then Tramp's barking sounded muffled. Through the rag, Jetsam let out a stifled yell. *Leave him alone!*

"Quiet!" A moment later, the captors lifted Jetsam to his feet and pulled a sack over his head. He writhed to break free, but his bonds cinched tighter, and his abductors shook and admonished him.

"Bloody stupid malt-worm! What are you doing here? Gonna rouse a humpback."

Jetsam tried to speak, but only muffled sounds came from his gagged mouth.

A firm hand smacked the back of his head, right where it had bounced off the stone floor.

"Enough! Not another sound." Scalp stinging, Jetsam trudged along, and his throbbing head muddled his senses. Jetsam complied with his captors for now, though he had no choice. He heard Tramp squirming against whatever restraint they'd bound him with. *He's got more fight than me.*

A trickle of blood coalesced on Jetsam's scalp and gained enough volume to run through his hair. The crimson stream streaked down his neck as his blind march dragged on interminably. *Where are they taking us?* He recalled Seryn's tale about being captured outside the School of Sorcery. *That* story bought him no measure of comfort.

Why's life such a horrible struggle? His hooded head slunk lower and his legs lagged. *In a city full of food, I had to steal not to starve.* His captors dragged him now. *And that was before things got hard.*

"Ouch! Blasted mutt got me again!" Jetsam cracked a smile. The sound of Tramp getting whacked flipped the grin upside down, and lit his fire. *That's enough feeling sorry for myself.* He began plotting his escape as a drop of blood raced over his bony spine.

Jetsam twisted his wrists in a methodical repetition against his rope bonds. His skin chaffed and burned as his hands flexed and stretched, trying to wiggle free. *They tie a good knot.*

Then they stopped.

Tap-tap tap. Tap. Tap-tap. The sound of knuckle on oak. The knocking repeated in the exact cadence and rhythm. *Tap-tap tap. Tap. Tap-tap.*

A dead-bolt slid open with a *thunk* and rusty hinges creaked. Despite the hood, Jetsam detected just enough light to know they were entering a room. *At least I don't smell knuckle-draggers.*

Inside the lit chamber, Jetsam felt a slack in his captor's grip. *It's now or never.* A slippery fish, Jetsam stiffened, lurched, and escaped the grasp of his captors. Eyes covered and hands tied, he whirled and spun toward the doorway.

He ran straight into the jamb, bounced off, and before he regained his balance, was tackled once more.

"Bloody butter-fingers," someone said from across the room. "Hold on to him."

Rough hands pulled Jetsam to his feet.

"What 'ave ye got here?" The voice sounded familiar.

"Found him rummaging around the old camp. Figured he was trouble."

"Bring him here."

The sack on his head was yanked off, and Jetsam squinted into the harsh glare, discerning shadowy forms.

"Jetsam?"

Before his blue eyes adjusted to the light, he was wrapped in a bear hug and lifted off his feet.

"Ratboy?"

"Untie him," the familiar voice said. "And let Tramp go!" Jetsam stared his old friend in the face. Ten months had aged the lad. His cheeks sprouted stubble and his brown eyes carried a weariness that belied his age. *He's grown an inch, too.*

"What in the devil are ye doin' back here?" Ratboy hugged him again, before Jetsam formulated a response. When Tramp's four paws hit the floor, he sounded two fierce barks at his former captors, then raced to Jetsam's legs. He sniffed Ratboy's ankle, and let out a knowing bark.

"Where do I begin?" Jetsam asked as he soaked in his surroundings. He stood in a Dwarven hall, only this room was no debris-strewn, cobweb-coated, ransacked relic. *This room's restored.* Filled with burning oil, cressets illuminated the immense hall and rebuilt Dwarven furniture filled the room—benches, tables, and a stout armoire, while the hearth burned a warming fire.

"Come, sit," Ratboy instructed, strolling toward the fireplace. A broad bench rested in front of the roaring fire. Jetsam noticed fresh nails and unmatched legs. Still, it proved a comfortable seat. He sat, while fingering the new scab on his scalp. Tramp jumped in his lap.

"So good to see ye," Ratboy gushed, sitting next to him and rubbing Tramp behind the ears. "Ye've no idea." Another lad handed each a stone tankard of mead. Jetsam took a sip, winced, and shook his head. "Good, nay?" Ratboy asked. "Now, tell me everything."

After taking another sip, Jetsam began his story. "So our raft crashed against the grating and dumped us into the Jade... "

Wide-eyed Ratboy hung on every word of his tale. As Jetsam modestly detailed his path from Dwim-Halloe and back again, his audience grew. Familiar faces greeted him briefly, not daring to interrupt the tale. *Rooster, Biter, and Pike.* And as morning rolled in, more orphans returned from their nocturnal scavenging.

Jetsam regaled his old friends with stories of forest nymphs and gypsies, bounty hunters and rushing rivers, knights and squires, sorcerers and rogues, ogres, goblins, and *more* trolls. And of course, a dragon.

Reluctantly, he told them of Drahkang-roth, and his ride upon the magnificent beast. He feared this tale would push the limits of their belief. *I can't believe it myself!* But, by now, his audience sat entranced.

By the time Jetsam finished, old friends, who were now acquainted with his new problem, surrounded him. Lil' Pete, Blister, Cricket, and Stinger clustered with the rest, awed by Jetsam's adventure.

"I like the new place," Jetsam said. "Why'd you leave the old cavern?"

"After ye left, things got worse. Ye were right about the reward on yer head. We'd more than a few would-be bounty hunters pokin' around down here." Ratboy swallowed hard. "We lost Mole to 'em."

Jetsam's heart sank at the news. "My fault." A tear came to Jetsam's eye, and he wondered how many others were gone.

"Nay—not yer fault. Seemed every dim-wit guard in Dwim-Halloe saw yer poster and figured they could earn easy coin. But that wasn't the worst of it—the humpbacks were."

"*More* trolls?"

"Aye, don't know where they came from, but once they sniffed out the camp, we were on the run. We lost a few new ones to 'em. Youngsters that came after ye left." Ratboy shook his head and stared at his feet.

"How'd you find this place?"

"By luck, mostly. We were runnin' like scared coneys, in whatever direction was away from the knuckle-draggers. Some left back above ground, and we ain't seen 'em since. Rest of us kept goin' deeper and deeper. Came upon these ruins and made a stand."

"And the trolls left you alone?"

"Nay, but we've learned a few tricks to keep 'em at bay."

"The mirrors?" Jetsam asked, recalling the trickle of sunlight that froze the troll chasing him yesterday.

"Genious, aye? We use the mirrors to catch light from the old minin' vents, and bounce the sunlight all around these tunnels. Course, only helps in the day—but least we get some sleep."

"What do you do at night?"

"We steal oil from the blacksmiths and chisel little troughs in the passages around our base. Humpbacks get too close, we set flame to 'em."

"There seems to be more of you, now."

"Aye, they keep comin' from above, and when we were on the run, we slammed into another bunch livin' down here. Took us a while to work out our differences, but we were smart enough to realize there was safety in numbers. Turns out we learned a few things from 'em, too."

"I need your help," Jetsam said.

"Figured as much. Not sure how we can keep the king from executin' yer wizard."

"What do you know about that door near the underground river?"

"We've stumbled upon the river, but 'tis always thick with knuckle-draggers, so we've not seen this door of which ye speak."

"Do you have someone to look at it? Maybe get it open somehow?"

"Aye—got a few lads are real good with mechanicals. But ye know there'll be humpbacks guardin' it. Of that, I'm certain."

"I think I can help with that. Round up your lads and see if they can find that doorway. I'll give you directions as best I recall."

"Why don't ye just show us yerself?"

"Because I'm going to the Citadel."

Chapter Twelve

A full-body twitch awoke Seryn. *Spirits take me!* A lightning bolt of pain shot from the stump of his missing finger all the way to his shoulder, igniting each frayed nerve along the path. Seryn screamed into his gag. Every fiber of his abused body raged in agony as a painful current fired into his befuddled brain.

He forced his clenched eyelids to open a crack. *Can't see a bloody thing.* Blinking his watery eyes, Seryn realized a hood restrained him once more. Then he screamed again, and waited for the misery to subside. Memories of the torture flooded his mind, and his muscles twitched. *Was it real?* From his welted back to his burning knuckle to his broken nose, Seryn's body confirmed what his memory feared. *Must have blacked out.*

Sitting with his back to a wall, Seryn heard a buzz as a hungry horsefly landed on his wrist. Seryn shook his arm to dislodge the insect, and pain wracked his battered frame. His finger stump blazed as if a red-hot poker impaled his hand. He ground his molars and forced back the pain, just enough to think. *Wonder how long they beat me?* A second later, the resilient bug found its way through the back of Seryn's shredded tunic and administered a stinging bite. Seryn twisted in response, igniting his searing arm in the process, and the bloodsucker retreated to the air. *Can it get any sodding worse?* With a conservation of movement, Seryn stretched his cramping legs, and his bare feet slammed against the opposite wall. He roared into his gag once more and relented, sitting as still as he could. With every breath and heartbeat, his injuries screamed in defiance.

Seryn couldn't guess how long laid motionless against the stone before he mustered the courage to move again. He inhaled a breath through his crusty nostrils and clenched his jaw. *Slowly.* Legs outstretched, he explored the fortification with his toes. *Hewn stone.* Beneath his sweaty hood, Seryn's greasy brow furrowed. *Where the devil am I now?*

With icy feet and shredded shoulders, Seryn tested the limits of his confinement. Slower than a tortoise, he rotated on his troll-bitten rump, and the maneuver peeled his crusted trouser seat from the fresh scab. *Devil's luck, that hurts.* More flies buzzed toward the seeping blood. He shifted his weight to the uninjured buttock and slid his feet along the cylindrical cell walls. While the insects taunted him, he completed two revolutions with his blood-stained soles finding naught but solid rock. *No door, not even a crack.* Seryn slumped between his bent knees and blew a sigh through his swollen nose, chasing away another horsefly. *I'm in a hole.* Old tales of the Dwim-Halloe dungeons provided a disconcerting thought.

The oubliette.

Seryn tried to stand, despite his better judgment. His finger stump burned hotter than ever, demanding attention for every movement. He rose inch by inch, fearing slamming against a low ceiling. Yet, when he stood upright, with the wall's help, nothing smacked his head. He slid back to the slimy stone floor, and the bloodthirsty fliers joined him.

There's no way out of here. And it reeks. Seryn caught a whiff of his shredded tunic and soiled breeches—dirty, sweaty, and bloody. I *reek.*

A sob escaped from his chest.

Will Valin leave me here to die? Claustrophobia picked at his overwhelmed brain. *Or drag me out and behead me in the square?* Seryn's weary head bobbed, and the resulting tension ignited a spasm from his nape to his knees. *Either way, Valin wins.*

In the cramped, fly-infested dark, Seryn huddled with his thoughts, while wrestling with pain and fear. *Someone cast a spell back in that tunnel. A* powerful *spell. But who?* He pulled his shivering feet beneath him, hiding them from his winged attackers, and sat cross-legged in his buzzing tomb. *It couldn't have been Jetsam, could it?* Seryn remembered the magical sensations he experienced underground. *With the lad's fury, and the amplifying aura to draw from?* Seryn contemplated the possibility of Jetsam releasing such an incantation, but dismissed the idea. *The lad's good, but not that good.*

Seryn recalled the fate of Jetsam's talented illuminae parents. *I pray the lad didn't follow me. I've got enough of his family's blood on my hands.* His head slunk, chin to his chest. *Does he think I'm the reason his parents are dead?* Seryn remembered the night he told Jetsam the story of his mother's heroics. *I had to tell the truth—it was my obligation.* He swallowed hard, submitting to the guilt gnawing at him. *I did all I could for the lad, and still it wasn't enough.* He ground his teeth and sighed. *I swear, if I make it out of this, I'll do right by him.*

Spurred by this flicker of determination, Seryn reconsidered the commotion at the tunnel door. *Valin must have other enemies.* He recalled his brother's torturous line of questioning. *Wizards—and he thinks I know them.* He remembered Valin crushing the magic rebellion a decade ago. *Godspeed, whoever you are.*

Seryn's neglected stomach rumbled, and another horsefly broke his skin. *What options do I have?* He inhaled a calming breath and swallowed a wad of bloody snot. *Other than sit here and wait?* He tested his shackles once again and felt the scabs on his wrists crack against the iron. *Still no use.*

Seryn sucked in another stale breath. Even breathing proved laborious. *I'll not be rescued.* He recalled an image of his brother as a young man: strong, stubborn, and invincible. *Valin won't let me slip away again.* His mind wandered back to his first escape, a decade ago. *Maybe there's a hidden clue buried in my memories—a way to escape again.*

Eighteen-year-old Seryn cringed at the Oxbow guard lumbering toward him. It took Seryn a second to remember he was invisible. *And naked.* He scrutinized the approaching soldier. *Did he hear the alarm?* The unknowing sentry passed within inches of him, heading straight for the door Seryn just closed. *He smells of wine, too.* As the watchman disappeared behind the portal, Seryn realized news of his escape was imminent. *Word will spread like wildfire.* With a whispered Elven phrase, he sealed the door with an incantation to buy himself time.

With his head swiveling, Seryn assessed his surroundings, and presumed he stood inside Dwim-Halloe's northern curtain wall. *Odd that they took me so far from the Citadel. Why drag me way up here, when there's a dungeon beneath the Wizard's Tower?*

Vellae's whisper interrupted his contemplation. Her warm hand graced his shivering biceps. Her fingers found their way past his elbow and forearm to his hand and pulled him toward her.

"We're to meet Mírdaen," she explained. "He went to the Citadel to hear what news. We'll find him in Beggar's Alley."

Thunderous pounding and enraged shouting erupted from behind the magically-locked gatehouse door.

"The guards know I'm invisible," Seryn said.

The illuminae pulled Seryn forward and began to run. Unseen, they dodged empty market stalls and early-rising merchants, angling toward the alley where the homeless congregated in an ever-shifting conglomeration of the unwanted.

"They accused me of killing the king." He wished he could see her reaction. "Did you see who abducted me?"

"Dark forms—three men. They ushered you into a wagon and left. It was all I could do to keep up with them."

"Did they see you?"

"I think not. I disappeared as soon as they tossed you in the cart."

"Why here?"

"We've no time for questions—the spell won't last much longer." Seryn panted in the cool mountain air, lungs burning from the flight.

"There he is," Vellae said. She guided Seryn toward a lean man, hunched in a sheltered alcove. He peered out from a concealing hood.

Both of Mírdaen's feet left the ground when his wife's transparent hand touched his shoulder.

"Sorry—it's me," she said.

"You scared the life from me," Mírdaen Lothyrn said. Seryn

realized Beggar's Alley was the ideal place to talk to invisible folk. *Mumbling to oneself is ordinary here.*

"The news is grim," Mírdaen said, his shoulders slumping. "King Tygan is dead, murdered last eve. And talk is that Seryn's the killer."

The words released a shiver down Seryn's naked spine. "Impossible," he blurted, louder than he should have. Mírdaen glanced toward the sound of his voice.

"Keep quiet. Nargul has eyes and ears everywhere—even in Beggar's Alley."

"I'm being framed."

"I believe Vellae—*and* you," Mírdaen said, his voice devoid of hope. "But the high wizard said there were witnesses."

"Who?" Seryn implored.

"He couldn't say. 'Twas risky for him to speak at all. The Citadel's on alert. 'Tis utter chaos."

"Did you tell the high wizard I'm innocent?"

"I didn't tell him anything," Mírdaen said. "Until we know who's behind this, we trust no one."

As Seryn watched Mírdaen speak, Vellae materialized in front of his eyes. Still barely visible, she hid inside her hooded cloak, hair obscuring her face. Beneath the velvet covering, she wore an illuminae robe. *She must not have slept,* Seryn marveled, and suffered guilt pangs for his indulgent prison 'nap.'

"Your spell's worn off," Seryn whispered. Upon seeing Vellae in the flesh, he comprehended the immense gamble she'd taken to rescue him. *I wonder what they risk in aiding me—innocent though I am.* He felt humbled, and unworthy.

"You must flee the city. Your spell shall expire within the half-hour," Vellae warned. "And remember, you're naked." He noticed Mírdaen raise an eyebrow.

How could I forget? With nothing but thin fabric covering his groin, the morning air nipped at his skin.

"Go north," Mírdaen said, "and we shall send word once this conspiracy is solved."

"How will you find me?"

Husband and wife glanced at each other. After a moment of

silence, Vellae's eyes widened.

"Each day at noon, meditate and quest out your mind for as long as possible," she instructed. "If we bring news, we will scry for your presence, and seek you out."

"But keep yourself hidden," Mírdaen said. "And take no chances, whatsoever."

Seryn stared into her eyes as the direness of his predicament sunk in. *I'm a fugitive, fleeing into the wild, with winter but months away. Can it be that this is my best option?* Considering the unsettling events of the last half-day, he struggled to accept it. *I should stay and fight to clear my name.* But then he thought of Valin, and his lust for the throne. The notion ripped Seryn's heart to even contemplate it, yet he feared his own blood forsook him.

And so, Seryn hugged Vellae and shook Mírdaen's hand, though neither could see him.

"I owe you my life—I'm forever in your debt."

"Here," Mírdaen said, handing Seryn a stuffed backpack. "I filled it with everything I could think of—including a change of clothes." His gaze darted toward his wife. Seryn grabbed the sack, and it vanished. From beneath his long cloak, Mírdaen withdrew a silver short sword and held it in Seryn's direction. The morning sunlight reflected off the forged steel. "Take this. Now go."

As Seryn grasped the hilt, the weapon disappeared as well. His icy feet on the hard cobbles sent an urgent message to his brain. "But I've no boots."

"That won't do," said Vellae. She surveyed the yard. Across the alley slept a vagrant with shoddy shoes. She shook her head. "Give him yours," she told her husband. Mírdaen and Seryn stood roughly the same size. "'Tis better than stealing a flimsy pair from a beggar."

So Mírdaen Lothyrn removed his fine leather boots and stockings, and watched them disappear one at a time as Seryn donned them.

With his new belongings in hand and his former life evaporating, Seryn fell in behind a merchant wagon heading for the gatehouse. He watched the Lothyrns leave Beggar's Alley on foot.

As the cart horses plodded along with their rolling load, Seryn counted the minutes as his time trickled away. *Suspect the guards have escaped the gatehouse by now.* He glanced behind him, scanning for watchmen, then turned back toward the wagon. *Faster, you old gold-biter.*

When the creaky wagon finally reached the stoic gatehouse, the watchmen gave the cargo a thorough once-over and sent the familiar merchant on his way. A few steps behind, an invisible Seryn walked out of Dwim-Halloe in naught but new boots and underclothes.

Who knows when I'll return?

The past is gone, and I've naught left to glean from it. Seryn's tortured mind returned to the present, where he sat in the oubliette, seeping welts splashed across his back. Tenacious horseflies, both real and imagined, tormented him, and every twitch and turn brought more pain. Even his hood's fabric touch shot daggers up his crooked, swollen nose. *I must relegate myself to the inevitable.* He blew a gust of air through his damaged nostrils, pushing the offending cloth and its insect tenant from his nose.

How much longer will I last? His thumb absentmindedly moved toward his missing finger, finding an oozing nub that ignited at the touch. *No food or water since the caravan.* He wiped the puss onto his ring finger, rubbing the goo between thumb and fingertip until it dried and crumbled. *One way or another, I shall die soon.* Seryn swallowed a sliver of tickling mucous and suppressed a cough.

Will my dying thoughts be of regret? A bittersweet image of Ioma graced his imagination. *My true love thinks me a murderous, lying, lunatic.* Seryn rubbed his cracked thumbnail against his calloused index finger, flexing the keratin plate. *And I thought I could change that.* Through his gag, he grunted a sickly imitation of a chuckle. *What legacy will I leave?*

His thoughts turned to Jetsam. *Only the lad knows my tribulations,* he realized. *Though my hopes of rescue are futile, maybe someday, my true story will be told.* A quarter of his thumbnail creased and tore. Seryn didn't notice the pain. *Maybe someday the truth will reach Ioma's ears.* Tears welled in his crusty eyes.

I pray I taught you well, Jetsam. Seryn imagined his apprentice finding his way to the grotto. *The lad's smart and resourceful, and he has the terrier*, he assured himself. *They'll find their way back.* Seryn's mind inventoried his supply stock. *Jetsam will be safe there, like I was.* Seryn's empty stomach turned. *And then what? Another fugitive growing old in the wilderness until his luck runs out. I've left the boy naught but a roadmap to ruin.* A salty tear raced down Seryn's cheek.

The pit's stillness taunted him. *Curse the fates that dealt me such an unfair life. Were I born deaf and dumb, I should not have suffered as much.* A tinge of guilt poked Seryn as he digested this thought. *No, I would not have traded my time with Ioma for anything. Were the devil to offer me the world...*

An abrupt recollection unseated Seryn's lamentation. A corrupt idea, only spoken in whispers, of the vilest salvation. *There is a way.* His spine stiffened.

Grimwealder.

In desperation, Seryn's mind seized a favorite story from his youth, a book he'd read over and over. The ominous words resurrected in his tormented mind. *With his forces routed and kingdom lost, Grimwealder offered his soul to the dark art, summoning a demon spirit to save him from death.* Seryn shuddered. *I couldn't do it if I tried.* Cognizant of his bindings and restraints, he realized even if he submitted to such a temptation, the means were beyond him.

Or are they? The illuminae instilled a terror of black magic into their students with warnings of how easy it was to surrender to the dark power. *So easy, you don't have to try,* he recalled. *'Tis harder to resist than it is to submit.* Seryn noticed his body trembling. *Could I conjure the dark spirits with my mind alone?*

Visions of Ioma enticed him, as he imagined reclaiming everything he had lost. *Retribution, absolution, recompense.* Seryn saw himself on the throne, his queen by his side.

Revenge.

Seryn felt a trickle of blood flee his damaged nose and taunt his dry lips. *Could I cheat death, without losing my soul?* He remembered the price Grimwealder paid. *Once the demon entered his body, Averon Grimwealder existed no longer. A corporal shell, the spirit became one with the magician-king, and the Grimlord was spawned.*

Seryn sat in the oubliette, listening to his teeth grind.

No, that will not be my legacy. His jaw relaxed. *I will die with honor.*

Seryn thought of his heartless brother, and his resolve stiffened. *Death on my terms, not his.* He envisioned more torture and realized that taking his own life was the lesser of two evils. *I can at least steal that final victory from him.* Seryn imagined Valin's fury at finding his corpse in the oubliette. *No more torture, no answers to his questions, no public execution. I'll be dead, but Valin's paranoia will live.*

But how?

I can't rely on expiring—he could return any moment. Seryn struggled to his feet, blocking out the agony. With his shoulders, he rubbed the walls, spinning in a circle. *Smooth as glass. No protrusions of any sort.* He slid to the floor.

Strangle myself with my shackles?

Seryn arched his back against the wall and pushed his feet against the other side, lifting his rump enough to slide his bound hands beneath him. Despite his amputation's excruciating objection, he slipped his shackled wrists over his heels and toes and brought the chain to his neck. Fatigued and blinded, Seryn maneuvered in the hole, searching for a fatal position. He pushed his bonds against his throat, trying to crush his windpipe. His breathing labored and he felt lightheaded. With a snort, his limp hands fell to his lap.

Fates' fury, I'm too weak to kill myself.

Chapter Thirteen

Dwim-Halloe at night appeared as Jetsam remembered it. The white-capped Mirrored Peaks dwarfed the granite city, poking into the starry sky. Metalwork fumes floated on the air and a spring mountain breeze swirled the forge dust. Trees had not yet budded, and the landscape retained the earthen tones of winter. Full greenery was weeks away.

This concerned Jetsam, for he wondered if Giselle still strolled a flowerless garden. *If I can't find her, I'm doomed.* She was the only person he knew who might have heard something about Seryn. *It's a long-shot, but she's all I've got.*

He felt near invisible skirting the lamp light and heading to the Jade River. Modest homes clustered in long rows east and west of the curling waterway as it drained out of the mountains southward toward Calderi. *I don't relish another swim.* But crossing the Jade was his best way into the Citadel, short of strolling through the gates. And his odds of sneaking across a drawbridge and through a manned gatehouse were close to nil. *One more case where bloody invisibility would be a boon.*

For this venture, Jetsam left Tramp in Ratboy's care. He hated leaving the dog almost as much as he hated submitting him to a midnight swim in a fast river. Jetsam suspected Giselle would love seeing Tramp, but he also recognized the canine was a burden to his mission. Jetsam traveled light—no staff and no Regret. *My sling is my only defense this eve.*

Jetsam entered the river as if an otter, with nary a splash. This time of year, the water ran frigid—much colder than the underground river he splashed in yesterday. The spring thaw left the Jade flowing full, and the exhausted Jetsam panted when he reached the narrow inner bank. The stoic ashlar walls of the Citadel's outer curtain loomed above him. Rushlight fell from the crenellated towers bolstering the wall.

Hunched on a thin earthen lip beneath the wall's thick ivy, Jetsam shivered, dripping wet and panting. With trembling hands, he cast a spell to dry and warm himself. Jetsam whispered the incantation and drew symbols with his slick fingers. *Can't have my chattering teeth give me away.* With Seryn's lessons echoing in his mind, he used only enough magic to get the job done, and kept a reserve for more spells, should he need them. *Sure hope I don't.*

Gripping the ivy while tiptoeing to the drainage chute, Jetsam's eyes checked the guard towers above him. *Though I'm but a speck, being spotted by the sentry is a dangerous possibility.* As he climbed into the wall breach, the drainage chute pinched him tighter than ever. He'd grown both in height and width since the last time he wormed through this hole. Now, the muscle Seryn's cooking added over the winter made his entry challenging. *Almost too big for this,* he admitted, snaking through the filthy drain.

Damp and dirty, Jetsam feared his appearance would again offend Giselle, but he had no choice. *At least she'll recognize me—even with her eyes closed.* Jetsam squirmed from the orifice, regained his feet, and brushed himself off, shaking twigs, leaves, and worse from his tangled locks. Hunched low, he slunk across the cobblestone lane running beside the curtain and slipped into the royal stables. This late, the stable master and his minions slept along with the rest of Dwim-Halloe. *The stables are my best option for reaching the garden undetected.* To the east lay the open south bailey and the neighboring guard barracks. Jetsam stalked through the shadows, kept clear of the sentry, and wove his way past stalls and barns.

Hidden in a hedge row on the north edge of the stables, Jetsam gazed across another stony street. The thoroughfare and a line of trimmed whitebeam were all that separated him from the garden wall.

When Jetsam surveyed the stone barrier, he suffered the chills, but not from his river swim. The bittersweet memories of the garden played his emotions. He chased images of Elvar and Giselle from his mind and focused his senses on the inevitable sentry. With a few long strides, he crossed the road and stood beneath the tended trees.

Upon reaching the garden boundary, he discovered changes. For one, atop the stone wall he so easily climbed before was a cast-iron gate, replete with tightly-spaced bars and pointy finials. Jetsam scooted around the ashlar perimeter, then crept north toward the garden's entrance. He glanced at the conglomeration of nobles' estates to his right. Memories of himself and Elvar racing through the exclusive borough tortured him. He chased them away with a shake of his head.

In the gloom before him, Jetsam detected a stationed sentry outside the closed garden gate. *Don't need a crystal ball to tell me the gate's locked.* He scratched his moist scalp with dirty fingernails while glancing back to the wall.

All this because of little ol' me?

Jetsam backpedaled out of the guard's line of sight, then bit his lip and mulled his options. *Can't slip through the bars, and that sentry's not going away.* Again, Jetsam regretted not being able to turn invisible. *I swear, if I get Seryn out of this alive, it's the next spell I'll learn.*

Crouched in the shadows, he ran scenarios in his head. *Could cause a diversion, but I'd still have to pick the lock.* He shook his head and gazed up the fortified wall. *Guess I'm going over, spikes be damned.*

Jetsam backtracked to a shaded spot midway between wall torches and scrambled up the ashlar. *Just like old times.* He entertained second thoughts after examining the veritable wall of spears. *I'll skewer myself and bleed out before the guards find me.* Then an idea presented itself. *Why not?*

Jetsam braced himself atop the wall by hooking his arm around an iron bar. Knees bent, his bottom rested on the wall's flat top. With hands free, Jetsam whispered a spell. He focused his energy on the next picket in line and heated the metal. Akin to a magical forge, his spell softened the ductile metal. With the sole of his boot, he pushed the compromised rod, and it bowed just enough for him to slip though. Jetsam waited at the wall's top for the curved metal to cool. *Burning myself on red-hot iron's not what I had in mind.*

From his perch, Jetsam scanned the familiar park. Even fresh from the throes of winter, the garden retained a somber beauty. Enough conifers interspersed among the deciduous plants to maintain an emerald tone, the greenery brought to life even at night by flickering wall torches and pathway lamp posts. Spring-awakened bullfrogs and crickets serenaded within the pastoral retreat.

Jetsam licked his finger, and with a quick tap, tested the iron's temperature. *Cool enough.* He slithered through the metal fence.

"Ouch!" *Not cool enough. That's gonna blister.*

Through the fence and down the wall, Jetsam slunk into the garden, soft-stepping on dry foliage, trying to keep silent. *The leaves have other ideas.* Crunching, snapping and crumbling, the crispy leaves betrayed his stealthy efforts. *This won't do.* Jetsam abandoned this tactic, and crept out of the shrubbery. *I'll stick to the paths.* He followed the shadows, crouching on the flagstone walkways, but skirting the edges.

The garden was sprawling, and his ground-hugging advance proved fruitless. *Need a better view.* Toward the park's center, Jetsam spied a giant mulberry tree and angled toward it. Hand by hand, foot by foot, he climbed upward. After a minute, he'd put four fathoms between himself and the ground. A view of the expansive garden was his. *Now I watch and wait.*

From above, he admired the artistic designs cut by the flagstone paths. The walkways weren't just random meandering trails, but rather an ornate pattern, dissecting the foliage into precise shapes and repeating patterns. *Pretty from up here, but I don't see a soul.*

Jetsam craned and scanned until his neck became stiff. *My leg's falling asleep.* He twisted in the mulberry branches, trying to find a comfortable perch. *Maybe this wasn't such a good idea.* He ground his teeth as time crawled in the still garden. *What other choice do I have?*

Jetsam spotted movement on the periphery of his vision. He swung his head toward the motion and focused on a feminine form. *Giselle?* She roamed far away, walking toward the part of the garden abutting the Citadel's inner curtain. *Think it's her!* Jetsam wanted to shout, but that notion was folly. *Must be her.* He slid down the tree, jumping from the lowest branch and landing with a *plop* on his bottom as his wet boots slid out from beneath him. *As if I wasn't filthy enough.* He regained his feet and tiptoed in her direction. Between trees and shrubs and dormant flower beds, Jetsam darted, covering the ground nimbly. He heard the unmistakable sound of a door clicking shut.

There's a door?

When he reached the inner curtain where he spotted the lass, the garden was empty. *Bugger me raw.* Jetsam climbed through the brambles and ivy covering the wall, then ran his hands across the stone, searching for the portal he heard.

She must've gone inside the palace! He knew the Granite Palace housed the noblest of nobles—and royalty, of course. Jetsam had never set foot in the palace grounds, even as a youngster while his illuminae parents still lived. The dry branches grabbed and tugged at him as he worked his way along the wall. His fingers touched the door. Small, oaken, and reinforced with iron, the postern hid behind a thick ivy blanket. Jetsam took a deep breath and tried the handle. *Not locked!* He inched the portal open, peeking through the ever-widening crack, and blackness greeted him. Jetsam tiptoed into the void, and closed the door behind him. He stood inside the ashlar wall comprising the Citadel's inner curtain. Blindly using his hands, he tickled the close walls and rounded ceiling, just taller than his head. Four cautious steps forward, with arms outstretched, he discovered another fortified door, also unlocked.

They'll kill me for sure if I'm caught on palace grounds. Jetsam cast a *hush* spell on himself. Seryn taught him the incantation to use on Tramp, in the event that he found himself in a situation where barking was not appropriate. Jetsam hoped the spell would muffle any sound he might make. *Not that I plan on barking.*

Jetsam prepared for his grand entrance by wiping his sweaty palms on his dirty thighs. *As if that will help.* Delicately pushing the oaken door outward, he peered into the palace yard. *I must be behind the Great Hall.* He spotted a silhouette at the alley's end. The feminine form swung left, around the corner and out of his vision. As cautiously as he opened it, Jetsam closed the wooden door. He recognized guards manned the corner towers high above him, and that he'd have to cross their line of sight to follow Giselle. *I sure hope it's Giselle.*

The Great Hall and the keep sat side-by-side along the south part of the Citadel's curtain wall. Jetsam estimated ten paces separated the huge granite structures from the wall. *Until I reach the alley, I'll be exposed to the corner towers.*

In the heavens, a thin line of clouds approached the waning moon. Jetsam waited for the clouds to douse the lunar glow, and made a run for it. *Spirit, hide me.* The interminable sprint lasted mere seconds, but Jetsam felt naked to the world. In the alley betwixt the hall and keep, Jetsam clung to the Great Hall, his back flush to the stone. He held his breath, anticipating the sentry's clarion.

All remained quiet.

Jetsam released a sigh and slipped northward along the wall, eyes scanning the darkened windows of the flanking buildings. When he arrived at the corner Giselle disappeared behind, he craned his neck around the wall's edge.

No one in sight.

She must have gone inside the Great Hall. Jetsam scratched his head. *I would've seen her cross the bailey.* He chewed his lip and squinted. *Can't stroll through the Great Hall's front doors.* Even at this hour of the night, a posted guard was guaranteed, and the door was surely barred from inside. He slunk into the alley, contemplating his next move.

With his back to the quiet keep, he stared up at the structure, still in disbelief that Giselle lived inside the Granite Palace. He'd surmised she must live *somewhere* within the Citadel, but he imagined her the daughter of a noble or wealthy merchant—not *royalty*. Doubt gnawed at his intentions.

Then he spied a flicker through a fourth-floor window. A dot of light moved inside the room. *A candle?* The light stopped moving, then vanished. *Must be her.* Jetsam gazed up at the arched window and evaluated his options. *I pray it's her.*

The Great Hall sat ahead of him, a massive stone block: square, hard, and imposing. The building stood a fortress unto itself. A dusting of ivory on the hall's granite walls did little to soften the structure's demeanor.

Decorated in an arcade of repeating columns, blind arches took the place of first-floor windows. A lintel sat atop the colonnade, ringing the Great Hall at the top of the high-ceilinged ground floor. The second story displayed tall, narrow windows separated by thick mullions. *Like bars on a jail cell,* Jetsam mused, doubting he could squeeze between the thin openings, even if he broke the stained glass.

Above the daunting windows, a molded band wrapped the Great Hall between the second and third floor, which also had widows, impenetrable duplicates of those below them. The fourth floor architecture differed from that beneath, with the narrow arched windows interspersed with protruding oriels. It was from one of these windows Jetsam detected the light.

I can do it. If I'm not spotted.

Jetsam squinted at the crenellated battlements and corner towers. A patrol walked atop the walls. *I've got to avoid those eyes.* He watched the sentry pass high above him, adjacent to the Great Hall. As the soldier ambled out of his line of sight, Jetsam began to count. *Can I climb four stories before he makes it back around?* As Jetsam waited in the shadows, timing the guard's route, he scrutinized the lighting cast on the Great Hall, and noted the most shadowed section. *That's where I'll climb.*

Jetsam had just counted past two hundred and fifty seconds when the guard reappeared. *That's not much time.*

Jetsam waited until the guard was out of sight, then began his ascent at the base of a column. He started counting to gauge the patrol's return and used the ivy as a ladder and the pilaster block seams for toe-holds to scale the Great Hall's exterior. His outstretched fingertips gripped the top of a blind arch as a handhold, and he maneuvered to grasp a capital with his other hand. *This isn't so hard.*

His toes clinging to molding, Jetsam hoisted himself using the carved ribbon marking the start of the second floor. Although unnerving, grotesque window jamb figures offered decent climbing. *Ugly as sin. Thirty-four.* The nooks and crannies on the monstrous carvings provided him with enough protrusions to continue. Jetsam ignored gravity's whispered taunts and refused to look down.

The higher he climbed, the slower he moved. The confidence that inspired him at ground level vanished by the time he passed the second floor windows. *Ninety-two.* As he ascended, the ivy abandoned him. And he knew every second he spent on the building face was another moment to be spotted by the guards. *Don't look down.*

Time ticked away as he worked his way upward, relying on carved ballflowers to adhere him to the wall. Upon passing the third floor windows, he breathed a sigh of relief. *Almost there. One sixty-three.*

Above him sat the protruding windowsill where he noticed the candle light. He envisioned Seryn beneath the executioner's axe, and it spurred him on. *There's no going back now.*

By extending his hand to the ledge above, Jetsam pulled himself to the window. The ledge was wide enough for him to sit sideways as he peered through the glass. The room was dark inside, and he saw nothing. He tapped a scraped knuckle on the pane, and waited. *Two hundred.* A second time he knocked, louder than the first, and waited.

He heard a screech from inside the room and lost count.

Gods, no.

Jetsam glanced at the castle wall, searching for the patrol's return. He almost fell from his perch when the window creaked open.

"Jetsam?"

"Giselle!"

"What are you doing? Come in before you fall!" Her porcelain hands grabbed his damp tunic and pulled him into her room. Jetsam stumbled, finding his balance in just enough time to avoid an embarrassing tumble. His heart pounded while his skin flushed.

Jetsam had not seen Giselle since he'd fled Dwim-Halloe in mid-summer of last year, yet he recognized her instantly. *More lovely than I remember.* Moonlight trickled across her visage as he gazed into her glittering eyes. Her blond hair fell in long strands on her shoulders, covered by a silken robe she'd thrown on to cover her nightclothes. Her lips pursed as if to speak, but uttered not a sound. She lunged forward and kissed Jetsam on the cheek.

For a moment, his worries disappeared. *She feels so soft, smells so sweet.*

"You are damp!"

"I swam the moat," he said, inches from her face, her breath warm on his cheek.

"Why are you *here?*" she asked in a hushed voice.

"I need to talk to you—it's urgent," Jetsam whispered.

"They'll take your head if they find you here. It must be *very* important."

She took his hand and led him to her bed. "Sit, and tell me everything. You've been gone so long. I never thought I'd see you again."

As Jetsam sat on the down-filled mattress, his hands sunk in the fur cover. He scanned the chamber, lit only by the fireplace glow and a touch of moonlight. Though he held fond memories of his childhood home, the cozy bedroom he once shared with Elvar paled compared to this expansive retreat. *This room could hold our entire house!*

The luxurious canopy bed where he plopped his damp rump floated like a yacht in a crowded harbor. Embroidered tapestries covered the walls with pastoral scenes and domesticated animals. High-backed carved chairs pinned a bear-skin rug to the polished floor, while oak dressers and armoires anchored the bedroom's perimeter.

Jetsam pulled his gaze from the lavish room and turned toward his hostess. He wanted to repeat the story he told the orphans in all its glory, yet he knew time slipped away. *Those details must wait.* Jetsam told a truncated version of the tale he shared with Ratboy and the orphans the previous night. And like his prior audience, Giselle sat enraptured.

"And where's Tramp now?" she inquired, excited from hearing about the terrier.

"Left him with Ratboy—river's too perilous for him."

When Jetsam reached the part of his story about finding Seryn, he felt a lump in his throat. *The king sleeps under this same roof.* Jetsam was an intruder and a welcomed guest all at the same time.

"I found the wizard I sought."

"Where?"

"He lives in a cave, far north of here in the Kierawaith, near some Dwarven ruins."

"Tell me of him," she implored.

"He's a good man, an excellent teacher."

"What did you learn?"

"He taught me about herbs—how to brew potions and make salves. I know more of plants and roots and fungus than I thought possible."

Her wide eyes begged him to continue.

"I learned woodworking and alchemy, how to hunt and prepare game, to mend clothes and leather. Also worked on my reading a lot," Jetsam blurted. "After living in the underbelly, I figured I could survive in the wild, but without him, I'd have surely died."

"What of your scroll and of... *magic?*"

Her question unbalanced him. Jetsam longed to boast of his newfound skills: the spells he could cast, the magic he learned to sense around him and his ability to manipulate it. Yet, he hesitated. He was aware that in this building resided the king who outlawed sorcery. *The king who I offend by my very existence.* Though he recalled Giselle held no prejudice against magicians and their ilk, he feared lowering himself in her eyes with such revelations. He so desired to impress her that he subdued his enthusiasm.

"Aye, I learned that, too." He scrutinized her face, searching for any subtle change caused by his confession, but he noticed none.

"Who is this wizard of yours?"

"He is... *Seryn Vardan.*"

Jetsam watched her expression plummet. Her look of wonder evaporated and gravity weighed her eyelids and the corners of her supple mouth. Crestfallen, she spoke.

"The *kingslayer?* But... he killed my *grandfather!*"

Chapter Fourteen

A wretched silence suffocated Giselle's bedroom. The night air grew sticky and oppressive. Jetsam's heart pounded a kettle drum beat as the blood drained from his face. He longed to take back the words as his world unraveled before his eyes.

"Your *grand*father?"

Bulbous tears welled in the girl's green eyes. *It cannot be!* Giselle sat upright and inched away from Jetsam. Reality hit him with the force of a war mace. *Her father killed my parents!* Without conscious intent, Jetsam leaned further from her. Their closeness became a chasm. The escalating silence pushed them apart. *Why?* Jetsam lamented. *Why her?* He began to hyperventilate. *Why me?* He refused to look at Giselle. *How could one so cruel father one so kind?*

Giselle's icy voice broke the silence, but did nothing to close the gap. "Why'd you go to *him?*" she demanded, sounding more a princess than ever. "Seryn Vardan is *evil!*"

Jetsam restrained himself from a terse reply and considered the word: evil. Giselle's use of it made no sense. *Seryn is the least evil person I ever met.* "Didn't know who he was 'til I found him." Lightheaded, Jetsam gaped at the sprawling bed, feeling everything slip away. *Again.* "Seryn saved my life. He *didn't* kill King Tygan."

"Of course he did! *Everyone* knows that. Father saw him with his own eyes."

"Your father, the *king*." The word spat from Jetsam's mouth as if poisonous. He tried to stop himself, to eat his words, but they spilled like milk from a tipped urn.

"Your father *killed* my parents!"

Giselle flung herself from him, collapsing on the bed and burying her face in a pillow. Jetsam watched her convulse in sobs, and recalled telling her once that his parents were spellcasters. *She knew it then.* He ground his teeth until his ears popped. *Giselle knew I was orphaned because of her father.*

The goose-down muffled Giselle's sobbing, yet Jetsam feared her mournful caterwaul would rouse someone. *I'm the one who should be weeping.* The princess' crying raked his conscience. *Never heard a girl cry before—least that I remember.* Giselle had been the only lass he'd spoken to in years. *And now I've made her cry.*

Jetsam bit his dirty thumbnail while he stared at the princess. Though he tried to resist, he pitied her. *She has a horrible father.* Jetsam remembered his own father and the love he bore for him. *To have it otherwise would be torture.* Jetsam sat in the darkness contemplating the disconsolate princess. *The lonely princess, who wanders in the garden at night.* He recalled her speaking of her parents once, and the memory haunted him. *"Father's too busy to pay attention to me, and Mother's always sad."*

Hatred and sympathy wrestled for control of Jetsam's emotions. *I cannot believe the man responsible for ruining my life fathered Giselle.* A despicable notion somewhere deep in his core whispered that this lass presented an opportunity for revenge. *A way to get back at the king.* Cognizance of such an idea—even for a moment—shamed him. *That would be revenge, not vengeance,* he scolded himself. Even in his most uncontrollable rage, Jetsam could not envision lifting a finger against this girl.

Giselle was but a babe when her father killed my parents, he rationalized. Jetsam's fury retreated a reluctant step. *It's not her fault.* He remembered Seryn and his compassionate winter lessons. *I wish nothing more than to be back in that cave studying with Seryn.* He yearned to run away, to flee this dreadful tower, full of heartless souls. Jetsam calculated how many days to reach the hidden grotto on the creek bed.

Fruitless, he admonished himself, dispatching his fantasy. *Without Seryn, I've nothing.*

He gazed at Giselle, her ribcage rising in falling in rhythm with her sobs.

Giselle didn't kill our parents, Elvar whispered from a faraway place that Jetsam couldn't see or touch. *But she can help you save Seryn, brother,* Jetsam heard in his head, recognizing the silver lining in this black storm cloud.

Conflicted, Jetsam inhaled deeply, forcing the debilitating fury from his mind. *You're right, as always, Elvar.* Jetsam rubbed his fingertips across his sweaty palms and envisioned Tramp—thinking of the dog always calmed him. He recalled Seryn's words, and the directive was clear. Vengeance is not the answer. *Don't let emotion rule your logic,* he told himself, though the message was Seryn's. He swallowed hard and took another deep breath.

"Seryn was betrayed," Jetsam said in a trembling voice, lifting his eyes from the bed and onto her. "Someone framed him with treachery and evil magics." The last part proved difficult for him to say. Jetsam loved magic, but he recognized its potential for evil. *Enthran showed me that.*

Like a breeze-swept feather, he set his hand on her calf, and the princess recoiled.

"You should go," she whispered between gasps. Jetsam slid from her, ready to leave. *What now?* He stopped on the edge of the mattress. *This is all I've got.* He reached for an elusive calm.

"Don't you think it's possible," Jetsam cooed, "that Seryn *could* be innocent?" He waited for her reply. The hourglass dripped as if full of molasses. He decided not to budge, giving her time to consider the possibility. *Talk to her, Elvar,* he urged his brother. Another deep breath.

"Why do you care so much about this *assassin?*" Giselle leaned her head to speak, one ear still buried in the pillow. Her wet cheek glistened in the moonlight.

"Because he's all I have," Jetsam said, trying to pitch his voice in his most sympathetic tone, attempting to override his rollicking emotions. "And he's a noble man—honorable." He debated continuing for a moment, fearing he pushed too hard. But he held nothing back. "Seryn told me how he loved your mother."

"*Mother,*" she whispered. Giselle's petite form shook the mattress.

"Your father holds Seryn now. Had trolls capture him. I saw him taken away." The haunting image remained fresh in his mind.

"Thou saw my father with *trolls?*"

"With these," Jetsam put two fingers to his cheeks, pointing at his blue eyes.

Giselle sobbed again, but sat and faced Jetsam. The princess brushed the hair from her face, and their eyes met.

"It must be *him*, then," Giselle said. Jetsam furrowed his brow, as she explained. "There's a celebration feast tomorrow for the capture some infamous criminal, followed by a public beheading the next morning. It can be no other."

"*Beheading?*"

"Mid-morning," Giselle said. "Father's done bad things," she confessed. "He's cold, and hard, and loves *no one*. Not Mother." The princess inhaled a shaky breath, her nostrils flaring. "Not *me.*"

Jetsam watched the words sting her. Giselle appeared to be one breath from collapsing.

"Your father betrayed his own brother, and he wants to kill Seryn to keep the secret safe." Jetsam sniffled and wiped his nose with a dirty sleeve. "I *have* to save Seryn." Jetsam gazed unflinching into her watery eyes. "And I need help."

Her tongue stretched to lick her upper lip, catching a salty tear in the motion.

"I cannot aid a murderer."

Gods curse me, Elvar, how can I get through to her? Jetsam filled his lungs with castle air. "Don't help Seryn, then. Just help *me*, and let the gods decide our fate." Jetsam watched Giselle chew her lip. He burrowed his fingertips into his palms and waited for a reply.

"What am *I* to do?"

"Tell me how to get to the dungeon."

"I don't know how." Her voice trailed off in desperation.

Jetsam slumped. "How'm I supposed to rescue Seryn if I can't even *find* him?" he mumbled to himself, not expecting Giselle to hear.

"You are so certain this man's innocent that you'd risk your life to save him?"

"*My* mother helped Seryn escape," he explained. "She *knew* Seryn was innocent!"

Now Jetsam teetered on the verge of tears, while Gisele halted hers. They stared into each other's eyes. Into each other's souls. Cruel reality crushed their fairy tale puppy love in its infancy.

"Seryn's like a father to me," Jetsam offered. "Told me how he was framed, how he was betrayed. Why would he lie, and take me in, save me, and teach me magic?" Jetsam pondered his own words, and wondered if he could be wrong. His perspective was biased, but it was the only one he had. "An evil man would've ignored me—or *worse.*" As the painful memories floated in his head, he longed for the princess' icy resolve to melt.

Please, Elvar, help me.

"If he *has* been taken prisoner, Mother might know where he is," Giselle offered.

"Take me to her," Jetsam pleaded. For the first time since he crawled in this royal bedroom, he held hope.

"Mother may not even speak to you," Giselle warned. "A moody woman she is—and a sick one at that."

"Your mother's the only chance I've got."

Giselle wavered, biting her moist lip. "Mother could call the guardsman, have you beheaded with the kingslayer." The princess twisted away from Jetsam. "I shan't do it."

"Then what shall I do? Return to the wilds and die alone? Turn myself in for the murder of a guard I didn't kill? Or just cast a spell in the town square and let the guards take me away?"

The oppressive silence returned as Jetsam studied the girl while she deliberated. Giselle's brow fell and rose, and dipped again. Jetsam considered the inner turmoil she wrestled with. *If she refuses, I'll find the queen myself.*

"I shall wake Mother, and bring her here—*if* she's willing." Giselle wiped her eyes with the back of her hand. "Hide in my armoire 'til I return." Her silk robe bunched at the elbow, she pointed a thin arm at the ornate closet.

"Thank you," Jetsam said.

In the darkness, her blush escaped notice.

Jetsam hid in the armoire for an eternity. Giselle's clothes were soft and silky and smelled of rose petals, lavender, and chamomile. *And I smell of river slime and shite.* He rolled the fragrant fabric between his thumb and fingers. *What've I got myself into?*

When Giselle returned, Jetsam counted but one set of footsteps.

"Mother refuses to budge," Giselle said, holding open the door for Jetsam to exit. "I don't think she hears me. She's worse than ever."

Jetsam stepped from the armoire. "Is she with the king?" Jetsam fought the resilient urges of revenge. *If the king was dead, would Seryn have a chance to live?*

"Nay, Father's rarely in the Great Hall, and even rarer for him to spend a night in the solar."

Jetsam's eyebrows floated. *At least I won't be tempted by the king's sleeping throat.* Not that he could envision killing Giselle's father with her present. Though his hatred burned strong, Jetsam wasn't certain he could kill a slumbering man—even if it was the man who ordered his parents' execution.

"I told you Father doesn't love her," Giselle blurted. "Afraid he'll turn sick like her."

Jetsam pushed aside his thoughts of regicide. *Seryn's more important.*

"You must take me to her. I've come all this way, I can't turn back."

The princess nodded, her nose wrinkled. "Follow me, quiet as you can."

Little does she know, I can be as silent as a shadow when I wish.

Through a long, lightless hall, she led him past hanging tapestries and towering oak doors.

"In here."

The royal bedroom covered half of the Great Hall's fourth floor. Jetsam's jaw dropped as he scanned the luxurious room, setting his gaze upon an ornate bed. He entered the dim chamber on tiptoes, trying to focus on the task at hand. His damp boots made no sound as they sunk into a fur rug. *From what behemoth a hide this massive comes, I cannot imagine.*

Beside the barge-sized bed, Jetsam examined the queen, lying wide-eyed in the moonlight. *She's younger than I imagined, and beautiful, like her daughter.*

"Your Majesty?" he said, almost choking on the words. The woman swiveled her head slow as a turtle. The queen's gaze pierced him, settling on the vaulted ceiling. *Something's not right.*

"See," Giselle said, "she's having one of her spells."

"How often does she suffer them?"

"Often enough. Brother Tropf says she's of feeble constitution, and is wrought by visions. Never recovered from Grandfather's death."

Deep inside, Jetsam churned. A familiar aura tainted the room, vile wizardry he'd experienced before. *Enthran Ashvar!* Jetsam remembered how the warlock ensorcelled him, and hijacked his free will. The same black tendrils moved through the solar, invisible, yet tangible to Jetsam's sixth sense.

"She's under a spell," Jetsam whispered.

"I know," said Giselle, "'tis what I said."

"No, you don't understand." Jetsam shook his head. "Someone cast an incantation upon her."

"How do you know?"

"It happened once to *me*." Jetsam recalled how he struggled against Enthran's mental invasion, how after nearly submitting, he pushed the controlling thoughts from his mind.

"I'm going to try to help her." Jetsam reached out and grasped the queen's hand. *It's delicate, like Giselle's, but clammy.* His other hand delved into his pocket, where he kept the crystal shard he'd taken from the underground river. *I need every bit of power I can draw from this.* He clamped his eyes shut.

The black magic floated like a foul odor, unavoidable, yet elusive. Jetsam squeezed the queen's hand and his palm began to sweat. Mentally, he tried to force his magic into her. Sinister tendrils swatted him away. The task felt akin to threading a rope through a needle's eye. He recollected the agony of the warlock's unwanted intrusion, and how he focused to break free of his grip.

Teeth clenched, Jetsam exuded his energy, filling the room with his force, trying to chase out the intruding magic. *Unlike Enthran's spell, which controlled me from within, this magic feels like a blanket, smothering all beneath it.* As he tried to peel back the leaden cover, his power poured out of him and he weakened, knees buckling. With both hands, Giselle supported him under his arms.

Hang on, Jetsam urged his wobbling self. His body experienced a sensation akin to dragging his brother's corpse from the troll cave. *Elvar, please, I need your help again.* With every ounce of his magical energy, Jetsam tugged and pulled on the suffocating layer, trying to uncover the queen.

Then her hand twitched and squeezed his. A warmth returned to the queen's flesh that Jetsam hadn't noticed before his effort.

"I think the spell's broken," he told Giselle, not sure exactly how he accomplished the feat. Sweat coated his brow and a salty drop pinched his eyeball.

"Giselle?" the queen said. "What are you doing here?" The woman sounded sleepy, but coherent. "And who's this odorous lad?"

Though he'd just destroyed a powerful spell by sheer force of will, under the revived queen's gaze, Jetsam felt five years old.

"Mother, this is Jetsam." Giselle paused and glanced at him, dropping her hands from under his arms. He nodded encouragement. "Jetsam knows Seryn Vardan."

The blood drained from the queen's face and her jaw dropped. By her reaction, Jetsam feared the spell had returned.

"Seryn?" she asked, her gaze once again lifting toward the heavens. "He lives?"

"For now," Jetsam said. "But the king's captured him and he'll be executed soon."

"Oh, most certainly he will," Queen Ioma said. "As he *should.*"

Jetsam's knees buckled once more.

"Your Majesty, he was betrayed," Jetsam pleaded. "Seryn did not kill your father."

Queen Ioma scrutinized Jetsam, as if deciding his fate. *She'll never believe me.* The queen's eyes roved down and up, setting on his desperate gaze. *How can I convince a queen to believe a smelly orphan?*

"If only that were true, how things would be different," the queen confessed. "I loved him once."

"Seryn loves you still. Says deep inside, you know it's the truth."

The queen's gaze scorched Jetsam like the midday sun.

"No! I saw him flee my father's chamber. It could be no other."

"You *saw* Seryn?" The queen's revelation shook Jetsam's conviction.

"Every peasant in the Oxbow Kingdom knows my story, yet you do not?"

His face flush, Jetsam shook his bowing head.

Somber as a hanging judge, Ioma revealed her memory. "Valin and I were summoned to my father's room... and a man came running out, bloody dagger in hand. As he raced toward us, his hood fell, and I saw him. 'Twas Seryn. Even his own brother said so."

Jetsam's mind raced as he processed the information. *If Seryn can change to look like an old gypsy...* "It was dark magic," Jetsam said, then added "Your Majesty." He saw he held her attention. "Like that which enscorcelled you before I chased it away," he explained, without a trace of pride in his voice. *It must have been.* A twinge of doubt poked at him. "I've seen magic change a man's face, turn him from young to old and back again."

With narrowed eyes, the queen surveyed Jetsam. He stood still, aware of her penetrating inspection. *Yes, believe me—a dirty, stinky fugitive.* He would have laughed, were it not for the urge to cry. The queen turned her gaze upon her daughter.

"Giselle, where did you find this shameless urchin, and why did you bring him to me?"

"I met him in the garden, near a year ago. He's an orphan who lost his twin brother and his parents." Giselle paused and trembled. "They were wizards slain by Father's men."

"And you trust this outcast?"

Jetsam glanced at his feet, fighting the familiar urge to run.

"He banished your spell, Mother. I've never seen you so clearheaded."

Eyes wide, Jetsam waited for the queen to reply.

"Giselle—do you believe this outlandish story?"

"I trust Jetsam—he would not lie to me." Jetsam exhaled as his muscles relaxed. "And you seem alert now," Giselle said. "You look me in the eye, not through me." The princess leaned on the mattress and wrapped her arms around Ioma. "Oh, Mother, you have been sick for *so* long." Mother and child experienced a moment Jetsam hated to interrupt. Yet, he'd violated so much convention tonight, stopping now seemed pointless.

"Does it seem a coincidence that you were summoned right

before the murder?" he asked. Both mother and daughter pulled from their embrace to stare at him. Neither face appeared pleased with the inquiry. Undaunted, Jetsam pushed forward. Not only had he breached etiquette, but he'd cast it in the filth and trod upon it. "Seems someone *wanted* you to see Seryn."

"I never understood why he did it. Made no sense at all." Ioma shook her head. "Why would he kill Father? We had a future together— he would have been *king*." The queen glanced at Giselle and tears filled her eyes. "Nearly drove me insane. My nerves were destroyed—they had to medicate me."

"But he's innocent! Seryn told me how he was ambushed leaving the School of Sorcery."

"Why did he flee? Were there no witnesses to provide him an alibi?"

"The witness was killed." The words scathed Jetsam's throat as he spoke them. "Seryn knew he'd been framed."

As Queen Ioma mulled Jetsam's confounding words, Giselle chewed her thumbnail.

"And he's been living in the wilds all these years?"

"Dreaming of the day he could be with you again," Jetsam confirmed.

"So what do you want from me, shabby knave?" Queen Ioma asked. "My tongue hath no sway with my husband. I cannot halt the executioner's blade, even if I wanted to."

"Tell me how I might find Seryn."

"Then what? Arrange an escape? Get yourself killed is what you'll do."

"If I must, so be it."

"Such a willful youth!" The queen glanced to her daughter, then back to Jetsam. "Your presence has invigorated me. Tell me, why does Seryn mean so much to you?"

Jetsam told the queen his story, from meeting a disguised Seryn in Beggar's Alley to when Kandris Bayen and his minions handed him to the king. And with apprehension, he told her of Seryn's plan for a longevity potion.

"That sounds like the Seryn I once knew. Oh, how I wish it true—if he was innocent, how different things would have been." Queen

Ioma peered at Giselle, but looked away before her daughter caught her gaze. "Must have broken Seryn's heart to learn I married Valin."

"It did," Jetsam said.

The queen lowered her eyes, and released Giselle from her arms. Ioma stared at the quivering hands in her lap. "I didn't want to marry Valin. It was Nargul—he forced my hand, and with the medication, I wasn't thinking clearly, I—" the queen emitted a long sob, and gazed upon her daughter. "Oh, my poor, poor Giselle. Your life has been lived in lies and half-truths. I only wanted what was best for you."

"What do you mean?" Giselle sat straight as a post. "What did Chancellor Nargul do?"

"Darling, I'm so sorry. I never meant for you to find out—not like this."

"*Mother!*"

The queen spun from her daughter and peered at Jetsam with pleading eyes. He didn't understand why, and stood arms at his sides. Her chest heaving, Queen Ioma recomposed, and shifted toward Giselle. She placed her hands on the princess's shoulders.

"When your grandfather died in my arms, you were already in my womb," Ioma confessed, forcing the words from the pit of her soul. "Seryn and I—" she faltered, and Jetsam spied a tear race down her porcelain cheek. "We planned to wed—*Seryn* is your father."

Not moving a muscle, Jetsam stared at Giselle. The princess quivered as though she'd seen an apparition. She trembled, and the trembling changed to shaking, and the shaking to tears. Arms wide, Queen Ioma leaned toward her daughter.

Giselle launched from her mother's bed and bolted from the room.

Jetsam tore after her, with Queen Ioma following in their wake. *Devil take me, Elvar, the world's collapsing at my feet.* Jetsam found the shattered princess in bed, face buried, sobbing.

"I'm so sorry, Giselle," Ioma said.

"You lied! Lied to *me!*"

"I had no choice. I did it to protect you."

"Protect me with *lies?*"

Jetsam froze in his tracks. He didn't wish to be there, but he *was*, and with all he'd overheard, he had to stay.

"I was depressed—medicated—blackmailed! Nargul learned of my pregnancy and once Grandfather was killed, he forced me to marry Valin." The queen's voice rose in desperation. "Nargul swore Seryn didn't love me, that he only wanted the crown." Ioma gulped, filling her lungs. "Said if I married Valin, he'd never tell anyone Seryn was your father, and that one day you'd be queen."

The world raced past Jetsam faster than a shooting star, sucking the breath from him. Yet, necessity compelled him to speak.

"Who's this Tark Nargul?"

The queen swiveled to Jetsam as if he'd materialized from thin air. Giselle squirmed further from her mother, deeper into the goose-down.

"Nargul was my father's chancellor, and a friend of Valin's," Ioma told Jetsam. "Seryn didn't think well of him, though. I can see why."

"You shouldn't have listened to him!" shouted Giselle, striking like a coiled snake.

"Hush. We need no more audience for this conversation." She moved to her daughter's bed and sat beside her. "I wasn't well—grieving for your father, the loss of my fiancé. If Nargul revealed you were Seryn's child, I don't know what would have happened to you. As it was, he rushed Valin and me to the altar before I began to show, so Valin would think you his daughter."

Jetsam noticed Giselle's countenance soften, her skin eggshell white in the lunar glow. With the sleeve of her robe, she wiped her wet cheeks.

"I wonder," Ioma said, "if *that woman* told the truth."

"What woman?" Giselle questioned, spitting out the words between gasps.

"After Father died, a woman from the School of Sorcery came to me with Seryn's scroll case. Claimed he was innocent. I was furious and threw the case out the window. 'If he was innocent, why did he flee?' I screamed at her."

Jetsam beheld mother and daughter, silent now, contemplating the avalanche of emotions he ushered forth. *My mother?*

"They *loved* him at that school," Ioma said. "To them, he could do no wrong. Seryn was a prodigy—their most distinguished student."

Ioma paused as if her mind returned her to those heady days, though only for a second. "But I *saw* him, bloody dagger and all. I *know* what I saw." She glanced at her daughter, and then to Jetsam, as though for approval.

"Nargul said the killing blade was coated with a magical poison unknown to the royal healers. Said the magicians conspired against the king. Once we married and Valin was king, Nargul convinced him to close the school and ban sorcery altogether. How could I trust another wizard? I *loved* my father."

Giselle cleared her throat. "Mother, what if Jetsam speaks true, and you were deceived by wizardry?"

Yes, what if?

"Then I have forsaken my true love."

The words hung as mother and daughter paused. Jetsam spied an opening. "Help me give him another chance," he pleaded. "Tell me where he is." The queen looked to her daughter. *She's considering it!* Giselle nodded.

"If Valin has him, he'll be in the dungeon, probably the oubliette. But there's no way you'll save him."

"Tell me of the dungeon, and I'll do my best."

"The entrance is inside the old Wizard's Tower. It's been empty since Valin banished magic, but he keeps it locked and guarded. If you've seen an entrance by this underground river, my advice is to enter there."

"But that's guarded by humpbacks!"

"Trolls or the king's elite guard—either way, you're doomed with this foolhardy quest."

"I'll need much help and a lot of luck."

"I will help, however I can," said a teary-eyed Giselle.

"And I as well. You've given me much to ponder. I'll not turn my back on Seryn again, until it is proven that he did this evil he's accused of."

"I must go speak to Ratboy, and make plans. Time's not on our side." Jetsam whirled and strode toward the oriel.

"You shan't climb down the wall again," Giselle declared, part demand, part plea. "I'll sneak you out downstairs, through a rear window."

"I'll be fine climbing. Down is easier than up."

"Nay, 'tis a miracle the sentry didn't spot you," Giselle said. "We'll do it my way."

"Put servant's garb on him," Ioma instructed. "Should you be spotted, the guards may not take note."

Like mice in the castle hallway, Giselle led Jetsam to a closet where he donned a baggy tunic and breeches. From there, he followed his hostess through back stairways and into the kitchen, where she propped open a vent panel.

"Be careful," Giselle said. "I cannot bear losing you again." The princess wrapped him in a hug, and pecked his cheek. Jetsam slid through the wall, skittered to the postern gate, and exited via the garden. The whole while, his mind raced, searching for some desperate plan that may hold even a bleak hope of success.

The frigid moat numbed his body as he paddled through the moon-lit ripples. Fingers of dawn pulled at the horizon.

Only a day 'till the execution.

Chapter Fifteen

Inside the orphan-renovated Dwarven ruins, Jetsam stood near the hearth, warming his chilled frame while exchanging his wet clothes for dry, borrowed garments. He pulled a pair of Biter's trousers over his goose-fleshed legs. Ratboy paced nearby, his greasy brow furrowed.

"Impossible," Ratboy said, as he fiddled with his ragged tunic collar. The frayed woolen garment fit tightly on the sprouting lad. He wore the peasant-pilfered mismatched shirt and breeches that served as the underbelly orphans' unofficial uniform. Jetsam noticed Ratboy carried a long dagger sheathed at his waist, and his leather boots appeared newer and in better condition than Jetsam recalled.

"That's what you told me when I left for the north," Jetsam said. Hands above his head, he slipped on his silvery Dwarven hauberk. By now, Jetsam grew accustomed to the extra weight. He fastened the sheathed hand-and-a-half sword Regret around his midsection, then donned his russet cloak. After a few minor adjustments, Jetsam slung his holster over his shoulder and slid his gnarled hardwood staff into place on his back. *Ready as I'll ever be.*

"Ye've added some interestin' gear to yer inventory," Ratboy mused, while eyeing the late warlock's staff and the dead bounty hunter's sword. Mind if I look at the blade?" Jetsam nodded and slid Regret from its sheath. With both hands cradling the sword, he presented the weapon grip-forward to Ratboy. The elder orphan held the blade aloft, twisting it in the rushlight as he examined the sword. The blade gleamed, mirroring the fire's glow. "Tis feather-light," he said. "Wondered how ye handled a thing this long, but now I see." He flicked his thumb across the sharp edge. "Fine forged steel, it is." Ratboy ran his fingertips over the inlaid patterned etchings. "Like ta have one fer meself," he said, returning the sword.

With his attention from the sheathed weapon, Ratboy locked his gaze on Jetsam's blue eyes. "We scavenge every inch of Dwim-Halloe, 'cept for the Granite Palace. 'Tis folly for the mouse to enter the cat's lair," Ratboy said. "'Tis watched like a hawk and crawling with guards. In a hunnert tries, we'd not spring yer wizard that way." Ratboy attached a well-worn belt pouch to his buckled strap.

"Then we shall sneak in from below," Jetsam said.

"Past the bloody humpbacks? Ye know how vicious those sodding curs are, and near impossible to kill." Ratboy tossed another dry branch on the fire. "Besides, those tunnels ye speak of are unknown to us." An unruly stack of mismatched branches and broken scraps of salvaged Dwarven furniture awaited incineration.

"I can find the way back," Jetsam insisted.

"Still, don't like the idea of mixing unmapped tunnels with knuckle-draggers."

"I've a plan," Jetsam said. "But I need your help." Jetsam stared at his friend, who in return, eyed him up and down. "And some volunteers. And luck—lot's of it."

"We all die someday," Ratboy said. "Today's good as any."

The solemn orphans ventured deep into the nether reaches of Gwae Gierameth. Jetsam retraced his steps, leading a band of young outcasts at his heels. Along with Ratboy, Jetsam's old cronies, Lil' Pete, Biter, Blister, Cricket, Pike, Rooster, and Stinger, followed with some newer boys whose names Jetsam hadn't memorized. The urchin troops carried their weapons along with other gear. Their burgeoning organizational skills impressed Jetsam. Bolstered in number and weapons, these runaways strengthened out of necessity. *Adapt or die.*

Jetsam's path revealed another winding tunnel for the orphans to add to their underbelly cartography. They shimmied past the petrified carcasses of the two trolls who ran into the mirror-reflected sunlight as they chased Jetsam a short time ago. The pair of humpback statues now stood as warning of the mirrored light trap beyond. With their lanky forms filling most of the passage, they obstructed more knuckle-draggers from passing. The lads brandished satisfied smiles upon inspecting the 'frozen' beasts.

"The runawaifs who arrived after yer departure know yer story," Ratboy told him. The ragtag band proved eager to follow Jetsam's direction.

"This is where you'll set up," Jetsam instructed Lil' Pete. "Ratboy and I'll go on ahead."

Jetsam and his friend slunk further along the inky passageways, leaving the busy coterie behind. As the duo approached their destination, a glimmer of rushlight shone in the wormhole in front of them. *I'm walking toward humpbacks—on purpose!* Jetsam made a hushing sound and crept forward, guiding Ratboy by tugging on his woolen tunic.

"There they are," Jetsam whispered as they peered at four trolls and a human form. Jetsam's senses again tingled at the unusual magic residue emanating from the surrounding stone, as though the echoes of a once-extraordinary power lingered. *Bloody strange, it is.* He refrained mentioning it to Ratboy.

"The small one—ye know him?" Ratboy asked.

"It's Kandris Bayen, but he's different. Ensorcelled, I think."

"Looks dead," Ratboy said.

"He's not the same squire I knew, that's for sure. The old Kandris would lose his water and soil his breeches being that close to a knuckle-dragger. But this *new* Kandris, he shows no fear, and it's like the humpbacks *listen* to him."

"Evil magics, indeed," Ratboy said.

Jetsam appraised his friend with a solemn familiarity. They'd faced death before. *Much too often for boys our age.* "You ready?" Jetsam asked.

"Aye. Been good ta know ye, Jetsam. This one's for Flotsam." The pair shook hands and Ratboy pulled his friend into a half-hug.

After the melancholy farewell, Ratboy strode into the troll's line of sight. Jetsam glanced at his friend and spun the other way, retreating up the passage.

Ratboy slipped into character, acting the part of a disoriented, lost wanderer, he meandered toward the humpbacks. The trolls attuned to his presence, and with a nod and a grunt, they lumbered toward him.

Coated in a nervous sweat, Ratboy appeared not to notice the trolls. *I pray he's pretending,* Jetsam thought. With a choreographed flop, the orphan leader stumbled to the stone in shock, letting the trolls know he'd seen them. *Don't overdo it!* Ratboy's pratfall whetted their appetite, and the beasts charged full speed.

Spring-like, Ratboy jumped to his feet and tore back toward the tunnel whence he came. With the troglodytes in pursuit, he sprinted up the lightless passage as the creatures jostled for position, falling into single file in the narrow wormhole. The fastest pursuer closed the gap, its outstretched arm grazing Ratboy.

Curled up in a natural alcove in the cavern's ceiling, Jetsam viewed the procession speed past below him. *Run faster!* When the fourth and final troll passed beneath Jetsam's hidden perch, he waited a few seconds and dropped to the ground. With a glance behind at the trolls, he headed for the doorway, knowing Kandris Bayen stood in his way. He prayed Ratboy would be alright. *Of all the things in the world, I hate humpbacks most of all.*

When Jetsam reached the tunnel's mouth, he spotted the imposing door barring his way. Dimly lit by a flanking pair of low-burning torches, Jetsam detected no sign of Kandris. *Odd--I swear he didn't run past me.* The mystery of Kandris Bayen would wait. *I've a job to do.* With long strides, he covered the ground between the tunnel's end and the formidable doorway in a handful of steps. Scattered bones crunched under his soles. The waste appeared similar to the discarded remnants he'd find in town. Near the door sat a tipped-over bucket. Jetsam peeked inside and saw the wooden pail coated in blood, with bits of rancid meat festering on the bottom.

Is someone feeding the knuckle-draggers? His troubling thought presented an unnerving possibility. *That would explain them hanging around.*

Upon reaching the door, he surveyed the iron-reinforced barricade. *No handle, lock, or latch.* This door only opened from the inside. *Just what I feared.* After a quick glance around, he cast a spell.

Like the iron bars atop the garden wall, Jetsam undertook heating the door hinges. Two amplified fire bolts shot from his staff, each pouring heat into one of the resilient fixtures.

Jetsam maintained his focus, concentrating his magic to its maximum temperature. He watched his *V* of fire lay siege to the ironwork. As seconds ticked away, Jetsam recognized his magic depleting. The hinges were thick and strong, and he understood this was his one chance. Near the end of his magical reservoir, Jetsam noticed the hefty door shift, and the hinges began to fail under the massive weight.

With that, Jetsam ended the spell, holstered his staff, and leapt upon the door. His fingertips clutched the top, squeezing in the crack between wood and rock. With one foot planted on each side of the door, he pushed off. *Come on, you sodding bugger.*

The door wavered. By rocking his weight, Jetsam pulled harder. The hinges squealed and gave way. With Jetsam hanging on, the door fell on top of him, riding him to the cave floor. The weighty door knocked the wind from him. Sandwiched between the oaken slab and the unforgiving stone, Jetsam wheezed, trying to suck the stale cavern air into his hungry lungs. Pinned on his back, he observed an ominous form rise from the underground river.

Kandris!

Trapped by the dislodged door, Jetsam gaped as Kandris lumbered toward him. Lungs screaming, they couldn't fill fast enough. The dripping-wet Kandris Bayen trampled over him, moldy boots stomping across the door. His weight squeezed the air back out of Jetsam. With three steps, the squire strode past him and up the now-open passage.

Fobbing piss-pail!

It took Jetsam another minute to inflate his lungs and wiggle out from under the door. *That didn't work out like I planned.* On his feet, he peered into the portal he'd so painfully opened. A stone stairway lay in front of him, rising upward. With a longing glance behind at the tunnel where the trolls chased his dear friend, he bolted for the stairs.

The passage loomed dark, but not pure black. Periodic cressets cast a gloomy glow throughout the winding stairway. There was only one way to go, and Jetsam clambered up the granite steps, still wet from Kandris' dripping form. Two at time, Jetsam assaulted the stairs. As his thighs burned, so did his nostrils. *Smells like corpse.* The odor intensified the higher he climbed.

Relentless, Jetsam maintained the pace. He knew he ran faster than Kandris Bayen, and the wet steps told him he was on his trail. As the stairway curved around itself, spiraling upward, Jetsam winced at the stench while his legs begged for a reprieve. He heard footsteps above, and the sound of a door swinging open.

When Jetsam arrived at the doorway, he spied Kandris' slumped back, lumbering through a long corridor. *Barred cells line both sides of the hallway.*

Jetsam slowed his pace enough to check each cell as he ran past, swinging his head left and right. *Empty... empty... ugh—skeleton.* The human remains startled Jetsam for but a moment.

Ahead, Kandris opened another door at the corridor's end and disappeared. By the time Jetsam reached the portal, he'd seen several other bony captives—all dead. *But no Seryn.*

The room beyond was round and vaulted, but it held no prison cells. Across the wide chamber, Jetsam spotted Kandris fleeing through another doorway. Between him and the squire sat a variety of contraptions. Iron thumbscrews, floor-chained shackles, a blood-stained turning-wheel rack, sharp-toothed crocodile shears, and a strange, A-shaped, hinged metal rack.

The bone-cracking, flesh-tearing devices filled him with unsettling chills. Then he spied the wobbly table. Atop the rusty plane sat bloody shears and a severed finger. Jetsam gasped and rubbed his hands, thankful for all ten of his digits. *I can't get out of this room fast enough.*

As the unnerved Jetsam raced past a pillory and padlocked wooden stocks, his feet landed on a grate. He stopped on the iron framework, and glanced beneath his boots. Far below sat a hooded man, with hands behind his back, dressed in a plain tunic and trousers.

The oubliette!

"Seryn!" Jetsam shouted. The hooded head snapped upward. Jetsam stepped off the grate, crouched, and gripped the bars. With a tug, he pulled.

Locked.

"How do I unlock it?" he hollered to Seryn, his heart pounding. He heard a muffled grunt in reply. Jetsam inspected the grate, but located no lock or keyhole.

Perplexed, he surveyed the chamber as the seconds slipped away. Kandris was heading somewhere, and wherever the destination, it spelled trouble for the escape. Jetsam listened to murmuring from ahead. *Someone* had been roused, and was aware something was afoot. Panic poked at Jetsam, trying to unnerve him. He noticed a small desk, and ran to it. With frantic hands, he pushed the papers off, opened each drawer, even checked underneath it. He found keys. *But there's no keyhole,* he realized, glancing back at the floor grate. Jetsam pocketed them anyway.

From the cells, he heard an incomprehensible voice. *That'll alert the guards.*

Hands on hips, Jetsam became flustered. *I don't have enough left in me to melt those bars, not for a few hours, at least.*

The unseen prisoner's voice grew louder, and Jetsam fumed. As he strode toward the doorway, ready to admonish the captive, the words sunk in.

"Pull the lever on the wall."

Jetsam swiveled and scanned the dim room.

Chains... ropes... weapon racks...

Lever!

Jetsam raced to the handle and pulled, but the rusty lever resisted. *Fobbing rot.* He repositioned himself, straddling the lever, crouched to push off with his thighs. Hand over hand, he grasped the handle, and with all his might, yanked again. His whole body strained as he wrestled with the lever. *Come on, you bastard.* His thighs burned and hands blistered as he tapped his last bit of strength. With a loud creak and a following clank, the floor grate flapped open. *Finally!*

Jetsam grabbed a rope from the wall. *It's wet.* He saw red on his hands. *Blood.*

He wiped his hands on his trousers, then tied the rope to the grate. With the slippery cord as an aid, he lowered himself into Seryn's smooth-walled oubliette. Barefoot in the narrow hole, Seryn wobbled before him, blind and mute. The back of his tunic was shredded and red welts swathed his shoulder blades and ribs. *Purely for sport,* Jetsam surmised. *For what could Seryn tell the king he didn't already know?*

In a matter of seconds, Jetsam removed the hood—and gasped. Seryn's nose sat crooked and swollen, both eyes black. A week-old beard covered his cheeks and chin. With the gag still in place, the captive grunted, snapping Jetsam from his gawking trance. Jetsam's nimble fingers relieved Seryn of the restraint. The battered mage released a prolonged sigh. If possible, Seryn appeared even more surprised than Jetsam.

"Jetsam! How in the world—"

Jetsam raised a finger to his lips. "Your face?" he whispered.

"Trolls aren't the gentlest handlers," Seryn said just as quietly. "Can you unbind me?"

Jetsam's eyes popped wide as he viewed Seryn's hands.

"Your finger!"

Jetsam gaped at a scabby stump where Seryn's little finger used to be. Dried blood coated the injured hand.

"Naught I can do about it now—just set me free."

Jetsam snapped from his stupor and remembered the desk keys jangling in his pocket.

He fumbled with each of the pilfered keys, discarding the wrong ones until finally the manacles opened. He peered at Seryn's wrists, chaffed raw and bleeding. The captive caught his gaze and shook him off. "I'm fine—don't waste a spell healing *that*. Just get me out of here."

As Seryn clutched the suspended rope, Jetsam assisted the stiff sorcerer. *He's so weak.* Jetsam supported from beneath as Seryn climbed. With every pained movement, the wizard groaned. Jetsam stood on his tiptoes, pushing Seryn's bloody heels.

When Seryn reached the top, he tried to stand, faltered, and crumpled to the floor. On knees and elbows, the sorcerer gasped.

Jetsam scrambled up behind him and hovered over his struggling mentor. "I must heal you."

Seryn shook his head and grunted, but Jetsam ignored him and began a restorative incantation. Within moments of finishing the spell, Seryn raised his head and met Jetsam's gaze.

"Thank you," Seryn said as he regained his feet. "You've learned well."

"I had a good teacher."

"What now?" Seryn asked, stretching his shoulders.

"Kandris Bayen went that way," Jetsam pointed.

"He's no longer Kandris, I fear," said Seryn. "Malefic wizardry animates his corpse, but Kandris is no more."

"So he's dead?" Jetsam cocked an eyebrow. "I don't understand."

"Yes, I fear poor Kandris encountered some fell evil after we sent him on his way. His soul is gone, yet his body remains animated, possessed by a sprit, or controlled by necromantic means."

"Necromantic?"

"Dark sorcery, like the Grimlord wealds. I feel the grimion raiders and this undead Kandris portent the Grimlord extending his reach further southward. But that's not our worry at the moment."

"We can escape this way." Jetsam pointed to the opposite doorway.

"There's evil afoot in this castle, and I shall run no more. We'll follow the walking corpse, and see where he leads." Seryn hobbled to one of the weapon racks, and took a small sharp blade. Without his staff and belongings, his spells and this knife would serve as his weaponry.

Jetsam stood back, surprised by this course of action. The Seryn he knew was conservative, deliberate, calculating. *I like this change.*

They left the torture room via the same door as Kandris Bayen's shambling corpse. Beyond the portal sat another long row of cells. Jetsam wasn't concerned with the contents of these cubes, and hurried past, aware that Kandris built a sizeable lead. He assumed Seryn ran right behind him, but when Jetsam reached the opposite end door, he stood alone. His heart skipped a beat as he spun around.

Twenty paces behind him, Seryn lingered, transfixed on the resident of a certain dank cell. *The voice that spoke of the lever!* Jetsam trotted back to his teacher and listened to them talking.

"What sort of trick is this?" Seryn interrogated the captive, waving a warning finger. Jetsam noticed his master's pursed lips and furrowed brow. Befuddled, he stopped behind Seryn and peered into the cell.

Jetsam scrutinized the man behind bars. He wore tattered prison garb, gray and threadbare, his matching hair long and tangled. Yet, his visage resembled the regally-dressed man at the underground river—the man he'd seen Kandris Bayen hand Seryn over to. Gray eyes, auburn hair, oval face. *Almost like Seryn.*

This man looks like the king.

"'Tis all part of the same trick, brother," the captive said. *They even have the same voice,* Jetsam realized.

"What are you doing locked up?" Seryn asked. "What happened since you dropped me in the hole?"

"'Twasn't me that plunked you in the oubliette." Jetsam watched the prisoner shake his head, his hands floating palm-up in front of him. "'Twas the shapechanger."

"Shapechanger? What do you mean?"

"Figured a magician like you would be able to tell," the captive said. "Tark Nargul is not a man—he's a doppelganger."

Seryn wobbled like a flimsy door hit by a battering ram. He put a hand to the cell bar to steady himself.

"Aye—he fooled us all, brother. Formed himself in your image and convinced Ioma and me you killed Tygan. Believed it, too, until he locked me in here." The man waved his arms, displaying his prison. Dirty long fingernails attested to his interment. "Bastard's been parading as me ever since. You were right about him, all those years ago. I was just too blind with ambition to see it."

Seryn crinkled his nose, his eyes slits, despite the dim environs. Jetsam chewed his lip and watched the mage deliberate. *I don't like this.*

"So you didn't plot against me?"

Ashen, the captive stared at the floor. "I didn't know what Nargul intended. He only promised he'd 'take care' of you—and I let him. Never did I imagine he conspired to kill Tygan and frame you. Only after I was locked in here did I realize his true power, and began to suspect how he deceived us all."

With inquisitive eyes, Jetsam compared the two men, separated by the cell bars. *They* could *be brothers.*

"Yet, you married Ioma, so guilt-ridden were you."

"I didn't know then that Nargul was a doppelganger, nor that he'd framed you for the murder."

"He locked me up for regicide." Jetsam noticed Seryn's voice rising.

"Still, you escaped. For that, I'm glad."

"I suppose now you want me to help *you* escape?"

"I'd run if I were you. Get as far away as you can, before they take your head. But first let me out." The prisoner leaned forward, eyes wide and pleading. "And if you can't bring yourself to do that, put me out of my misery. I'd rather be dead than spend another day in here."

A fly on the wall, Jetsam almost believed him.

"Part of me has wished you dead for a long time," Seryn said.

"Don't blame you. I hated you once, too. Feared you'd stop me from becoming king. And then I figured you lost your mind, pickled by your sorcery," the inmate said. "But I got what I wanted." His eyes dropped to his feet. "Be careful what you wish for."

"Ioma?" Seryn implored.

The captive raised his heavy head and his somber gaze met Seryn's. "She always loved you—I won the throne, but you won her heart."

"So you didn't love her, yet you still wed, just for the throne."

"Men have done worse to wear a crown." The prisoner picked at his stubble with curving nails. "I fear Nargul played a part in it. Think he picked me for his victim. I suspect he knew he could use me."

"Why you?" Seryn asked. "Why not me?"

"Because I was weak-minded—susceptible to his tricks, and blinded by a thirst for power. But you—he feared your magic. Don't think he could see inside your head like he did—does—mine."

"What do you mean?"

"When we were courting Ioma, I *was* truly fond of her. Who wouldn't be? She was beautiful, charming, and *royalty*. And Nargul surely saw I yearned for her, but my sentiments weren't returned. So he planted seeds, made me jealous of you, told me she *did* favor me. That I was the *king's* choice. Told me *I* should be king, convinced me you used wizardry to win her over."

"You *believed* this rubbish?"

"I did. Perhaps I was ensorcelled, too."

Seryn ran his five-fingered hand through his stringy hair, while Jetsam idled behind him, paralyzed with indecision.

"When did this start?" Seryn inquired.

"The night of the harvest ball, I think. I talked much with Nargul that eve, and savored a confidence in his presence. Suspect he got inside my mind that very night."

Jetsam eyed the captive with utmost scrutiny. *A tall tale, indeed.* Yet, to Jetsam, it rang true, despite his misgivings. He wondered if Seryn suspected the same. *True or not, I don't trust him,* Jetsam decided.

"But you'd unnerved Nargul," the prisoner said. "When Ioma began falling for you, he saw his plan unraveling. You were the fly in his ointment."

"Where's Ioma now?"

"Haven't seen her in years." He shook his scraggly head. "Part of her died the day Tygan was killed." He met Seryn's eyes, and Jetsam swore he detected pity in the prisoner's gaze. "After that, she hated you more than she loved you. Can't say I blame her. I was convinced you were the killer as well."

Seryn blinked as his jaw dropped.

"How could you believe I murdered the king?"

"I swear, it was you. When the hood came off and you looked at us, I had no doubt. But never did I believe a doppelganger was anything more than a myth."

"So, now you believe I'm innocent?"

"I do, yes. Not that it'll do you any good. I'm no more the king than your urchin sidekick." He pointed to Jetsam, whose anger neared the boiling point. *I'm tired of all this talk,* he thought. *Brother or no, this man is no ally of ours.* Jetsam trembled with rage.

"You murdered my parents, you bastard!" Jetsam shouted. "If Seryn won't kill you, *I will!*"

Jetsam took a step toward the cell door. With the melodic keening of steel on leather, he unsheathed Regret.

"Jetsam!" Seryn turned to him with a shattered expression.

"I didn't kill them any more than Seryn killed the king," the prisoner said, unflinching, yet sliding away from the bars. "Day after the coronation, Nargul tricked me into this cell, and I've been here ever since."

Jetsam glimpsed the mage's open palm outstretched in his path, eyes pleading. The gesture proved enough to redirect his fury. Jetsam's sword-hand dropped to his side, the tip of his blade tickling the floor. "Then we must kill this Nargul," Jetsam said, recalling Queen Ioma's story. "For he's ruined *all* our lives."

The three shared a moment of contemplation, and neither Vardan brother outwardly disagreed with Jetsam. With reluctant resignation and a shaking hand, he returned his sword to its sheath.

"If you truly are my brother," Seryn postulated, "tell me this: why do you remain alive? Seems Nargul would have finished you long ago."

"He can't—not if he wants to keep looking like me. That's the rub of being a doppelganger. They need to see the person they're copying, so he keeps me alive, studies me as I age, pries information from me. In exchange for my life."

"Let's get you out of here—then we'll take care of Nargul."

Jetsam shook his head. *That's not a good idea.*

"I fear it's too late," the prisoner said. "That walking dead has surely alerted him by now. Nargul's no fool—he's got an army behind him, and Ioma in a trance. She'll be of no help to us."

"I broke her spell!" Jetsam blurted. "She told me how to find you—she'll help us."

The prisoner appeared crestfallen. His reaction baffled Jetsam.

"Oh, lad, if she's out of her trance, Nargul will *know*. And that can't bode well for her."

Jetsam's eyes grew wide. *Or Giselle!*

He whirled and ran.

Chapter Sixteen

Gaping at his estranged brother, wasting away in a dungeon cell, Seryn marveled at how wrong he'd been. While fleeing Dwim-Halloe as his world collapsed around him, Seryn pieced together the scraps of clues he learned about his betrayal. He was convinced his sibling sacrificed him for the throne. *Who stood to gain the most? Who beat me to a bloody pulp? Who knew my daily routines?* Every question provided Seryn the same answer. After the pummeling he received in the library at Valin's hands, Seryn thought his brother capable of the vilest treachery. *Valin was as much a victim as me.*

Valin's cell was dim, with a thick curtain hanging outside the bars. His cell was the only one featuring such adornment. Inside, rubble ashlar covered the remaining three walls, topped with a coarse lintel supporting a vaulted ceiling. Seryn noticed a bed and a full bookshelf, along with a small table and a wash basin. A few anemic candles flickered and a threadbare rug covered the stone floor. Though still a cell, some effort had been taken to make it habitable.

For a prisoner, his brother appeared well-fed, though he no longer looked the muscular specimen Seryn remembered. *Thin and sloop-shouldered, he looks as if he abandoned exercise years ago.* He carried a paunch, poking out from his plain threadbare tunic. Though oddly clean-shaven, his graying hair hung long and tangled, and his skin was as pale as a dwarf. *And he smells like a prisoner.*

Head reeling, Seryn tried to rearrange the facts. *Nargul kidnapped me—not my brother.* This idea struck him as foreign, yet it took hold. For years he agonized over his brother's accomplices, wondering what royal commission he promised them for their complicity. Now Seryn realized his brother's relationship to the conspirators existed solely in his imagination. *They were Nargul's men— if they were men at all,* he pondered, recalling the animated corpse of Kandris Bayen.

I was already locked up when Nargul impersonated me and killed Tygan. Seryn understood that as he sat captive, the royal murder unfolded. *Nargul stole any chance of an alibi.* He imagined Nargul changing form as he sprinted past Valin and Ioma, only to return as the Lord High Chamberlain, feigning shock and horror at his handiwork. *Surely he took credit for my capture as well.* Seryn shook his head.

Nargul could not have found two more perfect witnesses in all the world. For if Seryn was identified by his own blood and his own love, what witness or evidence could trump that? *And even more convincing, who would stand against the queen's word?* For upon Tygan's death, his daughter, who testified through a river of tears that Seryn Vardan killed her father, inherited the throne.

The idea that this imposter mimicked him so convincingly as to fool his brother and lover chilled Seryn. Even his mastery of magic found this ability unnerving. The image of Ioma watching this replica flee her dying father with the murder weapon in hand sickened him. That his beloved failed to discern him from the imposter added a heaping of nausea on his churning internals.

Despite his revulsion, the intricacy of the plot impressed Seryn. Nargul had been cunning in his ruse. *Every angle was covered.*

Except one.

Illuminae Lothyrn—and now she's dead. Because she believed in me. Seryn recalled his new apprentice, and pictured how young Jetsam was when his parents were murdered. Seryn's heart grieved for the youth. His friendship with the Lothyrns helped him understand the teen's unrelenting fury. Seryn began to taste it himself. *Seems everyone I know was ensnared in this vile web.*

And yet his mind second-guessed fate, allowing him to imagine a world where the Lothyrns lived, and he was vindicated by their testimony. *Everything would be different.* He shook off the bittersweet daydream. *What odds did the illuminae hold against the insurmountable false evidence Nargul assembled? She was right to insist I flee. I stood no chance.*

Seryn's melancholy thoughts drifted to his father. *I wonder if he harbored even the slightest doubt that his son was a murderer?* He'd not seen his father since his flight those many years ago. He granted Daelis the benefit of the doubt. *What could he do? With his golden child and the queen identifying me as a killer, he had no recourse.* Deep inside, Seryn hoped his father held an inclination that his youngest was incapable of such an atrocity.

Poor Father. Does he not realize the king's an imposter? Can he not discern his own flesh and blood from the mimic? He peered at his frail sibling, comprehending the sorrow Daelis Vardan would feel if he learned his favorite wasted away like a bird in a covered cage. *He resembles Father now.* The same gaunt skin weighed down by gravity's pull. *The same stern look in his adamant eyes.* Though Seryn owed his father no sympathy, he carried it nonetheless.

"What of Father?"

Before Valin uttered a word, Seryn read his ominous expression.

"Father's dead," Valin said, barely above a whisper, spitting the razor-sharp words. Both brothers swallowed hard, mirroring each other. "Heard it from Nargul." Valin's eyes turned glossy. "He may have poisoned him, too. I fear he always suspected Father would know he wasn't me."

"I'm certain he would have," Seryn lied. He conceded Valin's bond with Daelis was something he'd never experience, yet the jealousy over this treatment had dissipated, replaced with sympathy for his sibling. *For a moment, the world was his,* Seryn reflected, imagining his brother as king, and the shared pride of father and son. *Then it was snatched away, leaving him but a taste of the life he'd never have.* Compared to his own horrible fate, Seryn would not trade places with his sibling for anything. Just speaking of Daelis shrunk Valin even further from the vibrant image Seryn remembered. *I cannot let sorrow delay us,* Seryn reminded himself.

"So you talk to him—Nargul, I mean?"

"He talks to *me*. The only man—or *thing*—I've seen in years. And, yes, I suppose I talk to him, too. Though I'm not sure between his poisons and wizardry, how much control over my mind I actually have."

"And Ioma—" Saying her name aloud chilled Seryn, and he paused to dispel the demons. "Does she know a doppelganger has taken your place?"

"Cannot imagine she does. It would serve no purpose for Nargul," Valin said with a tone suggesting he'd mulled this question before.

"I've been back to Dwim-Halloe a few times—in disguise," Seryn said. "Rumors are she's not well."

"Imagine Nargul keeps her on a short leash. After Tygan was killed, they began medicating her. I'm sure he had a hand in that, and from what I sense, he still does."

"I must save her."

"I agree, her and your child."

"*My* child?"

"You don't know?" Valin paused, realizing his inadvertent revelation. His gray eyes softened as his posture straightened. "Ioma was with child when Tygan died. *Your* child."

Seryn faltered, grasping for words. His mouth hung wide enough to catch the flies lingering near Valin's waste as he wrestled with the possibility. His mind returned to that afternoon in his bedroom, when Ioma called on him while he convalesced from Valin's attack. *That was the happiest day of my life. And yet she didn't tell me?*

"She may not have yet known," Valin said, as if reading his brother's mind. "Told me when I proposed. Said you were the father. With her grief and her medication, I scarce believed her, and I wavered."

"What then?" Seryn asked, with no trace of compassion in his voice.

"Nargul convinced me I must marry her, and pretend the child was mine. He promised Ioma would keep the secret."

"And you went along with this, though you knew she loved me and carried my child?"

"I did." Valin nodded, a flood of shame washing his visage. "But do not forget, I thought you killed Tygan," Valin said in a weary voice, hoarse with regret. "I should've had more faith in you—questioned my own eyes. But, by then, I was in too deep. The throne was mine—all I had to do was wed her." Valin swallowed hard and met his brother's gaze. "So I did."

"Lad or lass?"

"I know not," Valin said, with honesty in his steely eyes. "Nargul speaks not of the child, yet I know it was born."

"And you and Ioma?" Seryn let the sentence hang. Valin paused to comprehend the inference. The once-king shook his head.

"No—of course not. I told you, as soon as the wedding and coronation finished, Nargul drugged me and threw me in here."

"That was *eleven* years ago."

"Feels like *a hundred* and eleven."

"Nargul thinks he can keep you here the rest of his days while he parades as a king?"

"I suspect Nargul serves a greater power," Valin said. Seryn pondered his brother's words for but a moment. There was only one figure Seryn had ever heard of that powerful—and evil.

"The Grimlord?"

"'Tis my fear."

"What makes you think it?" Seryn hoped he'd misconstrued the portents of the unnatural monstrosities banding in the southern Oxbows, but now his brother echoed the same suspicions.

"Nargul strikes me as a puppet," Valin said. "Ask yourself, why would a doppelganger want to be king?"

"There is little written lore on these beings, even in Eh' liel Ev' Narron," Seryn said. "But I suppose for riches and power—like any man."

"I see no motive for him to *continue* the ruse. He could've disappeared with Dwim-Halloe's gold years ago and still lived the life of a king. But he stays here, year after year, pretending to rule. *Toiling* as the king. He quizzes me on policy and protocol, as if controlling the kingdom were an obsession. As though he were afraid to *fail*."

"I agree, it's odd." Seryn said. "But why does that make you suspect the Grimlord?"

"Nargul hates magic. Despises it. *Fears* it. Plots of ways to rid it from Dwim-Halloe—from Tythania."

"So *he* outlawed magic—not you?"

"Of course. He cast the lord high wizard out of the tower and made it his personal prison. For me."

"And the wizards of Dwim-Halloe turned back the Grimlord's minions all those years ago."

"So they say," Valin responded, cracking the slightest of smiles. "Though Father left me with a different slant on the history," Valin said.

Seryn bit his tongue. *I will not speak ill of the departed.*

"With magic gone from the Oxbow Kingdom, Dwim-Halloe is once again vulnerable to the Grimlord."

"Especially with his doppelganger on the throne." Seryn's brow furrowed, wrinkling his forehead. He reminisced on his cherished days in the family library, reading tales of Lord Averon Grimwealder. For every sliver of fact recorded about the enigmatic man, a pound of uncertainty muddled his elusive history. Seryn recalled studying the siege on Dwim-Halloe, and how even then, none but the vaguest descriptions of a ghastly figure on horseback tied the Grimlord to the hordes. Many unimaginative scholars dismissed the idea of a Grimlord-led army entirely.

But Seryn's teachers at Eh' liel Ev' Narron taught him otherwise. Illuminae Daystar lectured of the black sorcery propelling the raiders at Dwim-Halloe. The sage wizard described the demonic fury and uncharacteristic solidarity the grimions, ogres, and goblins possessed. The former battlemage detailed the vision of the lord high wizard, who scried into the horde's heart and discovered a despicable entity, filled with netherworld power. Whether this commander was once Averon Grimwealder was not determined, yet the lord high wizard named this being Grimlord.

"I had hoped the Grimlord passed from this world."

"I pray he has—yet I fear he lives. You understand far more of the powers of wizardry than I. Is it not possible to magically extend life?"

Seryn reflected on his own attempts at longevity. *It's not impossible to imagine the Grimlord succeeding.* "It is possible," Seryn admitted. "And, I've seen grimion war bands in the Oxbows."

"'Tis an ill harbinger, indeed," Valin said.

"And this walking dead minion," Seryn peered through the hallway where the former Kandris had fled. "Is certainly the product of powerful necromancy." A shiver of nervousness ran down his spine as he thought of his apprentice chasing this vile monstrosity. He knew he must hurry to catch up.

"Something malevolent infiltrated Dwim-Halloe and has taken root," Valin said.

"I cannot completely convince myself you're not part of it."

Shoulders drooping, Valin hung his head, his prickly chin resting on his chest. It pained Seryn to admit he couldn't decide whether his brother's despair was a charade. But, with Jetsam bolting headlong into more trouble, Seryn had no time to ponder.

Through his prison bars, Valin Vardan stared at his brother. *Never thought I'd see you again, Seryn.* Familiar feelings of guilt assaulted Valin. *You can't hide it, brother. I can see it in your eyes—you despise me. And rightly so.* As he watched his fugitive sibling deliberate, Valin recalled the day their nightmare began. *The day it all went to the devil.*

Valin closed his eyes as the painful images repeated from his memory. *I remember standing in Nargul's chamber, his double-doors closed. The cavernous room was empty, save the two of us.* Lord Nargul reclined behind a colossal oaken desk. A few scattered parchments tried in vain to cover the vast wooden plane. A round stone the size of a melon dominated his desk. Its cracked-open top revealed a crystal-filled inside. *The strange geode is mesmerizing.*

"Your father did the Vardan name proud when meeting with his majesty today," the Lord High Chamberlain said. "King Tygan favors you, and sees the value in an arrangement with your house."

Nargul's office was noteworthy for its lack of content. Stark and cold, Valin saw no personal items or mementos. The walls were bare, free of colorful tapestries, paintings, or other unnecessary adornment. Twin bookshelves languished dusty and unbothered, with a smattering of tomes likely unopened since Nargul's predecessor sat in the chair he now occupied.

"Your brother, however, saw the princess *again* today," the bristling Nargul said, placing his gloved hands palms-down on the oak. "*Embraced* her, even." His frigid eyes were bottomless.

"She speaks well of him," Valin conceded, rubbing the back of his tightening neck, staring at the Lord's leather-clad hands. Unlike discussions with his father, Valin's bravado abandoned him. *I cannot lie to Lord Nargul.* "I fear he has stolen her heart," Valin confessed.

The lord high chamberlain rose from his leather chair, pushing it aside with a squeak. In vivid contrast to his environs, Lord Nargul wore colorful finery, befitting a man of his stature, if not ostentatious. A velvet cape hung from golden clasps at his shoulders, layered over an amber tunic with brocade undersleeves. Ebony hose covered his thighs and poured into his shiny black boots, polished by his obedient page this and every morning.

"Stolen her heart with sorcery, no doubt," Nargul said, scratching his chin. He strode around the desk, his hand sweeping across the geode, and stopped within a breath of the young Vardan. Though Valin stood a touch taller, Nargul did not need to gaze up to penetrate his eyes. "I'd hoped you the master over your sibling," Nargul said. "He's become a nuisance." Valin's face reddened, his hands squeezing into fists. Nargul stared at Valin with icy eyes. "Worry not, Lord Vardan. I've decided *you* will be king."

Valin's brows floated weightless to the heavens as he watched Lord Nargul steeple his fingers. For once, words escaped him as gravity tugged his jaw.

"And since you seem incapable, *I* shall deal with your meddlesome brother."

Jetsam sprinted along the prison hallway, passing alternating intervals of iron bars and stone block. Cast-iron torch mounts hung from each arch cusp along the corridor, although few held torches, and fewer yet burned. Under the intermittent rushlight, he dallied not, avoiding even a quick glance into the gloomy cells. The passage loomed dim as a moonless night, and he risked not a misstep at the cost of his curiosity. As it were, the remaining cells sat empty, as he suspected by the ominous silence. *Quiet as the catacombs.*

Through an arched doorway, Jetsam ran into a small square room. A low-burning wall cresset provided the dim light seeping through the corridor and cast a timid amber glow in the chamber. Furnished with a desk, chair, empty weapon rack, and naught else, the room was unadorned. *He's not even closing the door behind him,* Jetsam considered the abomination Kandris Bayen had become. *Maybe he wants me to follow?* After an imperceptible pause to scan for danger and clues, Jetsam continued north, across the utilitarian chamber to another iron door—this one ajar as well.

Through the portal sat another stairway leading upward. The spiral staircase filled a long tube extending skyward. A thick tow rope hung in the spiral's center. Jetsam brushed the stringy hair from his eyes and discerned light at the top. He paused to catch his breath before the climb, and in the moment of stillness, heard faint, clumping footsteps on the stairs far above.

That's him, all right.

Visions of this vile monstrosity finding his fair Giselle terrorized him. Two steps at a time, Jetsam launched up the stairway, determined to catch the dead-walker before he reached the princess. The oaken planks beneath Jetsam's feet were well-worn and sunken in the middle. The wood creaked even under his meager weight. Each hurried step echoed his ascent, yet he slowed not. *I'll not forsake speed for stealth.*

After a furious start, Jetsam's thighs wearied, and he abandoned his two-step attack. Relegated to a pedestrian step at a time, Jetsam pushed to keep his pace. His right hand brushing against the rough stone, he clung to the outer wall. With no railing to keep him safe, the center pit deepened ominously with every hop.

The racket of his boots on the pinewood drowned out any chance of hearing Kandris above, yet Jetsam suspected he closed the gap. He gauged his nemesis' pace, and calculated the closing time in his swirling head. What he would do once he caught the fleeing corpse he'd not decided. He was grateful for Regret hanging at his side. Though he trusted his magic, Jetsam recognized the value of a sharp blade.

When the ascent reached its conclusion, he encountered another open doorway. With his first step through the portal, the heavy iron door swung toward him. The door accelerated into Jetsam, and his momentum surrendered to the speed and mass of the iron slab.

Stupid, he chided himself. *Should've listened for footsteps.*

The moving door slammed Jetsam backward, his boots slipping from under him. He impacted flat on his back as he tumbled feet over head onto the spiral staircase. The creaky wood punched his ribs as hard as marble. Jetsam completed his unintentional back-flip by landing on his unsteady feet. The blow's force rolled him to the staircase edge. For a moment, he hovered precariously, keeping his balance on the precipice, heels teetering over the void at the spiral's center. His fingers waved at the ends of his outstretched arms, though there was naught to grasp.

Then the door swung open and the being that was once Kandris lunged at Jetsam with a gleaming short sword. For a soulless corpse, the entity still possessed agility. The sword drove straight into Jetsam's sternum. He experienced the familiar momentary sensation of weightlessness before gravity claimed him.

Because of his Dwarven hauberk and his precarious position on the spiral stairway, the stab didn't penetrate his flesh. However, the impact provided more than enough impetus to knock him over the edge. Jetsam whirled in free-fall, his hands reaching for the tow rope behind him.

As he fell, Jetsam wrapped the rope around his flailing forearm, and his hand gripped the cord. Jetsam felt slack in the rope for but an instant. The rusty pulley squealed and stuck as the rope slipped onto the bolt, catching tight.

The coarse rope burned his palm as gravity yanked him. As the snaking twine wrapped around his wrist and forearm, friction took hold, and Jetsam stopped so abruptly his shoulder tore from its socket. Jetsam screamed, while his left hand grabbed the rope. With his free-fall halted, he contorted himself to take the pressure off his damaged shoulder as he bounced and swung in the stairwell void.

On the stairs beside him, Kandris descended toward him—hissing. Jetsam glimpsed the former squire. His tongue tip protruded grotesquely from the side of his mouth. The muscle's color matched that of his bloodless lips, pasted to his mustard teeth. Eyelids barren of lashes shriveled away from his bulbous orbs, the once-whites now coated a moldy gray and interlaced with ebony spider-web veins. The left eye rolled back, its gaze fixed blindly on the adjacent lacrimal bone. The flesh surrounding the faulty orb was blackened and split, memorializing the ocular injury. In his right eye, Kandris' pupil and iris bled into a single inky spot, devoid of any spark of comprehension.

As Kandris approached, Jetsam sensed an insidious emanation that reminded him of the late warlock Enthran Ashvar. The craven

Kandris Bayen that traveled the Kierawaith the prior autumn contained not a flicker of magical energy. *I'm sure of that.* The imminent danger allowed Jetsam no time to ponder this conundrum.

Jetsam saw the blade rise, and twisted his head from harm while bracing for impact. Another blow from the short sword struck his overextended right shoulder, and he lost his grip. With legs wrapped around the cord and his left hand still clinging, the strike propelled Jetsam into an accelerating slide. The rope seared his flesh as he dropped another fathom before stabilizing himself. He heard the boot stomps of his attacker approaching again.

His shoulder numb, Jetsam couldn't tell if the slash severed his armor. He hoped the ringmail left his shoulder unscathed, but for now, it remained a mystery. All he knew for certain was that his sword arm was useless.

Sodding, bloody—

Thwack!

His accursed enemy hit him again in his injured shoulder. Jetsam didn't feel the impact, only the resultant force of it and the slap of steel as the blade's recoil caught his cheek. This time, his left hand failed, and his legs clung to the rope as he flopped in an awkward death spiral. *Only the bottom can stop me now,* and he had no idea how far that was. When it arrived, the stone floor robbed him of consciousness and breath.

Undead Kandris shambled past Jetsam, back toward the dungeon—and Seryn.

Chapter Seventeen

Separated by dull bars, Seryn stared back at his brother—familiar and strange at the same time. Both bore the scars of ill-treatment, Seryn from being hauled as a troll captive then tortured, and Valin, by living as a prisoner these many years. White hairs interspersed amongst each sibling's auburn locks, though Valin showed a touch more gray than his younger brother. Wrinkled flesh bagged under Seryn's hazel eyes, mirroring the skin beneath Valin's steely orbs.

Seryn concentrated on an incantation to release the lock. He set the torturer's blade on the flat crossbar of the iron cell. His hands flitted in the air and an Elven phrase passed his lips. After a moment of uncertainty, he heard a metallic click, and the door sprang free. *Can't believe I'm letting him out.* Seryn swung the cage door open for his kin.

Valin snatched the idle blade.

Armed with the newly-acquired weapon, Valin stood wild-eyed and ready to strike. Now Seryn comprehended for certain that his brother had betrayed him. Valin pounced, blade raised high, flashing toward Seryn. Their bodies collided as Valin landed on his brother and they tumbled toward the floor.

Expecting the blade's sting and the stone floor's impact, Seryn experienced a softer landing.

Someone broke my fall! Seryn, Valin, and a third body landed in a heap. Sandwiched between his sibling and the unknown, Seryn listened to Valin moan and the body beneath him hiss, as if the air squeezed from its lungs. Seryn untangled himself from their arms and legs and slid to the side. As he escaped from beneath his brother, Seryn heard a groan from Valin's lips. First on hands and knees, Seryn scrambled to his feet and gazed at the two bodies on the floor.

The tip of a short sword protruded through Valin's back, while Kandris Bayen lay beneath him gripping the weapon with both pale hands. The former squire rolled Valin from atop him and withdrew the wet blade with a sickly sound. Blood flowed from Valin's chest. Seryn spied the grip of the 'borrowed' torturer's blade jutting out from Kandris' ribs.

Valin buried the dagger to the hilt.

The imprisoned former king lay crumpled on his side, motionless. Kandris Bayen, however, bolted upright and yanked the dagger from his chest with nary a flinch. No blood seeped from Kandris' wound. The only blood on the lifeless assailant belonged to Valin, smeared on his pasty fingers. A blade in each hand, the former squire lurched at Seryn, who crouched in shock at his brother's side.

With no time to cast a spell, Seryn rolled and covered his face with his forearms. But instead of the sharp piercing of honed steel, Seryn experienced a crackling wave of heat and the tingling sensation of magic. He uncovered his eyes, and saw Kandris Bayen writhing on the ground, enveloped in flames. *His withered flesh takes to flame like dry wood.* Arms and legs flailed as the body convulsed and hissed. *The long-dead corpse smells worse than a funeral pyre.*

At the hall's end stood a wobbly Jetsam, blood dripping from his forehead, staff in hand, ready to deliver another blast should the possessed creature rise again.

But it did not. As the flames burned away the tattered clothes and rotting flesh, the form stopped moving altogether. How the real Kandris Bayen died would remain a mystery, though his soulless corpse died like a troll.

A steaming crystal fell from the skull's blackened eye socket and rolled on the hard floor. *That stone's imbued with magic energy.* The oval gem stopped at a crack and rocked like an egg.

Jaw agape, Seryn hovered over the fallen body, until his brother spoke. Blood gurgling in his throat, Valin curled around his wound, arms and knees drawn to his cleaved chest.

"Sorry, brother," Valin said in a pained whisper. "Fell under Nargul's spell—too weak to resist." His tongue licked his lips, smearing them with his own blood. "Betrayed you for glory. Plotted with Nargul to steal your love." Valin labored with each painful word. "Never imagined he concocted such a nefarious plan. Prithee—forgive me."

Seryn watched his estranged brother's eyes flicker shut. *No! You'll not die now.* Despite his longtime misgivings, Seryn stood, and rushed into a healing spell. The conflicting feelings he held for Valin would never be sorted out, but regardless of their tumultuous past, they remained kin. *I will not allow you to die at my feet.*

"I was a horrible brother—always," Valin said, eyes closed, though Seryn's focus on his spell prevented him from absorbing the words. "Even turned Father against you." Valin coughed, spraying red spittle over his chin.

After completing his spell, Seryn again knelt beside his sibling. *Hold on, brother.* Seryn examined Valin's wound. *Broad and deep, yet my spell staunched the bleeding.* Kandris' blade had hit the mark, slipping between Valin's ribs.

Seryn tore Valin's tunic, salvaging an unbloodied strip from the fabric and used the ragged sash to bandage the wound. He put a hand to Valin's moist forehead and then to his neck, searching for a pulse.

He's just holding on.

"I don't understand," Seryn said to Jetsam. "That spell should've done more." Jetsam nodded, putting his numb right hand on Seryn's shoulder.

With his tattered cuff, Seryn wiped the blood from his brother's open mouth. He held the back of his good hand to Valin's lips. *I don't feel his breath.* Seryn placed his fingers on his brother's chest. *His heart still beats, but slow and weak.* Seryn adjusted his makeshift bandage, pulling the cloth tight across the wound to close the gash. Amidst the gore, Seryn noted the slightest sheen on the blood. He inhaled deeply, as if savoring the scent of death. His gazed drifted to Jetsam.

"Poison, I think," Seryn said. "Stronger than my magic."

"Is he dead?"

"No, but my most powerful spell wasn't enough to overcome the poison. I'm not sure what else to do."

"I'm sorry," said Jetsam. "He saved you from the blade, you know. Kandris was aiming for *you*. I couldn't cast fast enough."

"You did just fine. That was a powerful, accurate blast." Seryn spotted the blood on his student's forehead. "Are you hurt?" He peered at Jetsam in the poor light. The lad's breathing was shallow and sweat glistened on his pale skin. Jetsam's lips held a bluish hue, matching his glassy eyes.

"I'm all right," he mumbled. "Except for my shoulder, maybe. Bastard knocked me off the stairs."

"You're bleeding." Seryn assessed Jetsam's scalp, wet and sticky beneath his brown hair. "Quite a bump." Seryn dabbed the trickling blood off Jetsam's brow, then directed his attention back to Valin. *First things first.*

Seryn lifted his brother under his arms and dragged him back into the cell. He pulled Valin onto the bed and cast a thin blanket over his brother, and lingered for more than a moment, gasping with ragged breaths. *I'll come back for you, brother. Don't die on me now.*

Seryn closed the cell door behind him and shuffled toward Jetsam. "The longer they think him asleep, the more time we have," Seryn said. "We need to find the queen. Nargul is surely around. Once he learns his lackey is dead, we'll lose our advantage."

"What about him?" Jetsam inquired, nodding toward the smoldering corpse.

"I've just the place for him." Seryn panted, hunched with hands on hips. *Gods, I'm exhausted already.* Moving Valin to the bed depleted his remaining strength. "You well enough to help me drag him to the hole?"

Jetsam nodded, but winced as he bent to Kandris. Seryn noticed him wobble and struggle with his right hand. "Let me look," he said, reaching through the neck of Jetsam's hauberk. His fingers made their way around Jetsam's shoulder. "Swelling already. Your shoulder's out of socket."

"Not surprised," replied Jetsam. "Can you fix it?"

Seryn wrinkled his brow. "I can cast a spell to dull the pain and speed the healing, but I must place the arm back in manually. Come and sit." Seryn led Jetsam to a stool inside Valin's cell. "Try to relax and breathe deeply." Jetsam did as told, as best he could. *Given the circumstances, relaxing is no easy assignment,* Seryn realized.

Seryn cast a spell to numb Jetsam's entire body. If not for Seryn's quick reaction, Jetsam would have flopped off the stool. Taking his arm, Seryn manipulated the joint. He heard the grinding and popping of muscles and tendons, but saw that Jetsam suffered no outward discomfort. Jetsam's shaky left hand bounced against the stool and his head bobbed as Seryn worked the shoulder.

"There! I got it." Seryn lowered his apprentice to the floor and propped him in a corner for support. "I'll cast a spell to speed your healing," he said, and did. Seryn noticed the gratitude in Jetsam's eyes. "Sit here and rest while I dump this carcass in the oubliette," Seryn instructed.

With no choice but to comply, Jetsam sat idle beside the bedded Valin as Seryn dragged Kandris' lifeless body across the hallway. After a minute, a sickening thud echoed from the torture room as the burned corpse hit the pit bottom. By the time Seryn returned, Jetsam stood on his own, cradling his damaged limb.

"Giselle's your daughter," Jetsam blurted.

Eyes wide with slack arms at his sides, Seryn took a step back.

"*Your* Giselle? *My* daughter? How can it be everyone knew but me?"

Jetsam shrugged and bit his cheek. "She's in danger, too."

"I'm afraid you're right."

"I'm ready to go," Jetsam said, though he did not look the part. Seryn contemplated leaving the boy with Valin. *But I can't protect him if he's not by my side, and I'll be damned if I lose them both.*

"I suspect we're near the surface," Seryn said. "If we're spotted leaving the dungeon, the guards will be on us posthaste."

Jetsam nodded. *He's still groggy and suffering the effects of my spell,* Seryn determined. "Follow me, but tell me if you can't keep up. You're still a ways from whole."

Seryn's finger stub burned as he girded his weary body for the climb. *I'll rest when I'm dead.* Trailing Seryn, Jetsam again ascended the stairs, clinging to the exterior stone wall the entire way.

"You all right?"

"Good enough," Jetsam replied. "Your spell helped a lot."

You just healed him and now you're leading him into danger. Seryn shot a protective glance back at the wobbly orphan. *He's safer with me than in the dungeon,* Seryn tried to convince himself. But he wasn't sure he believed it. *A motley pair, we are. I pray I'm not marching us to our deaths.*

At the top, they entered the room where Kandris ambushed Jetsam. The irregularly-shaped chamber sat devoid of any furniture or trappings. Silvery spider-work clung to the ceilings and corners, as a handful of arachnid craftsmen eyed the human intruders warily.

"I think we're in the Wizard's Tower," Seryn said as he tiptoed toward a closed door opposite the one they breached. He tried to open it. "Locked." He glanced at Jetsam. "I've not taught you a spell to break locks. I feared that may be too tempting a trick for a young lad." He faced the door again and began to cast. Seconds later, the lock clicked open. "I didn't want to use all my magic before we found Ioma, but I fear we must not be seen to succeed. Stand still, and I'll make us invisible."

Jetsam recognized the Elven words as the same Seryn uttered on the slope above the caravan, when Jetsam charged into the fray. *Now the tables are turned,* he realized, watching the determined Seryn taking decisive action.

A moment later, they both vanished. He could still hear Seryn, though.

"Follow me."

They crept through a narrow hallway. Another closed door blocked their path at the far end. This second door, however, was not locked. Jetsam jumped as the door opened by itself, before he recognized it was Seryn. *Being invisible takes some getting used to.*

This modest room was shaped like the first and Jetsam now comprehended the curved outer walls formed the cylindrical tower's frame. Dusty and cobwebbed, this neglected room appeared to have once served as an entrance foyer. When Seryn unlocked and opened the door leading outside the tower, he did so painstakingly slow, and only enough for he and Jetsam to slip through the crack. As Seryn inched the door closed behind them, Jetsam viewed the royal bailey, and across it the Granite Palace's Great Hall and adjacent keep. The setting sun drifted toward the western Mirrored Peak, casting the entire courtyard in the eerie half-light between daylight and darkness.

Royal guards stood their posts and a few nobles milled about. Everyone looked to be acting normally. *So far so good.* Jetsam jumped again when he felt Seryn's hand groping for his wrist.

"Stay close," the sorcerer whispered. "We must wait till the Great Hall doors are opened, then hurry in."

Jetsam studied the two door guards beside the imposing entrance, rigid and bored. *A door opening by itself will be noticed.* "I know how we can sneak into the kitchen," Jetsam suggested.

"Let's go."

They made their way to the rear of the Great Hall. Within moments of their undetected arrival, the kitchen door swung open as a cook carried out a pail of scraps. The underbelly boy in Jetsam drooled at the discarded edibles. *It is true! Nobles throw away better food than the townsfolk eat!*

Jetsam and Seryn slipped inside before the door swung shut. Jetsam maneuvered invisibly around the busy kitchen staff and resisted the urge to reach out and grab someone, just to scare the daylights out of them. Fortunately, Seryn still held his hand, and moved too quickly for Jetsam to be tempted by any shenanigans.

Wonder how long this spell will last? They exited the bustling kitchen and stood in the Great Hall's dining room, on the same marble where Seryn once danced with Princess Ioma. Upon glimpsing the gustatory spread, Jetsam's jaw hit the floor. The feast exceeded every one of his lavish mental images. The great trestle table overflowed with aromatic dishes, the scents of which nearly floored the hungry Jetsam. *More food than an und'orphan eats in a year!* And yet, an army of cream-clad servants delivered more to the gaudy buffet.

As he languished over the royal meal, his ears delighted to the musical notes swirling around the Great Hall. The Granite Palace minstrel led an ensemble of troubadours in a stirring ballad that, on an ordinary day, would have soothed Jetsam's frayed nerves. As it was, the melody emanating from the lutes and flutes distracted him from the dinner table long enough to peek at the colorful musicians.

As Jetsam's gaze floated in wonderment to the towering arched ceilings and glowing chandeliers, he remembered his purpose. *Look for*

Giselle and the queen. The high-backed chairs seated noble diners dressed as exquisitely as the minstrels and troubadours. The ornate chairs on the royal dais, however, sat empty—no doppelganger king, no Queen Ioma, no Princess Giselle.

"She's not here," Jetsam whispered, snapping from his daze. Distracted momentarily, he caught peripheral movement and side-stepped a cup-bearer with a brimming flagon. The harried lass rushed a fresh serving of Calderian vintage to the thirsty diners.

That was close!

"I know where their rooms are," Jetsam said, tugging at Seryn, oblivious to the fact that the Great Hall was not foreign territory to any Vardan. The mage allowed Jetsam to lead anyway. Across the chamber they strode, grasping each other's arm, past the crimson and cream banner cloaking the wall and to a sprawling landing. They ascended the sweeping stairs like a breeze flowing up a hillside, and were just as visible.

Hurry! Jetsam heard in the center of his mind. *Danger.* For two invisible men, he and Seryn attacked the stairs as fast as possible. Nonetheless, his spirits fell when he recognized Elvar's warning. *Surely it's Elvar.* By now, there was no mistaking his brother's otherworldly messages. There was nothing he could tell Seryn, so he kept silent and pressed forward. He climbed faster, forcing the tired wizard to speed up to maintain the quickened pace.

From stairway to landing to stairway again the connected pair raced. When they reached the fourth floor, Jetsam led Seryn to the cavernous corridor with the royal bedrooms. They passed Giselle's room first, and Jetsam's heart stuck his throat. He strained from the mage's grasp to peek in the princess' chamber, but alas, it sat empty. With a gentle tug, Seryn urged him toward the solar. When they arrived at the regal room, the magnificent double-doors sat ajar. Jetsam gasped at the sight in front of him.

Elvar was right!

Queen Ioma lay on the floor next to the royal bed. Her silken dinner gown was torn and blood-stained. Seryn nearly knocked Jetsam over as he sprinted to her side. Stunned, Jetsam watched the mage materialize from thin air as his spell dissipated. Seryn began casting another spell. Ioma's eyes were open, unblinking.

"Seryn?" she mumbled.

Jetsam hushed her as politely as an orphan boy could mute a wounded queen. His now-visible hands moved in vain to relay that Seryn was casting a spell. Moments later, the frantic sorcerer completed his incantation.

"What happened?" Seryn beseeched the queen, his voice trembling as he fell to his knees beside her.

She coughed up bloody spittle. With probing fingertips, the distressed spellcaster examined her abdomen. She'd been stabbed. Her lifeblood pooled in her lap and spilled across her hips, onto the bearskin rug upon which she lay.

"Don't worry—I cast a healing spell on you."

She choked out a sentence. "Betrayed by my vile husband—your *brother*."

Despite his healing incantation, blood still seeped from the queen's torso. The slippery fluid covered his fingers. Seryn tore a sheet from the massive bed and used the fabric to staunch the bleeding.

"It wasn't Valin," Seryn corrected. "Nargul's a doppelganger. He's been masquerading as the king since your—" Seryn halted at the words *wedding day*. "Since the coronation."

"A doppelganger? Like in fairy stories? You can't expect—"

"It's true—he fooled even me, and now Valin lies dying in the dungeon."

The glassy-eyed queen sucked in a ragged breath and followed it with a painful sob.

"Oh, my poor Seryn," she lamented, her voice frail and strained. "How I failed you."

"You couldn't have known," Seryn replied, his voice cracking. The battered wizard held her trembling hand. "Her pulse is weak," he said to Jetsam, who stood idle, scanning the room.

Uneasiness assailed Jetsam as he turned his gaze upon the former lovers. *Seryn's spell should be taking hold.*

"So what of Valin?" asked Ioma, frail as a morning breeze.

"He's lived as a prisoner all these years, and this very afternoon was stabbed with poisoned blade."

"No," she said. "Like my father." She coughed again and crimson saliva ran over her lips.

The realization struck Jetsam, though he spoke not a word. He watched the blood drain from Seryn's bearded face. The wizard's lips mouthed the word '*no*.'

Queen Ioma is not reacting to his spell.

"Jetsam, that spell depleted me," he said. "I have naught left for another. You know the spell. Do your best."

Jetsam feared his effort was in vain, yet he focused as fiercely as he could. *If Seryn couldn't heal her, how will I?* His battered body ached and pleaded for rest, threatening to fail him. Deep in the back of his consciousness, his concern for Giselle grew unbearable. Despite his obstacles, Jetsam cast a healing spell to do Seryn proud.

Jetsam waited with desperate eyes, understanding Seryn's hopes rested in his healing incantation. Reflecting their fading chances, the last sliver of the bloated sun sank behind the mountain peaks, hiding its glow from the royal chamber. As the seconds slipped away, so did Jetsam's final grains of optimism.

As did Seryn's before it, Jetsam's spell failed to revive the queen.

"I'm poisoned, too, aren't I?"

Seryn swallowed hard, and only managed to nod. On his knees in the bedroom that was almost his, Seryn cradled Ioma, pulling her broken frame close, setting his head next to hers.

Tears ran across Jetsam's cheeks, mirroring those of his mentor. He had to ask.

"What of Giselle?"

Ioma's eyes sparked for an instant.

"Protect her from Valin—" she beseeched, her face contorted in pain. "Nay—*Nargul*."

Chapter Eighteen

The solar faded in the gloaming, the skeletal candle-trees stood ready with their wax sticks, but no candles carried flame. Interlaced woven tapestries covered the oak-paneled walls, depicting hunts and battles, yet none bore a scene so horrific as that which played out in front of the textile art. Glass eyes stared blindly from a grizzly's mounted head, unable to see the events that transpired below their unseeing gaze. A painting of King Tygan sat on a hand-carved overmantle above the hearth. The dead monarch's pigment eyes saw no more than the taxidermist's bear.

In the chamber's center, lavish sheets, pillows, quilts, and coverlets graced the largest feather mattress in Dwim-Halloe, which sat encased inside a canopied frame. A six-board chest anchored the vast bed at its foot. Like caravels and carracks surrounding a mighty galley, stools and setting chairs floated around the massive bed, dwarfed by its enormity.

Three muffling floors below the decorated solar, unaware diners devoured their feast, oblivious to the atrocity committed under the very same roof. Queen Ioma Vardan was stabbed with a quick thrust of a poison-coated blade, precisely aimed and cruelly twisted by a charlatan she assumed was her husband. As night fell across Dwim-Halloe, Queen Ioma slipped from consciousness in the arms of her one true love.

Jetsam peered at Seryn, hunched over the queen, his head buried in her bosom, while his own chest heaved. Jetsam saw the wizard sob, and it broke his own scarred heart. *Giselle's mother is going to die.* The thought brought Giselle to the forefront of Jetsam's mind. As fears filled his aching head, he agonized over where she was. *I cannot stand idle another second.* "Master," he said to Seryn, his pubescent voice croaking. "We cannot be found with the dying queen—they'll kill us both."

Seryn gently lifted his beloved and set her upon the bed. He watched her for a moment as though she slumbered, before covering her with a fur blanket. The color of his eyes matched the welts on his back. From the other side of the bed escaped a stifled sneeze.

Jetsam raced around the bed and discovered an elderly woman cowered against an armchair, trying to remain unseen. Even in the twilight, her frightened eyes averted Jetsam.

Her presence roused the somber mage from his daze.

"Woman! What did you see?"

"I, I," she stuttered, trembling with terror.

"Spit it out." The sorcerer retained none of his characteristic patience.

"The king—he, he stabbed her majesty, and left as if he'd just said goodnight." Jetsam's head swiveled from the woman to the wizard and back again. His feet itched to run, yet he knew not where.

"What were you doing here?" Seryn demanded.

"I'm Gentlewoman of Her Majesty's Bedchamber," the woman said, now regaining her composure. "I fear I fainted."

Tight-lipped, Jetsam knelt beside her, offering a hand to help her rise as Seryn continued his interrogation. "You saw her attacked?"

"Indeed I did," she said, while taking Jetsam's hand. "His majesty drove the blade into her womb. They'd been arguing, but I had no idea he'd react like that." Aged knees popping, the gentlewoman regained her feet, though she wobbled. Jetsam rose with her, and stood beside her for support, still holding her wrinkled hand.

"Continue," Seryn instructed.

"To my shame, I fainted, and saw nothing more." Her head drooped to her bosom. "Is she—is she dead?"

"No," Seryn said, "I will not let her die. We must find help, posthaste."

"The royal healer sups below us. And we must inform the princess."

"She's not in her room, nor at dinner," Jetsam said, his heart plummeting.

"Oh, dear," the gentlewoman said. "I saw m'lady in her bedroom only minutes before I entered the solar. Do you think *he* took her?" The three shared a pensive glance.

"Or stabbed her, too?" Jetsam blurted, putting to words the fear they all shared. A sudden nausea assailed him. His head pounded and he felt the urge to vomit. "She might be in the garden, though," Jetsam offered, despite his doubt. *Her one place of refuge.*

"We must get help at once," Seryn declared, turning to the queen's attendant. "Retrieve the healer, and tell him she's been poisoned."

"Poison? But I thought—"

"The *blade*, woman. It was poisoned. Our spells should've revived her."

The startled attendant glanced at Seryn and Jetsam, her jaw agape.

"Oh, dear, I shall fetch Brother Tropf and Lord High Chamberlain Nargul posthaste," she said and started for the door.

Nargul? A sickening feeling groped at Jetsam as he shared a wordless glance with Seryn.

"You'll not find Nargul now, for that was who stabbed the queen—*not* Valin," the wizard explained, grasping the wide-eyed matron by the arm. "Nargul is a doppelganger."

"Oh, dear. I can scarce believe it." A freckled hand covered her mouth and tears welled in her stunned eyes.

"Go look for Nargul, then. I guarantee he'll not be found."

The shocked woman's brows raised and her hand slipped to her chin.

"Now that you mention it," she said, as if realizing it for the first time, "I found it odd never seeing his majesty and the chancellor together." She squinted in the dark, as though waiting for a cue. With a nod, Seryn bade her continue. "'Twas for security, they always said, but vexing I found it." For a moment, the three stood in indecision, looking to each other for direction.

"Just fetch the healer, and no one else," Seryn instructed the gentlewoman. "Nargul is still around."

"No one will believe us," Jetsam said. The gentlewoman jumped at the sound of his voice and hurried toward the door. "They'll think we did it."

The tattered sorcerer grimaced. "We've a valid witness," Seryn said, eyeing the fleeing gentlewoman. "I'll take my chances. But I won't risk them taking you."

Jetsam peered at Seryn, perplexed. "Search the garden—find Giselle," the wizard instructed.

"And if she's not there?" Jetsam asked, fearing the worst.

"Then find your clan," Seryn said. "Put the word out. Get eyes on the streets. A missing king and princess cannot go unnoticed. Someone will see them."

Jetsam needed no further urging. *I fear I'll have to pull him out of the hole again,* he lamented as he strode to the window. *Soon as the guards see him, he'll be back in the oubliette.*

"What are you doing?" Seryn asked, looking strangely at Jetsam.

"Going to the garden," he replied, "through the window."

"You'll not scale the wall with that shoulder, nor the bump on your noggin," Seryn said. Jetsam shrugged, and stared at Seryn with a questioning look.

"Let me make you invisible again," the sorcerer offered. "I think I can do it."

Seryn concentrated and released the spell, and Jetsam faded.

"It will not last long. Run like the wind."

Jetsam gladly abandoned his plan to scale the Great Hall's exterior and exited the solar by the traditional method. On his way out, he slipped into Giselle's bedroom and grabbed a scarf from atop her dresser. *This'll help Tramp.* Every step he took in exiting the Great Hall, Jetsam searched for his young friend, but he spotted no sign of her. The royal dining table remained empty, though the rest of the room bustled.

By the time Seryn's invisibility spell wore off, Jetsam was inside Giselle's garden. When he saw his hands and feet materialize, he returned to his stealthy ways, vigilant of the ever-present sentry. By now, Jetsam was an expert at secretly navigating this garden, but as he searched every nook and cranny of the lush park, he found no sign of the princess. *She's not here,* he lamented. *I can feel it.* Despite his gut, he completed a thorough scouring of the entire garden, whispering her name to no avail. As a last resort, he climbed the tall mulberry tree once again and surveyed the grounds from his impromptu crow's nest. From his perch, he spied the sentry, but no one else.

Disheartened, Jetsam resigned himself to swimming the moat. Down the tree and over the wall, across the alley and through the stables, into and out of the drainage chute, Jetsam entered the Jade River without a witness. He favored his damaged shoulder, more from memory reflex than actual pain. *Seryn's incantation worked wonders.*

Yet, Jetsam maintained doubts about Seryn's instructions. *None of the lads even know what the king looks like. And what if he changes form again? He could look like anyone.* Jetsam tried to take his mind off Giselle, but it was fruitless. Right now, he didn't care what became of Nargul, as long as *she* was safe. A deep fear gnawed at him that the doppelganger and the princess were together—wherever they were. *I pray she yet lives.*

Soaked to the bone, Jetsam hit the shore running. *Until I've a better idea, I'll go with Seryn's plan.* The possibility of Giselle in danger chilled him to his core. On winged feet he ran to the orphan lair, not knowing Ratboy's fate.

I pray I've not lost them both.

When the ebony troll claw grazed the back of Ratboy's skull, it took a sliver of his scalp and sandy hair with it. *Fobbing shite, that hurts!* Ratboy staggered and stumbled, but kept his flying feet beneath him. In four hurried steps, he regained his balance. Ratboy tapped into the resulting adrenaline surge to sprint even faster. His hand shot to his stinging head and found a wet, bleeding bald spot. *That was too sodding close.*

As a stream of blood ran down his nape, Ratboy felt a *woosh* of air on the open wound from the troll's next swing. This time, the knuckle-dragger missed by inches. *Devil take you, stinky bugger.* Ratboy's long legs stretched and churned. He dipped a shoulder to the left and cut right, hoping to gain a step with the feint. His boot sole slid on a slick stone and the maneuver nearly backfired. He saved himself with an outstretched hand to the wall. *Fob it, straight ahead, fast as I can.*

In the tunnel in front of him, Ratboy spied a glimmer of light from a low-burning cresset. *One I lit on my trip to the troll den.* Now he scanned for the rope he had looped over the nook between the cresset and the wall. *Ye'd better find yer stinkin' sorcerer, Jetsam.*

As blood seeped into his tunic collar, Ratboy eyed the rope and reached up as far as he could before taking hold. *Like a swing over a country pond,* he reassured himself. *Not that I've ever been to the country. Or swung over a pond.* He shook his bleeding head and grasped the dangling rope mid-stride, not losing a step to the trailing troll. With his hands clamped tight, he swung from the rope he'd secured to a beam. Launching in an arc, he pulled his legs to his chest. *Oh, shite.* As it was, when he reached the midpoint of his swing, his bottom slid across the pitch-coated floor.

Bugger me greasy arse!

At the peak of his momentum, Ratboy released the rope and flew through the tunnel. *I'm flying!* He hit the stone floor in a roll, tumbling past Lil' Pete, who crouched, torch in hand, against the wall at the edge of the pitch. *That was bloody fun!*

"Light it!" Ratboy yelled as he slid to a stop. He clapped his hand over his clawed scalp, his hair sticky with blood. *Another inch and the bugger had me.* He sucked in a deep breath as he watched his cohorts jump to action.

Lil' Pete dropped the flaming brand to the floor, and the oil ignited with a flourish. A wave of heat slapped Ratboy as the corridor behind him became an inferno. As the trolls' feet slipped and slid on the greasy floor, the tunnel erupted.

'Tis bloody hot! Ratboy jumped back from the flames. *Feels like I'm sodding burning.* He spun around, searching for the heat roasting the back of his thighs.

"Ratboy! Yer on fire!" Lil' Pete shouted.

Fobbing piss. Ratboy slapped his rump and legs, trying to extinguish the pitch on his trouser seat. His efforts worsened the problem, as the hot pitch clung to his burning fingers and spread down his pant legs. He wiped his blistering hands on the front of his thighs and kicked off his boots. As the flames consumed his trousers, he slithered out of them as fast as he could. *I just stole those last week.*

Sitting barefoot in his smallclothes, Ratboy cracked a smile as he surveyed the chaotic scene before him, while his trousers burned at his feet. *Knuckle-draggers are faring much worse.* By the time the racing flames reached the first troglodyte, the brute had tried to stop, only to have its pitch-coated feet slide out from it. *Take that, ye pus-filled devil!* The knuckle-dragger's pratfall elicited a chorus of laughter from the orphans. *Least they're not laughing at me.*

Lemming-like, the three creatures tumble-crashed into their leader as the sticky pitch coated their flesh and set them aflame. *'Tis sodding perfect!* As the four trolls struggled, a line of orphans stepped past Ratboy and Lil' Pete to the edge of the burning grease. The urchin archers shot flaming bolts and incendiary arrows from stolen bows and arbalests. More orphans complimented this barrage with a steady rain of fiery sling-stones. A row of pikemen brandishing sharp wooden spikes stood interspersed with the bowmen, ready to defend them from swinging troll claws. The orphans had set their trap at the bottom of a decline, with the greased floor sloping downward, making retreat a slippery uphill climb.

The sound of wailing trolls, crackling flames, and shouting boys filled the smoky corridor. *Give 'em hell, lads!* A surge of pride lifted Ratboy to his feet as he watched his troops rain fire on their adversaries. *This one's fer Mole.*

Like frenzied pigs in mud, black pitch coated the disoriented, sprawling knuckle-draggers. Long legs and sinewy arms entangled in a mass of squirming, flaming, panicked flesh. Fiery bolts and arrows stuck them like ugly pincushions. By the time the dim-witted monsters tried to retreat from the onslaught of projectiles, the flames had crisped their skin. The beasts never made it back up the passageway.

"We did it!" Ratboy shouted. "We bloody burned 'em all!"

As Ratboy's words echoed through the tunnel, the fallen troll leader twitched its smoking head. With a desperate lunge, the wounded creature launched itself into the line of orphans, tumbling them like a haystack in a whirlwind.

Ratboy gaped at the chaos of flailing arms and legs as scrambling bodies tried to regain their feet. The snarling humpback crouched on all fours, its scorched hide hissing and popping. One of its eyes was no more than a blackened scar, yet the carnivore honed in on a target. Lil' Pete lunged out of the way as the beast's snapping maw clamped the smoky air.

Ratboy grabbed a wooden stake at his feet, hurdled Lil' Pete, and leapt toward the monster. With smoldering arrows peppering its rubbery skin, the troll turned its slavering head toward Ratboy and opened its toothy mouth wide. Ratboy pounced, his arm swinging, cutting the air like a catapult. His stake planted deep in the troll's eye, the point driven to the back of the beast's skull.

The troll collapsed screeching and clawing at the buried stake. A swarm of regrouped orphans assaulted the writhing monster, stabbing and hacking it to death. Juvenile war cries filled the smoky cavern as the final knuckle-dragger breathed its last. Ratboy dumped the rest of the pitch bucket on the mangled corpse and Lil' Pete set it ablaze once again.

As the tunnel filled with the acrid scent of burning troll, the coughing, jubilant orphans waited until the four carcasses turned to ash. Then they whooped and hollered in celebration all the way to their lair.

Hope Jetsam was as lucky, Ratboy prayed. *He'd be proud of us.*

The orphan boys were still celebrating when the exhausted Jetsam arrived. Mead flowed and songs filled the air. Upon seeing Tramp, his heart flooded with joy, but emptied when he didn't spot his friend.

"Where's Ratboy?"

A trio of arms pointed to the corner, where their leader sat with a bandaged head and borrowed baggy trousers. The blood-soaked band circled his head.

"What happened, Rats?" Jetsam asked, him mouth agape. "Are you all right?"

"I'm fine—just a little haircut," he said with a half-smile, regaining his feet. "Knuckle-draggers make shitty barbers."

Jetsam rushed to his friend and wrapped him in a hug. "Thank the gods you're alive." *He risked his life for me, yet again. I pray it was worth it.*

Faster than Ratboy could listen, Jetsam spewed forth the current dilemma, as Tramp danced, pawing at Jetsam's thighs as he bounced on hind legs.

"Takin' her to the Grimlord, I bet," Ratboy said. The urchin spun from Jetsam and raised a hand to his cheek. "To the north gate," he shouted. "Lil' Pete, Pike, Biter—get everyone topside. A man and a girl fleeing the city. Delay them at all cost!"

"They're dressed like royalty," Jetsam said. "The girl's hair is long and blond, and she answers to Giselle." The orphans' abrupt transition from celebration to urgency astounded Jetsam.

"She has green eyes," he added, but the lads were already moving. The main hall cleared in record speed.

"Come on," Ratboy urged. "I'll get us to the gate as fast as possible." With that, Jetsam and Tramp chased Ratboy as he navigated the shortest distance to Dwim-Halloe's northern gatehouse. Part of Jetsam hoped Ratboy was right, and part of him didn't.

Not the Grimlord.

As they ran through the familiar dark paths of the underbelly, once again Jetsam heard the subtle whispers of his dead brother. And as they often did, they brought him to a halt.

Underground river.

"We must turn around," Jetsam shouted to Ratboy, several paces in front. Tramp stopped along with Jetsam.

"Why?"

"Elvar—*Flotsam* told me he took the underground river."

"What?"

"He speaks to me from the other side."

Ratboy cocked his head and chuckled.

"Yer a bloody odd bird, Jetsam, but I'll be damned if I doubt ye. Let's turn 'round, then."

And so they did.

"I'm going with ye this time," Ratboy told Jetsam.

"Are you sure? You've built a home here."

"Aye, but 'tis my time. Plenty of other good lads to carry on while I'm gone."

"This time I won't talk you out of it."

"Ye couldn't if ye tried. Figure 'tis my one chance ta talk to a princess. Mebbe I can convince her to change the laws on orphans."

"You should let the lads know you're leaving."

"I'd leave 'em a note," Ratboy said. "'Cept I can't write."

"Seryn started teaching me to write," Jetsam offered.

"Bet yer wizard didn't teach the lads how to *read*."

Both chuckled at their shared misfortune.

"They're smart enough. They'll figure it out. But we should stock up before we go. Might take a while to catch up with their head start."

The trio stopped on their way past the underbelly lair. Jetsam cast a healing spell on the unknowing Ratboy while he rummaged through the orphans' supplies.

"What the devil was that?"

"Just a little something to fix your head," Jetsam said. "Don't worry about it."

"Kinda tingles," Ratboy said, while fingering his scalp.

Jetsam and Ratboy loaded up from the orphans' communal supply. Warm blankets and clothes, dried coney, a waterskin, sling stones, and other essentials were scavenged by the departing duo.

"They'll understand," Ratboy said. "They can refill the larder while I'm gone. Give 'em somethin' to do."

While retracing their steps through the Gwae Gierameth tunnels filled with petrified and charred trolls, they avoided encountering any other humpbacks. Jetsam gazed at the passage door he unhinged, and berated himself. *Of course he'd go this way. No one would see him. No one even knows of it.*

Besides me.

Jetsam let Tramp sniff Giselle's scarf. He realized it would prove difficult for the canine to find the scent in these water-filled tunnels, but he also knew not to underestimate the terrier. True to form, Tramp picked up a scent and followed it to the water's edge. Only the dog knew if the scent he tracked was Giselle's, but for better or worse, Jetsam felt more certain they were on the right path.

The trio continued north into the wet cavern. When they located the raft Jetsam built, Ratboy burst out laughing at his friend's lack of craftsmanship.

"I'd take on less water floatin' on my back," he goaded. "Let me show you a few things about skiffs." Ratboy proceeded to tighten, adjust, reinforce, and re-balance the craft, all while offering Jetsam unwanted tutoring on raft construction.

"When'd you become a sailor?"

"Been building a lot of things lately," Ratboy said. "That new lair needed a lot of fixin' and turns out I'm a pretty good carpenter."

"Not me—I nearly lost both thumbs trying to help Seryn make a bed frame."

"'Tis good there's at least one thing I'm better'n ye at. Now there, that ought ta keep us outa the drink."

Jetsam navigated the skiff back the route he took to Dwim-Halloe. This time, he stayed drier. The friends took turns pushing the raft with Jetsam's staff, while Tramp napped the entire journey. Though Seryn healed Jetsam after his fall, his body was tired and sore, and relished sleep. Despite his own head wound, Ratboy let Jetsam rest for much of the trip.

Jetsam was asleep with his terrier when Ratboy ran the raft aground. Upon awaking at the sound of wood scraping rock beneath his head, Jetsam recognized the cavern. They stashed the watercraft in an obscure nook, resolved to finish the journey on foot.

"Come here," he instructed Ratboy. "Got to show you something." Jetsam led his partner to the underground dock filled with barrels. With Ratboy holding the torch, Jetsam opened the barrel containing the Dwim-Halloe weapons.

"Ah, these are fine!" Ratboy said. He returned the brand to Jetsam and sorted through the weapons. "I'd take 'em all if I could." He retrieved a hand axe and offered it to Jetsam, handle-first. "We'll need axes," he said. "Let's each take one." Ratboy swapped out his dagger for a new, razor-sharp one, and claimed a short sword as well. "Now I'm properly armed," he said. "Never had weapons like this before." Jetsam acknowledged his friend's excitement.

They left the dock, lamenting the abandoned goods, and skirted the cavern's perimeter until they reached dry footing. Jetsam pulled Giselle's scarf from his pocket and let Tramp inhale to his heart's content. When Jetsam figured the dog's tail would drop from wagging, he put the scarf back. Tramp's snout moved to the floor and he began to sniff. The canine's pace increased, and his black nose inhaled in short, quick bursts. After a minute of following his nose around the cavern floor, Tramp slowed. He inhaled deeply, and followed with another long sniff. He glanced at Jetsam, and aimed straight for the steep passage Jetsam had carried him down on their journey in, sniffing the entire way.

"Think he's got her scent," Jetsam said.

By the time the trio emerged from the narrow crevasse Jetsam and Tramp entered days ago, daylight broke across the Oxbow Mountains. Nose to the ground, Tramp locked in on the scent, and headed north, toward the Kierawaith.

Chapter Nineteen

Cloaked in shadows, standing barefoot on the bloody bedroom floor, wearing the same trousers and tunic—what was left of it—from the caravan attack, Seryn hovered over Ioma. He'd not shaven in a ten-day and his mahogany hair sat matted and tangled. His odor was gravely inappropriate for the royal solar.

My love and my brother, both fighting for their lives against a poison that resists my power.

The healer bust into the solar, wild-eyed and panting. The gentlewoman of her majesty's bedchamber shuffled several paces behind him. Seryn scrutinized the robed man then glanced at the gentlewoman. She met Seryn's gaze and nodded, and he stepped aside to allow the healer access to the royal bed. *Doesn't miss a meal, this one. Still has goose sauce on his lips.*

"This wound is fresh?" The healer gaped at Seryn.

"Yes—I cast a healing spell on her. Stopped the bleeding, but it should have revived her."

"You're a—a *spellcaster?*" The healer scanned Seryn from his battered face to his bare feet and back again. "But I—"

"I fear she's been poisoned."

The healer peered at the gentlewoman, his face revealing confusion.

"Please, Brother Tropf, attend her majesty," she pleaded.

The healer nodded and began his examination, while Seryn hovered.

"Lord Vardan, we must get you a robe and shoes," she said, leading him from the bed. "You cannot be seen in the palace looking like a prisoner."

"You *know* me?"

"Aye, Lord Seryn," she confirmed. "Even with your black eyes and crooked nose. I remember when you courted Ioma—I served her mother Queen Venneth. You've not changed much. And though I can scare believe it, what I've seen today, I fear we did wrong by you."

"Lady Darksparrow?"

"'Tis I," she replied.

"I *do* remember you," Seryn said. "Ioma adored you." Lady Darksparrow had not aged as well as he, and he recalled her more by deduction than the familiarity of her face. The memory of her pulled his mind to days past, but the healer's interruption forced it to the present.

"Weak pulse," the healer said. "Shallow breathing, dilated pupils, blue lips, cold hands, and a strange odor on her breath."

"The poison," Seryn replied. "Already in her blood."

"I don't recognize the scent," the healer replied. "I fear I won't identify the poison with my nose."

"Can you do anything?" Seryn asked.

"I shall prepare unguents and tonics, and pray for the best. King Valin must be informed posthaste."

"The king lies stricken in the dungeon, poisoned as well."

"Oh, dear, I must attend his majesty at once!" The blood drained from the healer's face as he stared at the gentlewoman. "Lady Darksparrow, this is chaos! We must alert the high justice, the guards—and what of the princess?" The portly man trembled with sweating brow. "And *I* must see the king!"

Lady Darksparrow turned to Seryn. "Please, take him to your brother. I shall secure the solar and alert Lord High Justice Bainbridge."

"His brother? No, we must go to his majesty posthaste!" the healer said. "Who is this man that you trust him to escort me? He looks as though he escaped the dungeon himself!"

"I did. Valin *is* my brother."

Hand to his heart, the healer gasped and stepped back.

"The kingslayer!" The healer spun and strode toward the door. Seryn grabbed his robe before he completed his second step.

"Calm down, man. I've killed no one. Lady Darksparrow saw the queen attacked." Seryn glanced at the gentlewoman. "Tell him."

"Brother Tropf, please listen," she said. "I saw a man I swear was his majesty stab the queen, and yet Lord Seryn insists it was a mimic, masquerading as the king."

"A doppelganger," Seryn explained.

"Surely, you jest! You're both mad!" The healer struggled to get away, but Seryn's grip held firm.

"Come with me, then. I'll show you the king and you can decide for yourself. We're wasting precious time."

Brother Tropf inhaled and wiped his brow.

"Please," Lady Darksparrow pleaded.

The healer shook his head and turned to Seryn. "Gods help us. Take me to his majesty."

"Here." Lady Darksparrow thrust an armful of clothes at Seryn.

He consented to the gentlewoman and donned some of his brother's less extravagant clothing, turning his bloodied backside as his only show of modesty. Navy satin trousers, black leather boots, a wide-sleeved tunic, and an ebony cloak completed his outfit. Seryn pulled up the hood to shade his scraggly appearance.

"Go to the lord high justice," Seryn instructed the gentlewoman. He knew his own execution likely resided as the high justice's top priority. "Confess what you saw, and alert the guards that a doppelganger masquerades as king, and the princess is missing." Seryn turned to address the healer. "And, Tropf, is it?"

The monk nodded.

"To the Wizard's Tower. I'll follow you, lest we draw attention."

Tropf nodded again and strode out of the solar. *He's swift for a big man.* Without a word, Seryn flanked the healer through the Great Hall and out into the bailey. The lantern lights drew his memory back to the night of the harvest ball. He shook off the bittersweet recollection.

Seryn ground his teeth when he spotted the sentry outside the Wizard's Tower entrance. *Wish I could disappear again.* After trying to heal Ioma, he'd exhausted his last bit of magic turning Jetsam invisible.

A good night's sleep stands between me and another spell.

"He's not going to let us in, is he?" Seryn whispered over Brother Tropf's shoulder. The healer slowed to a stop feet from the idle watchman. "He'd better," Tropf replied. "I'll do the talking." Hands on hips, slouched and panting, the healer steadied his breathing before addressing the guard.

"Stand aside, soldier."

In the dark, with his visor shut, Seryn observed no response from the stoic sentry.

"Stand aside, he said," Seryn snapped. He strode past Tropf and shoved the guard's shoulder. As the healer gasped at the brazen move, the watchman slid off the door and landed with a crash.

Seryn glanced at Tropf for a moment and they both returned their attention to the guard, prone and motionless at their feet.

"Gods," murmured Tropf.

Seryn knelt and opened the visor. The man's eyes were wide and unblinking.

"Think he's dead."

Tropf knelt beside Seryn and began a hurried inspection. As the healer checked the body, Seryn noticed the blood seeping from the man's armor.

"Stabbed," Tropf said before Seryn could voice his observation. "Stabbed dead."

Seryn stood and hopped over the corpse. He twisted the tower door handle and rattled the door on its hinges. It refused to open.

"Locked."

Still on his knees, Brother Tropf's hands found the watchman's belt pouch. A moment later, he handed Seryn a hefty key ring.

"This'll do," Seryn mumbled as the third key he tried turned the lock. "Let's go." Seryn removed the burning torch from above the door and breached the tower. Brother Tropf shuffled behind him.

"Never been in here before," Tropf confessed.

"How long have you been the royal healer?"

"Years," he said between gasps.

"And you've never had to attend a prisoner?"

"Didn't know there *were* prisoners in the tower."

"*Beneath* the tower," Seryn said.

"After the rebellion, King Valin sealed it."

Torch in hand, Seryn backtracked to his brother's cell with Tropf close behind. Valin remained as Seryn left him. "He's not budged," he informed the healer.

Brother Tropf sat on the edge of the thin prison bed and began his inspection. By now, Seryn grew familiar with the routine. He knew the healer's diagnosis before it left his lips.

"I'm sorry—same as the queen."

"I know."

"We must get him out of here. He needs to be in the solar, where I can treat them together."

Seryn wavered at the thought of carrying his brother, even with the healer's help. With his adrenaline spent, fatigue undermined his depleted strength. "Fetch some guards," Seryn instructed. "Trusted ones. I'll stay with him till you return." Tropf frowned, but did as told. Seryn plopped next to his brother and grimaced from the pain in his hindquarters. *Gods, Valin, the whole world turned upside down.*

"For a decade, you've been all but dead to me," Seryn whispered to his unconscious brother. He brushed a strand of hair from Valin's forehead. "You're so cold." *What is this vile poison that resists the strongest magic I know?* Seryn slumped to the floor beside the bed, his hand resting on Valin's arm. Exhausted and battered, Seryn dozed.

A chorus of stomping boots snapped Seryn from his brief slumber. His reclining form jerked to attention at the noise. He craned from the cell wall he'd slept against and his stiff neck popped as his pain returned. The sight of royal guards produced a lump in his throat.

"Good gods," said the captain, "it *is* his majesty. He looks horrible."

Seryn gritted his teeth. *I'm not the only one who notices.*

"Place him on the cot," Brother Tropf instructed. "*Gently!* To the solar." The two soldiers obliged, stepping around Seryn to reach Valin's bed.

"He's been stabbed in the chest," Seryn said to the guards. "Don't anger the wound."

"Lord Vardan," Tropf said to Seryn, still sitting on the floor.

"You need rest. There's nothing more you can do this eve." The healer extended a meaty paw to Seryn, who grasped it and rose, thankful for the aid.

"I'm fine," he lied, while stretching his cramped muscles.

Seryn followed the somber procession from the dungeon, through the tower and across the bailey to the Great Hall, his attention on Valin the entire way. His sibling never twitched.

"Place him with the queen," Brother Tropf instructed the guards carrying Valin. "I must go to my study and prepare treatments. Ensure no one but Lady Darksparrow enters the solar." The healer held the door as the guards carried the king inside the chamber. Seryn took a step toward the entrance, but Brother Tropf placed a hand on his arm.

"Lord Vardan, if you could manage, I could benefit from your knowledge." Seryn stared at the sweating monk.

"I must be with Ioma." He stepped forward, and Tropf's grip tightened.

"Will you try another spell?"

"I'm afraid I'm spent." Seryn glared at the unwanted hand on his biceps. "It'll be hours before I can cast again."

"Then come with me." Brother Tropf removed his hand from Seryn and stood pleading, palms at his side. "Two minds are better than one when tackling a mystery such as this."

Though loathe to admit it, Seryn understood the healer's logic. *There's nothing else I can do. For now.* He nodded at Brother Tropf.

"Lead the way."

By the time they arrived at Brother Tropf's study, Seryn's head bobbed and his feet dragged. He plopped into a chair as the healer rummaged through his tomes. Seryn discerned the monk talking, but in his state of exhaustion, the words echoed foreign and incomprehensible. When Seryn slumped back and succumbed to the inevitable sleep, a nightmarish morass of failure, pain, and betrayal tormented his slumbering mind.

Seryn awoke to the dawn pouring through the window. His first movement triggered an onslaught of agony. Seryn's grunt caught Lady Darksparrow's attention. He licked his cracked lips, squinting at her.

"Where am I?"

"You're in Brother Tropf's chambers. After you fell asleep, he put you to bed."

"Ioma?"

"Still hanging on. Brother Tropf is with her and his majesty now. He's been up all night working on elixirs."

"I must go to them." Seryn struggled to sit, and grimaced as the scabs on his back cracked open. He'd slept in his brother's clothes and they absorbed his reek. Seryn swung his tired legs out of bed.

"In a moment, Lord Vardan," Lady Darksparrow said. "High Justice Bainbridge wishes a word with you."

Seryn noticed two royal soldiers flanking the exit. The gentlewoman signaled them with her hand.

The door opened and the lord high justice strode inside the bedroom. Gray hair covered his balding head and he wore a pained expression. Not a handsome man, his wide mouth and pig nose dominated his pear-shaped head. He scrutinized Seryn, gazing at his scruffy, battered face.

"By the gods, it *is* you." Lord Bainbridge's eyes widened. "How'd you escape the oubliette?" The high justice's brows furrowed. "You're scheduled to be executed this morning."

"You've more important matters to attend to, my lord." Seryn slipped on the king's boots. "As do I."

"Indeed." Ire rose in the high justice's raspy voice. "Tell me your story, Lord Vardan."

"Not now. I must see the queen." Seryn rose from the bed and strained to stand upright. Bainbridge turned and nodded to the guards, who closed the chamber door.

Fists clenched, Seryn filled his lungs. "There'll be plenty of time for questions later. Ioma and Valin need me." Seryn wobbled past the scowling Bainbridge, but before he reached the door, the two guards blocked his way.

"Lord Vardan, your stay of execution rests in my judgment. I suggest you humor me." Seryn met the gaze of each guard in succession, then turned back toward Bainbridge.

"Fine," he replied as he eased into a squeaky chair, favoring his troll bite. Despite Jetsam's healing spell, the captivity and torture had

ravaged Seryn's strength and stamina. *I'll be damned if I let it show.*
"But understand, Lord Bainbridge, you delay the one who may be able to save your king and queen."

"Lady Darksparrow claims she saw his majesty stab the queen and flee."

"You've seen his majesty this day, I assume," Seryn said. Bainbridge nodded. "And what conclusion did you draw?"

"His majesty is not well. He's a shell of the man I spoke with yesterday."

"My brother did not stab Ioma. It was the doppelganger, Tark Nargul."

"A doppelganger?" Bainbridge's voice escalated as his eyes narrowed. "I scarce believe you are in your proper mind, *kingslayer.*"

"I do not recall standing trial for that charge."

"Fugitives cast their own sentence," Bainbridge said. "And now you return with your illegal sorcery and superstitious tales of mythical creatures. Lady Darksparrow may be swayed by your guile, but not I, Lord Vardan."

"Nargul's a mimic. He's had Valin imprisoned since the coronation."

"A fantastical yarn. But what of the truth?"

"Is Nargul available to refute my accusation?" Seryn watched the man struggle to stay calm, but he detected a tremor in the high justice's tightened jaw. *Thick-skulled bureaucrat, use your pea-brain and think.*

"No. Nargul's nowhere to be found." Bainbridge's gaze dropped to his feet. "Nor is the princess."

Seryn's spirits plummeted. *Jetsam hasn't found her.*

"Lord Seryn tried to save her majesty," Lady Darksparrow said. *And failed. Miserably.*

"I have no choice but to keep you in custody until this is sorted out," Bainbridge said. "Guards, bind him and gag him before he ensorcels us!" The guards did as ordered, restraining Seryn by the arms. They bound his hands behind him and gagged his mouth with his crumpled hood. Seryn listened to the gentlewoman object, but her exact words eluded him.

Devil take you, Bainbridge!

"Lock him up," the high justice said.

Back to the sodding dungeon.

The bedroom door swung open and Brother Tropf burst into his crowded chambers.

"What is this?" the healer asked, first glancing at Seryn, then glaring at Bainbridge.

"They're locking him up!" Lady Darksparrow blurted.

"Unacceptable," said Brother Tropf. The healer appeared distraught and the bags beneath his eyes attested to a sleepless night.

"Brother Tropf, may I remind you he is a wanted fugitive," said Bainbridge. "I can't release him based on an outlandish tale."

"My treatments had no effect," the healer confessed. "Lord Vardan's spells may be the only way to keep them alive."

"What do you mean, Tropf? Healing is your *job.*"

"Nothing I've tried had any effect. They're hanging by a thread. Fear they shan't last the day."

Bainbridge and Tropf stared at each other while the guards held firm. Seryn tried to speak through his gag, but emitted a muffled moan. Lady Darksparrow's hand shot to his lips and pulled the fabric from his mouth.

"Take me to them," Seryn demanded. "Detain me if you must, but let me try to keep them alive."

"Devil's folly, Bainbridge, listen to them," the gentlewoman implored.

The lord high justice sighed and dropped his head. "Fine. We'll all go," he said. "Unbind him," he instructed the guards, "but follow him like a shadow. He's not to leave your sight."

"The princess is missing, and time is fleeting. The doppelganger is real," Seryn said. "I hope you have the rest of the king's men scouring the city for them." Bainbridge offered no reply as Seryn flexed his free hands.

The group trudged to the solar in silence. *What if they don't respond to my spell?* Seryn shot a glance at Bainbridge. *Will he accuse me of killing them, too? One royal or three, the sentence is the same.*

"Lord Vardan," Brother Tropf said, interrupting Seryn's thoughts. "I tried every antidote I know of, and fear it made things worse. I don't know what else to do."

Seryn chewed his lip. *Nor do I.*

The solar sat dim and warm, secured by a pair of royal knights both inside and outside the closed doors. After a word from Lord Bainbridge, the double-doors opened for Seryn and his entourage. A fire crackled in the hearth and the air smelled of incense herbs. *Tropf has this place smelling like a Calderian pipe den.*

Hands on hips, Seryn bit his cheek while surveying the somber scene. The king and queen lay on each side of the expansive canopy bed. *Devil take me, she's so pale and lifeless.* Across the mattress, he studied his brother. *Valin looks even worse, if that's possible.*

"What do you need of us?" asked Brother Tropf.

"Silence and a bit of space." Seryn waved a hand as Tropf and Bainbridge shuffled backward. *I only have to cast the most powerful spell I've ever attempted.* Seryn inhaled a smoky breath and swallowed. He rolled his shoulders and tilted his head until his neck released an audible pop. His conscience gnawed at him and guilt's icy fingers pressed against his jugular. *Forgive me, brother, for what I'm about to do.* With Ioma on the bed beneath him, Seryn began his incantation. Ancient words filled the room as his hands moved in fluid rhythm. Beads of sweat coalesced on his scalp.

And then he finished.

Wake up, damn it.

Brother Tropf stepped next to Seryn as he slunk in exhaustion.

"May I?" Tropf asked. Seryn nodded, and the healer knelt to examine her majesty. Seryn stepped back and slumped into a chair. *I did the best I could. Were I not so fatigued.*

"Her heart beats stronger," Tropf said, with his bald head to her bosom.

"It worked?" asked Bainbridge.

"It helped," replied the healer. "Her breathing's improved, too."

"She should be awake," Seryn mumbled, running his four-fingered hand through his hair.

"Now, aid his majesty," instructed Bainbridge.

Seryn chewed his cheek. *I poured everything I had into that spell and still she sleeps.*

"Lord Vardan?" the healer asked. "Your spell is stabilizing. It buys us time. Please," Tropf said, with a wave of his hand, "the king."

Seryn held up a finger and cleared his throat. "A moment, please." *I put my brother in peril to save my love, and it's all for naught.* Seryn rose and strode to the opposite side of the bed. *I'm afraid this will be for show, Valin.* He stared at his brother's stubbly face and saw his father. *Maybe I was the bad brother all along.* He took another deep breath, and coughed from the burning hassuck grass. *Not that all my power did much for Ioma, other than prolong the inevitable.*

Perchance Father was right.

Magic couldn't save Mother.

I am the bad son.

Lord Bainbridge's coughing snapped Seryn from his melancholy daze. He glanced across the bed at his murmuring audience and raised his index finger to his lips. All eyes were upon him, faces filled with doubt and hope. And fear.

Why finish this charade? Tell Bainbridge I used all my power on Ioma, and left my brother to die. Let him lock me up. I deserve it.

Seryn's thumb flicked at his missing finger, trying to scratch a phantom itch. When his nail scraped the stub, it sent a shiver of pain to his elbow. He winced, and noticed Lady Darksparrow's eyes widen. He cracked the faintest of reassuring smiles in her direction.

I wish Jetsam were here. He could actually cast a spell on Valin, and not just pretend. Seryn's mind wandered once again, this time to his apprentice. *And my daughter. I pray Jetsam's faring better than I. What a bloody mess I've led him into.*

Seryn set his feet apart and leaned over the royal bed. He glimpsed Valin's closed eyelids as shame washed over him. *What if I don't fake it? What if I dig deeper and try to find more magic? It's what Jetsam would do.* Seryn wiped his brow with his forearm and centered himself. He shut his eyes and listened to his pulse beating behind his eardrums. *Here goes nothing.*

When Seryn awoke, he was back in Brother Tropf's bed. He sat and slid his feet over the side while his wounds screamed for attention. *What the devil happened?* "Tropf?"

"Ah, finally awake," the monk said. "That spell sucked the life from you."

"I passed out?"

"Straight to the floor, a sack of flour."

"And Ioma? Valin?"

"They both yet live," Tropf said. "You've bought them another day, at least. Still, I'm no closer to finding an antidote."

"What have you tried?"

"Everything—flushes, purgatives, vinegar-boiled mulberry, ashes, incense." The healer handed Seryn a cup of tea. "I'm afraid I'm making them worse." Tropf dropped his head into his hands. "Your spellcasting is the only thing having any effect."

"And it's not enough." Though it scorched his chapped lips and burned his dry throat, Seryn finished the tea in two gulps. He raised his eyebrows at Tropf while wiggling the empty cup in the air.

"More?"

"Yes, please."

"What if you concentrated your energy on a single spell?" the monk asked as he poured more tea. Seryn swallowed hard and squinted at his feet. "You tried that, didn't you?"

"How'd you guess?"

"The queen's reaction to your spell was much more noticeable than the king's."

"I couldn't hold back from trying to save Ioma," Seryn said, his gaze still on the floor. "The fear of losing her was too great, and yet, guilt assails me for Valin."

"But you did your best, didn't you? You were out for hours."

"I gave him everything I had left, which wasn't much."

"I know little of sorcery, but it seems a dangerous thing to do."

"It was."

"Please, take no offense, but is there another who could cast a more powerful spell than you?"

"None still alive, that I know of."

"Ah, yes," Tropf mumbled, lowering his gaze to the floor as well, "troubled times, indeed."

Seryn thought of Jetsam, and how his healing spell hadn't restored Ioma, either. *I can't risk exposing the lad as a spellcaster, and devil knows where he is now, anyway.*

"Are you rested enough to cast again?"

"I think so. Though, a bite to eat couldn't hurt."

"Of course! I imagine you're famished. Let me bring you something." Tropf left the room and returned with bread, cheese and a ripe pear. "We should go to the solar as soon as you're finished." Seryn devoured the food in minutes, then departed for the royal chambers with Brother Tropf, followed by his pair of shadowing guards.

"Any news of Gis—the princess?" Seryn asked Brother Tropf. *Watch your tongue,* Seryn admonished himself. *Things are dire enough for the lass without me revealing I'm her father.*

"Nay," Tropf said. "Not a trace of her or Nargul, I'm afraid. Nor your underbelly boy."

Foolishness, Seryn thought, glancing back at his twin shadows. *Two able-bodied men who should be out looking for Giselle. And Jetsam. I could use the lad's help.* Seryn strode alongside Brother Tropf, past a congregation of kneeling supplicants surrounding the outer stairway and through the heavily-guarded front doors of the Great Hall. Their footsteps echoed in the hushed main hall and up the stairs to the solar. Dim and humid, the chamber reminded Seryn more of an infirmary than a royal bedroom. Lady Darksparrow maintained her vigil, holding Queen Ioma's hand. Somber and reserved, the gentlewoman greeted him with a nod and a forced smile.

"I'm so glad you're here," she said. "They need your healing again. It's all that sustains them."

Seryn placed his hand on her shoulder as she rose from the bedside. Prone wax statues, the king and queen anchored the mattress. *I can't just keep casting spells to keep them hanging by a thread.* Yet, Seryn cast his healing incantations on the royal couple, pushing himself to the limits of consciousness, not saving a drop of energy. He stepped away from the bed and allowed Brother Tropf to perform his familiar routine. Seryn eased himself into a chair, his wounds throbbing and clouded head pounding. *If I didn't have to use all my power to keep them alive, I could scry for Jetsam.* Seryn chewed his dry lips. *Gods, keep him safe, and send him and Giselle back soon.*

"The same as yesterday," Tropf said. "Your spells are sustaining them."

"They're no more than breathing corpses." Seryn waved his hand in disgust.

"The poison will not relent its hold," Brother Tropf said.

"We don't even know what we're up against."

"If only there was a method to intensify your healing power," Tropf pondered.

The nudge sent Seryn's mind racing. His hazel eyes widened.

"Did you treat them with powdered gemstones?"

"Yes, yes, of course. To no avail."

"Which ones?"

"Emerald and amethyst."

"What about Eidulaar stone?"

"Why, no, I haven't tried that. It's not a powder known for healing."

Seryn rubbed his stubbled chin with his four-fingered hand. "By chance, do you have Sylallian pine sap and elderberry pollen in your apothecary?"

"I'm not sure—I may. Have to check."

"Please do—posthaste."

Tropf scurried from the bedchamber.

Seryn rose and appraised Ioma and Valin. *Pray, you can hold on till tomorrow.* A salty tear slipped from his eye and disappeared into a maze of whiskers. *I just may have something to save you, after all.* Seryn wiped his cheek with his cuff. "Lady Darksparrow, thank you for your vigilance. You must rest yourself, for we have no healing to spare." She smiled and nodded as Seryn took his leave.

When he arrived at Brother Tropf's chambers, Seryn found the monk rummaging through his wares. He joined Tropf at his counter, while the healer sifted through a myriad of jars and bottles.

"Any luck?"

"Yes—elderberry pollen—plenty of that." He slid a jar toward Seryn. "And a pinch of Eidulaar powder left, too. Now, for the other. Sylallian pine sap, you said?"

"Yes, even just a bit."

"Maybe, just maybe," Tropf mumbled as he lifted a bottle to the light. "No, not that one." Seryn opened the jar of elderberry pollen and examined the contents. *This'll do just fine.*

"Ah, here we go," Tropf said. "Half a bottle of Sylallian pine sap."

"Is there any chance you have a drop of elf blood."

Tropf chuckled and shook his head. "Elf blood?"

Seryn nodded.

"No, no chance at all."

"No matter. I think I know where to find some."

"So, now what?" asked Tropf.

"We need to return to the dungeon."

"But why?"

"I'll explain on the way."

"The guards will insist on accompanying us."

"Down there, we'll need all the help we can get."

May the spirits guide you, Jetsam. It's up to you to save my daughter.

To be continued in
Warlock & Wyrm
Book III of
The Oxbow Kingdom Trilogy

Glossary

Aht-ir Aht-ir [ˈæt-ɪɔr æt-ˈɪɔr / **aht**-eer aht-**eer**] - An ancient ebony dragon who attacked and routed the Dwarves of Asigonn. It is rumored that after defeating the Dwarves, the great wyrm made his lair in Asigonn's great hall.

Asigonn - Asigonn is an ancient Dwarven city, long abandoned. Legends tell of an evil dragon routing the Dwarves and chasing them from their subterranean home.

Av-erif unan umine - An Elven phrase that, along with the proper focus and gesture, releases the fire ribbon spell. This incantation sends a bolt of scorching flame from the caster's staff or fingertips with enough energy to cook an ox.

Av-kier epira gwedath - An Elven phrase that, along with the proper focus and gesture, releases the sunblink spell. This incantation instantly floods the area around the caster with a blinding white light.

Calderi - Calderi is the next large city on the Serpentine Pass south of Dwim-Halloe.

Citadel, The - The Citadel is the central castle of Dwim-Halloe, which houses the Granite Palace; the residence of the Oxbow King. The Citadel proper consists of a moated, double-walled castle, with north and south gate houses. The Jade River has been routed to encircle the Citadel, serving as its moat as it flows southward. The castle sits atop a revetted motte, to withstand the eroding surges of the Jade.

The circular outer castle wall contains 12 towers, spaced like numbers on a clock. The outer curtain has a barbican with a drawbridged gate house on both its north and south sides. These defensive structures provide the only entrances across the Jade into the castle. Within the outer curtain lies the rectangular inner curtain. The higher inner wall surrounds the Oxbow King's Granite Palace and has four prominent guard towers at each corner, with gate houses on the east and west walls. If one were to look down from the Mirrored Peaks, the Citadel's curtains would appear as a small rectangle inside a circle.

Drahkang-roth - The emerald dragon who helped Jetsam defeat the bounty hunter Yduk Thiern.

Dwim-Dwaeroch [dwɪm dˈwā-räk] - A famous Oxbow Mountain landmark in the Kierawaith, west of the Drwarven ruins of Asigonn. Dwim-Dwaeroch is the Dwarven name of a double-edged mountain peak that juts like a knife with a broken tip.

Dwim-Halloe [ˈdwɪm ˌhal-oh] - The capital city of the Oxbow Kingdom, located midway along the Serpentine Pass through the Oxbow Mountains, near the Jade River. Named in the days when a Dwarven king ruled beneath the city while a human king ruled above, Dwim-Halloe was Old Tongue for City of Two Kings, although it had long been misinterpreted as Vale of the Twins, in reference to the Mirrored Peaks.

Dwim-Halloe is protected by the Mirrored Peaks to the east and west, and massive stone ramparts which extended completely across the pass north and south of town, intersecting the steep mountain faces rising on each side of the valley. At its lofty elevation, Dwim-Halloe sits near the top of the Oxbow Mountain timberline, at an elevation of approximately 6,000 feet. North of the city, the terrain rises above the evergreens, providing an unobstructed view for leagues. To the south, the Serpentine Pass winds lower into the green foothills. These natural features make Dwim-Halloe a crucial military defense point for the southern Freelords in protecting their border from any northern threat.

Major buildings in Dwim-Halloe include The Citadel, the city's royal fortification, and The Granite Palace, a double-walled castle that resides inside The Citadel. Dwim-Halloe's general populace lives outside The Citadel's outer curtain, but are still protected by Dwim-Halloe's boundary ramparts.

Eidryn Lothyrn [ˈaɪd rɪn ˈloʊ θrɪn / **ahyd**-rin **loh**-thrin] - The birth name of Flotsam's brother, Jetsam.

Eidulaar stone - A rare, crimson stone with orange veins that is only found deep underground.

Eh' liel Ev' Narron - Dwim-Halloe's School of Sorcery (Eh' liel Ev' Narron in Elvish) was built shortly after the city's construction began. The building itself is constructed of the finest Dwarven granite, mined from, and shaped within, the Oxbow Mountains.

Eh' liel Ev' Narron grew to become Tythania's premiere institution for the teaching and learning of magic; specifically, elemental magic, which most wizards maintained was the foundation for all magic known to Elven-kind. In the early days, every Eh' liel Ev' Narron instructor, or illuminae, was Elven. After many generations of learning, the faculty became sprinkled with half-elves, and even a few humans. In the school's final days, only a few instructors were half-Elven, and the rest human. The full-blooded Elves had long since moved on, mostly westward.

Forsaking the Elven pronunciation, most Dwim-Halloe residents now refer to the academy by the simplified—and less than precisely translated—School of Sorcery.

Elvar Lothyrn - The birth name of Jetsam's brother, Flotsam.

Enthran Ashvar - A surly wizard and former member of Sir Prentice Imoor's band of dragon hunters. Enthran died in Asigonn during a dragon battle. Jetsam now possesses his staff.

Fathom - A distance of 6 feet or approximately 1.8 meters, predominantly used to measure the depth of water.

Flotsam - The underbelly orphans' nickname for Elvar Lothyrn, Jetsam's deceased twin brother.

Furlong - A distance equal to 220 yards or approximately 604 meters.

Gaalf River [gahf riv-er] - The meandering waterway bleeds the Kierawaith of meltwater as it snakes northward. Cutting a turbulent path through the rocky foothills, the river runs all the way to the Badlands, draining into the vast desolate swampland north of the Oxbow Mountains.

Giselle - A green-eyed, blond-haired girl who lives in The Citadel and wanders the gardens at night.

Granite Palace, The - The palace of the Oxbow King sits in The Citadel in Dwim-Halloe. The Granite Palace consists of several buildings; the Great Hall, lesser hall, the keep, chapel, royal storehouse, and the now-vacant Wizard's Tower. In the center of the royal grounds sits the royal bailey.

Gwae Gierameth [ˌgweɪ ˈgɪər ɑ mɛθ / gwey **geer** ah meth] - The ruins of the Dwarven mountain stronghold beneath Dwim-Halloe. The underground Dwarven city was built hundreds of years ago, before mankind inhabited in the Serpentine Pass. The Dwarves mined the Oxbow Mountains for precious metal and stone.

In 899, an earthquake devastated Gwae Gierameth and caused innumerable fatalities. Although the quake caused severe damage to Dwim-Halloe, the destruction paled in comparison to the havoc wreaked in the Dwarven stronghold. As the mountains heaved and shook, even the exceptional subterranean architecture crumbled and collapsed, killing thousands of unsuspecting Dwarves, thus ending the reign of Gwae Gierameth.

Rather than attempt the impossible task of rebuilding their ravaged city, the surviving Dwarves moved on. Further west they migrated, deeper into the Oxbow range, away from the painful memories etched inside the mountain's core.

Illuminae - The title bestowed upon a wizard who taught at Eh' liel Ev'

Narron; Dwim-Halloe's School of Sorcery.

Jade River - This large river is formed north of Dwim-Halloe, at the confluence of three mountain streams fed by the meltwaters of the Mirrored Peaks. Near the Dwim-Halloe, the Jade is still small, but expands in width and depth as the Oxbow watershed feeds it on its southward journey to the Horned Sea. The Jade River runs through barred cutholes at the base of the north and south outer walls of Dwim-Halloe, flowing southward around The Citadel.

Jetsam - The underbelly orphans' nickname for Eidryn Lothyrn.

Kierawaith [kɪər ah weyth] - The region of the Oxbow Mountain foothills on the northern face of the mountain range, located northwest of Dwim-Halloe and the Serpentine Pass. The Kierawaith is noted for its rough terrain and harsh environment, especially in comparison to the foothills on the southern face of the Oxbows. The Gaalf River runs through the middle of the the the Kierawaith and drains the region's meltwaters into the fetid marshes of the Badlands.

Kandris Bayen - The former squire of the late Sir Prentice Imoor of Calderi.

League - A distance equal to three miles or approximately 4.8 kilometers.

Lohon Threll - A redheaded member of Sir Prentice Imoor's band of dragon hunters. Lohon died in Asigonn during a battle with the resident dragon.

Mirdaen Lothyrn – Husband of Vellae Lothyrn and father of Flotsam (Elvar) and Jetsam (Eidryn), a former illuminae at Eh' liel Ev' Narron.

Mirrored Peaks - The near-identical mountain summits sit on each side of the Serpentine Pass, near the midpoint of the Oxbow Mountains. The snow-capped peaks rise sharply above the timberline near the city of Dwim-Halloe. The peaks are similar in shape, size, and height, rising nearly 12,000 feet above sea level.

Mole - A skinny, squeaky-voiced 14-year-old underbelly orphan boy.

Oxbow Mountains - This range crosses the continent of Tythania, separating the northern part of the continent from the larger southern portion. From the northwestern coast of Tythania, the Oxbow rises out of the sea from a series of jutting islands and curves southeast to its southernmost point, mid-continent, near the Serpentine Pass. From there, the Oxbow begins to curve northeast, eventually disappearing into the ocean on the northeast edge of Tythania. From end to end, the Oxbow roams nearly 2,000 miles, spanning the entire width of the continent. The mountains can be divided into three principal sections; the Northwestern Oxbow, the Southern oxbow, and the Northeastern Oxbow. The Northeastern Oxbow contains the range's highest point, Devil's Peak, rising 15,000 feet above sea level. The Oxbow is widest in the Northwest, stretching nearly 160 miles, and ranges to about 90 miles at its narrowest region near the Mirrored Peaks.

Pike - An underbelly orphan boy, Pike is one of the three youths who get lost in Gwae Gierameth. He also gives Jetsam a tunic as a gift.

Ratboy - A brown-eyed underbelly orphan boy, Ratboy has tangled, end-curled, sandy hair. Ratboy unofficially founded the underbelly orphans and is its senior member and father-figure to the younger orphan boys.

Rooster - An underbelly orphan boy, Rooster is one of the three youths who get lost in Gwae Gierameth. He also gives Jetsam a paring knife as a gift.

Serpentine Pass - The snaking mountain path cuts a curving, 100-mile, north-south swath through the midpoint of the Oxbow Mountains. The pass is the major route between the northern and southern portions of the Tythania, being the only horse-accessible crossing near Dwim-Halloe for hundreds of miles.

At Dwim-Halloe, the Serpentine Pass spans nearly two miles at its widest part. At its northern and southern narrow points, walls span east to west, connecting to the rocky slopes of the Mirrored Peaks. Each wall has a large, two-towered gatehouse, providing entrance to the northern and southern portions of the town. Bastions are set near each end of each wall, alongside the peak slopes. These walls provide Dwim-Halloe's first line of defense.

Seryn Vardan - The fugitive accused of killing King Ulodonn Tygan.

Sir Prentice Imoor - A Calderian Knight who rescued Jetsam from the Gaalf River and was killed by Yduk Thiern inside Asigonn.

Stinger - An underbelly orphan boy.

Sylallian - The region of the Oxbow Mountain foothills on the southern face of the mountain range, located west of Dwim-Halloe and the Serpentine Pass. The Sylallian is noted for its green, alpine environment, especially in comparison to the foothills on the northern face of the Oxbows. The Sylallian has long been rumored to be an enchanted forest.

Tythania - Is the name of the continent where Dwim-Halloe and the Oxbow Mountains are located. The events of Mirrors & Mist take place entirely within Tythania.

Ulodonn Tygan [ˈu-lɔu-dɒn ˈtaɪ-gɪn / **Yoo**-loh-don **Tahy**-gin] - The previous Oxbow King, who was assassinated in the year 1004. King Ulodonn Tygan was followed by the current King; Valin Vardan.

Underbelly - The storm sewers of Dwim-Halloe serve as a makeshift home for the orphan clans, and are nicknamed the "underbelly." Hewn by the Dwarves centuries ago, the subterranean conduits were cut to harness the fury of the Oxbow Mountain thaws. Humans expanded these sewers in later times to channel storm waters away from the walled town and Citadel. Connected to the surface throughout Dwim-Halloe, the sewer drains provide the orphans access into town.

Unnatural - A term used to describe otherworldly or magically-influenced creatures, such as spirits, undead, and ghosts, as well as trolls, grimions, goblins and the like. It is also a slang derogatory term for one who uses magic, such as wizards, mages, and spellcasters.

Vellae Lothyrn – Wife of Mírdaen Lothyrn and mother of Flotsam (Elvar) and Jetsam (Eidryn), a former illuminae at Eh' liel Ev' Narron.

ABOUT THE AUTHOR

C. M. Skiera currently lives in Southern California, a long way from Michigan, where he grew up, graduated from Michigan State University, and started a career as an environmental engineer. He and his wife are devoted dog-lovers who share their home with rescue dogs. *Mirrors & Mist* is his second epic fantasy novel following his 2012 debut; *Crimson & Cream*. The third and final book of The Oxbow Kingdom Trilogy is titled *Warlock & Wyrm*.

Introducing an excerpt from

Warlock & Wyrm

Book III of The Oxbow Kingdom Trilogy:

Prologue

With an ear to her bedroom wall, Giselle eavesdropped on her parents' argument. The royal disagreement had turned to shouting before piquing her curiosity. Giselle held her breath until the yelling stopped, though she couldn't understand a thing the king and queen said. She pressed closer to the wall and strained to pick up more conversation.

As minutes passed, she listened to the silence, her blood pulsing behind her eardrum. When the double doors of the royal solar slammed shut, she jumped. With her heart pounding, she shot from her incriminating post and aimed for the safety of her bed.

Before Giselle threw back the comforter, King Valin burst into her bedroom and clamped her wrist. His steely eyes bore through her. With her mother's startling revelation of her genuine parentage still fresh in her mind, Giselle knew this man was not her real father. Her true father was a fugitive wizard wanted for murdering her grandfather.

The king yanked Giselle into the hallway and toward the stairway opposite the closed solar doors.

"Where are you taking me?"

"Keep your mouth shut, if you know what's good for you," said the man who was no longer her father. *He never acted like my father.*

The king wore a velvet mantle atop an ivory tunic, with a

gemstone-studded belt fastening striped breeches. Giselle's soles clicked on the marble stairs as they descended. Heaviness pressed on her chest as they reached the ground floor. *Mother wouldn't tell him about my real father, would she?*

King Valin gripped Giselle's hand and led her through the Great Hall, striding with purpose, his ermine cape fluttering along with the feather on his royal cap. With Giselle in tow, the king avoided the dining room and veered through the kitchen. The servants' eyes grew wide as they stepped back to clear a path. A startled cook knocked over a kettle, spilling steaming stew onto the floor.

Why is he making a scene? Giselle quivered and recalled her mother's words—*Seryn is your father.* Her gaze followed King Valin's arm from his shoulder to his elbow to the hand gripping hers. Giselle's long strides failed to keep pace with him. She jogged with her petite hand crushed inside the king's, her wrist aching from the pull.

With the king not her father, Giselle wondered if she was still a princess. He pulled her from the palace kitchen, into the alley behind the Great Keep—the same alley she had snuck Jetsam through yesterday. The king's glistening black boots clacked heel to pointy toe as he rushed toward the royal bailey.

Of course I'm still a princess—my mother's the queen! She stared at the back of his head, his auburn hair speckled with gray. *I have royal blood, and he's just some noble they forced her to wed.*

The Granite Palace's courtyard sat empty in the twilight as the nobility dined inside the Great Hall and bored guards squinted in the fading light. Giselle scanned the grounds, searching for anyone to make eye contact, someone to offer a clue as to what was happening.

Giselle's sovereign chaperone led her to the Wizard's Tower. A soldier with a closed visor stood guard at the tower door. The man who was no longer her father slowed as he approached the watchman. The king released Giselle's clammy hand, his gray eyes filled with fury.

"Stay," he said, and waved a stained finger toward her nose. Giselle swallowed and stood trembling, hands at her sides. *Is that blood on his hand?*

She twisted her dinner dress between her fingers as Dwim-Halloe's evening breeze chilled her. Giselle yearned to race back to her mother, but fear paralyzed her while curiosity kept her gaze fixed on the two men. The guard greeted his majesty, who stepped close to the sentry and placed a royal hand on his pauldron. The king slipped an object under the watchman's hauberk while his other hand slid from the guard's shoulder to his neck.

Was that a blade?

The soldier grunted and lurched, but the king pinned him to the wall and thrust once more at his abdomen.

"No," Giselle whispered through her shaky fingers.

The guard gurgled and struggled, but his boots no longer touched the ground.

Giselle spun and broke for the Great Hall.

Three steps into her flight, her head snapped back and her feet flew out from under her. She screamed and hung by her hair. Before Giselle caught her breath, the king yanked her through the tower's door and slammed it behind her.

"Quiet, girl! There are *assassins* in the palace." The king set her down and released her golden locks, then pushed her from the entrance.

"Assassins?"

As Giselle stumbled backward trying not to land on her rump, the king locked the door and pocketed the key. Giselle wobbled and frowned. He grabbed her wrist and spun her toward him. The king glared, leaning so close, his warm breath mingled with her frightened gasps.

"That traitor would have killed us both had I not finished him first."

Giselle's heart pounded against her ribcage as she met the man's gaze. "The guard was a traitor?" The king squinted, his face tight and nostrils flaring. His ivory tunic dampened with perspiration. *He didn't look like a traitor.* "How could you tell?"

"The guards betrayed us, and he was one of them. I'll not grant him the chance to strike first."

"So you just killed him?" Giselle's pink mouth hung open as she inched away from him, testing his iron grip.

"An assassin murdered your *mother.* Do you want to be next?"

"Mother's dead?" Giselle's eyes filled with tears, and she sobbed. "She *can't* be dead." Her limbs trembled and her heart turned to lead. "*You* were with her!" She glared at him. "You were arguing!"

The king released her wrist and stepped toward a round table with a lantern. Her chest ached and her shoulder throbbed. "I must go to Mother."

As he focused on lighting the lamp, Giselle examined the exit. *How can I unlock the door if he has the key?* Her gaze drifted to the floor, where her shiny shoes bore the scuffs of her ordeal. *I'm trapped with him, for good or ill.*

"We weren't arguing with each *other*," the King said. "An intruder stabbed the queen before I could reach her. I chased him off, but your mother was already dead." He held the flickering lantern to illuminate the dim chamber. "We can't trust anyone in the palace, so I'm taking you somewhere safe."

You're not my father. "You lie! Mother can't be dead!" The words scraped out hoarse and wild, and then her breath abandoned her.

"I wish it wasn't true," the king said while facing forward and tugging her through the tower. "I wish I'd arrived a moment sooner. Then the assassin would be dead instead of Ioma."

Dizzy and gasping for air, Giselle wept as her feet moved only for the sake of not being dragged. *Mother, no! You were finally getting well.* She recalled Jetsam using his magic to pull the bed-ridden queen from a stupor. *You can't be gone.*

Giselle's stomach roiled as the word assassin rattled in her head. An assassin had killed her grandfather. *It couldn't have been the same man, could it?* Guilt gnawed at her for suspecting someone Jetsam trusted. Someone her mother once loved. Someone who was her real father. She felt like a traitor for thinking it.

"Was it—" Giselle's chest heaved as she struggled to force out the words. "—your brother?"

"Hush. And watch your step—we're going down stairs. A lot of them."

Giselle sniffled and licked her lip. Her shoe slipped on a stair and she stumbled and fell. Her knees smacked the granite steps as she hung from the king's arm. *Now I'm a traitor for speaking it.*

"Get up. Pull yourself together. Behave like the royalty you are."

The king halted and faced her. She wiped her nose and found her footing. Tears streaked her damp cheeks.

"Yes, my vile sibling killed Ioma." He gazed through her with unflinching eyes. "Seryn escaped from the dungeon and snuck into the palace to murder us all."

"It can't be true. It can't." Her fingernails dug into her sweaty palm. "How'd he escape?" Giselle waited for the words she feared.

"I told you—the guards conspired against us. No man could escape without aid."

"Was there anyone else involved?" *Not Jetsam. Please, not Jetsam.*

"Do you mean the orphan? Yes, the lad was complicit. You and I were next if we hadn't escaped."

Jetsam helped Seryn escape and then he murdered my mother? And I helped him! The pain in Giselle's arm spread to her head and wracked her skull as she held back tears. She failed to comprehend why Jetsam would revive the queen from her magical illness, only to help kill her. "Why would someone do this?" Giselle wheezed and wiped her wet cheek.

"Why? For power, of course, and to return the wicked practice of magic to the kingdom." The king's reddening face scowled and his grip tightened. "Seryn and his wizards are behind this treachery. Now, hold your breath and pinch your nose."

Giselle did as instructed as they passed through a room that she recognized as a torture chamber. *Could my real father have tricked Jetsam—or ensorcelled him?* A wisp of rank air wormed into her closed nostril, and she gagged.

"Told you not to breathe." The king hurried her past a hole in the floor where the stench emanated.

The horrid malodor forced Giselle to swallow her bile as saliva seeped from the corners of her clenched mouth. She glanced back at the oubliette. *There must be a dead body in there.* Her eyes watered and lungs stung as she refused to inhale inside the rancid room. *Another one of the king's victims?*

She held her breath until he led her from the chamber and though a corridor lined with cells. *Or just another traitor?* When she relented and gasped for air, the stink subsided to a tolerable level. *Whichever it may be, I shall never forget that odor.*

Made in the USA
San Bernardino, CA
01 September 2018